Turtle
Belly

AMERICAN INDIAN LITERATURE
AND CRITICAL STUDIES SERIES

Gerald Vizenor, General Editor

Turtle Belly

A Novel by
Joel Monture

University of Oklahoma Press : Norman

This is a work of fiction. Names, characters, places and incidents are either the product of the author's imagination or are used fictitiously, and any resemblance to actual events, locales, or persons, living or dead, is entirely coincidental.

Excerpts from this book have been previously published as follows: "Over a Hundred Miles an Hour," in Hamline University's *Voiceprint*, Spring 1991; "Corn Soup," in Cornell University's *Northeast Indian Quarterly*, Fall 1991.

Library of Congress Cataloging-in-Publication Data

Monture, Joel.
    Turtle belly : a novel / by Joel Monture.
        p.   cm. — (American Indian literature and critical studies series ; v. 25)
    ISBN 0–8061–3010–5 (cloth)
    ISBN 0–8061–3332–5 (paper)
    1. Mohawk Indians—Fiction.   I. Title.   II. Series.
PS3563.05465T87   1998
813'.54—dc21   97–38309
                                                                      CIP

Text is set in Palatino with displays in Post Antiqua.
Text design by Alicia Hembekides.

Turtle Belly: A Novel is Volume 25 in the AMERICAN INDIAN LITERATURE AND CRITICAL STUDIES SERIES.

The paper in this book meets the guidelines for permanence and durability of the Committee on Production Guidelines for Book Longevity of the Council on Library Resources, Inc. ∞

2   3   4   5   6   7   8   9   10

For
Audre and Carole,
You make the night stars bright

Special thanks to A:rosen
Konnarohn:kwa

Contents

Turtle
Belly

I
Arrive

I Arrive

We came in a car, driving all night, beneath a water moon that hung upside down against a sky of obsidian clarity. The moon was like the lowered horns of a bison, dumping out all those stars. The moon was charging out of the sky, and the stars were crying because they had been thrown out alone in the darkness. Everything was fixed in the sky, as if the Creator had spiked the universe in place with diamond nails. I was a child, about six years old, faking sleep in the backseat of the car, my face turned into the warm wool upholstery, peeking at the moon above my shoulder, the moon staying always by my shoulder, as we proceeded quickly toward our destination.

My mother, sitting up front, would reach back, stroking my hair or cupping her hand around the ball of my shoulder. When I stirred, she asked, "Are you thirsty?" or she said, "Sleep now, sleepy, sleepy boy," and the warmth of her hand and the motion of the car and the oily smell in the air made me sleep for a while. But when I woke I looked for the moon, and it was there behind us, *between* us and whatever it was that gave chase, as we hurried through the night, as though an animal followed.

When my mother had waked me in my bed in the city, carrying me down the long dark stairs, he was there, over my mother's shoulder, carrying suitcases. We were moving fast, and my mother kept saying, "Thank you . . . oh, thank you so much!" We were running along a hall, down more stairs, until we were outside in the bitter dark street. I saw another man there, near a black car, and I said, "Look at him!" My mother jerked around so fast. The man had a drooping face, all skin and grey wrinkles, and he was twisting his nose with his fingers into the gutter with a loud, wet snort. My mother said, "Never mind that man. He has no soul." I asked why not as she settled me into the backseat of the black car, and she said, "He is a lonely man with no friends because he blows his nose on the sidewalk." The other man with my mother started the car, and when we drove away the man with no soul leaned his sagging face into my window and smiled, and he had no teeth. I asked my mother "What is a soul?" and she leaned back saying, "It is God's proof that you exist." I did not understand. She said, "A soul is like a star. When you are born, the Creator puts a star inside you. When you die, the Creator takes the star and puts it in the sky." I said, "That man has a star inside him," and my mother said no, he had lost his star. Then she told me to sleep. She told me to be quiet. I curled into the seat and watched the city lights fade and give way to the stars. That is how I came to be in that car traveling through the night.

Dawn, grey like the wing of a dove, brought fast-moving shadows. The moon slipped below the trees. The stars faded away. The land was flat and unfamiliar, and I did not want to look at it. Row upon row of grapes sweetened in the dawn, their heavy vines tied up on wires strung between poles. I saw apple trees planted for miles and waves of tasseled corn so thick their amber tops made play yards for red-winged blackbirds, flitting and crying "We-are-here, We-are-here!"

Now I remember the name of the man driving. My mother said, "Jerry, turn left onto the next line." His name was Jerry. I do not know *who* Jerry was, but I have learned now to listen and to remember. I have learned to listen and to remember because sometimes the smallest phrase spoken out of turn, seemingly without real meaning, comes back from memory like a piece of a puzzle. It was Jerry who drove us through the night to the Reserve. It was Jerry who carried the luggage down the hallways and dark stairs, helping my mother. If Jerry had not helped us, all the stars in the sky would have re-arranged themselves. Life would be different. Now, I suddenly remember my mother calling him by name.

She said, "Jerry, turn in here, this is the place." She seemed to hold her breath, "God, look at this dump. It's no better. It hasn't changed a bit. *See* why I left?"

The windshield of the car was brassy yellow with sun-light. A commotion of dogs started up. They came around the car barking. One of them stood against the side of the car, rub-bing his wet nose against the window, leaving a puddle of fog.

The stern voice of a young woman called out, "Gayskite! Wiskite! Get out of there!" and the dogs slinked away to the early morning shade of a dying elm tree. I looked out of the car and saw her coming out of a small house made of square logs. She was dark, with watery black eyes and long black hair pulled back and tied up with a red ribbon. She was barefooted, wearing old blue jeans and a man's plaid flannel shirt, baggy and untucked. When she came up to the car, she looked at my mother and then at me. *"She:kon,"* she said, "Come on in."

My mother said, "We're here now, Honey. Let's go in." She left the car and came back for me, and she carried me past the dogs, a large black one and a smaller brown one with no tail. The dogs followed close to our heels, and behind them came the woman with two small suitcases. The man waited in the car.

The interior of the house was dark and cluttered, all one big room with a ladder-like staircase that rose up to a hole in the low ceiling. There was a wide doorway in the center of the back wall that led to a kitchen wing. I could see a squat black woodstove in the middle of the kitchen. The kettle on the woodstove steamed, and the steam rose up among a half dozen skinned horsetails hanging from a beam. The woman went to the stove and stood among the horsetails, and I was scared to see her there. When she looked back at me, still in my mother's arms, she had a nice wide smile. I looked away from her, I looked toward the door we had come in, and I saw the carved wooden faces on the wall. They were painted black or red, with twisted grimaces, and they had long horsetail hair. Some of the faces had missing teeth and noses bent over. They stared into the room with empty eyes, and I thought about the old man on the sidewalk who had lost his soul. Those wooden faces seemed like they might be lost souls, and they did not scare me. I looked back at the woman standing beneath the horsetails. She smiled at me again, and now she did not scare me either.

My mother said, "This is your cousin, Ellie."

Ellie said, "Are you hungry? Come here and eat."

My mother put me down, and I walked up to Ellie, and I was standing beneath those horsetails. Ellie scooped corn from a pan on the back of the stove with a long ladle and put it on a plate. I sat there on the floor by the stove, and Ellie gave me a spoon. Even though it was August, I was cold, and the stove warmed me. The corn had a smoky flavor, and I ate it quickly. Ellie gave me tea in a tin cup. She put her hand on my shoulder and said, "Sit here while I talk with your mother." Then she left me alone.

They talked quietly, but I could hear them.

My mother said, "Thank you so much," and Ellie said she was sorry my mother was having troubles. "He can stay as long as it takes for you to settle your troubles."

My mother said, "His father called on the phone and said he was coming to take him. Thank God for Jerry. We stopped on the highway to call. I don't know where else we would have gone."

"No need to explain," said Ellie. "Aunt Molly walked down when you called, and told us."

"In the middle of the night?"

"She's old. She don't sleep too much anymore."

My mother sighed. "I will send you some money."

Ellie said, "Take care of yourself first."

Then my mother got up from her chair and came into the kitchen. She picked me up and held me. "I have to go now," she said.

I started to cry, and my mother slowly rocked me. She began to sing:

Peter Peter pumpkin eater,
had a wife and couldn't keep her.
Put her in a pumpkin shell
and there he kept her very well.

Then she lowered her face and kissed me. "Momma loves you," she said. "Momma always loves you."

My mother began to cry without making a sound. She carried me to Ellie, who took me in her arms, and when I looked at my mother I saw that her face had become grey and blank, as if all the life had gone out of her. Ellie said, "Go now." My mother kissed me again and turned out the front door quickly. She pushed between the dogs, wiping her eyes with her hands, and when she got in the car I saw her lean into herself, quivering as she sobbed. The dogs began to bark when the car started up, and when it left they ran off down the road, howling until the car was out of sight. They soon came back panting and lay on the wooden stoop of the house, hot in the August sun.

Then I heard a small rasping cry, and Ellie put me down on a worn-out sofa, sat beside me, and uncovered a bundled baby that had been there silent all this time. She unbuttoned her shirt and brought out a dark swollen breast streaked with blue veins and guided the brown nipple into the baby's puckered fish mouth. Then she wrapped her arm around me, holding me tight against her other breast, and softly sang a song of strange words, repeating them over and over again with such a gentle rhythm that I closed my eyes, making the world all dark. I sunk deeper and deeper into the darkness, hearing Ellie's warm song, until everything turned into a dreamless nothingness.

I
Awake

Turtle Belly

When consciousness slipped into me I found myself beneath a bright sunburst quilt, like a rainbow sun on a yellow sky. I looked down at the floor toward a cracking noise. A salt-and-pepper cat lay in a patch of sunlight eating a mouse. The cat's head was turned sideways in my direction, and his eyes were half-closed with happiness. The cat held the mouse between crossed paws and gnawed devotedly on it until the tail slipped into its mouth. I looked beyond the cat and saw a pair of dirty work boots and a black metal lunch pail. The toes of the boots were worn through, and shiny steel glinted in the sunlight from the window. Looking up the boots, I saw the silhouette of a man sitting in a wooden chair. "I'm your cousin, Tom," he said.

He got up and came over to me, and he picked up my hand, shaking it. "Do you like to ride horses?" he asked.

Ellie said, "There's time enough for that later. Let him get settled in."

I saw Ellie at the woodstove, and she asked me if I was hungry. I nodded, and she brought me another plate of corn.

Tom said, "Eat your corn, and you can come with me in the truck. Do you want to come in the truck with me?"

Ellie shook her head no, and then I shook my head no. Tom turned to her and laughed, and his face was round and full of happiness, like the cat's face. "Did you meet Eddie?" he asked. He reached past me and picked up the bundled baby, holding it in the air above him, bringing his son down until their noses touched. Then he sat on the couch beside me. "His name is Eddie after Ellie's brother. He was moose hunting in the fog up the line, and a semi truck hit him when he was crossing the road. You be careful on the road. You don't want to die like a dog on the road. You hear the dogs' names? *Gayskite. Wiskite.* Means fourteen and fifteen. The next one, after *they* get killed on the road will be *Yayskite*, Sixteen. So you hear me and be careful on the road." He reached over and rubbed my hair. I finished my plate of corn, and Ellie took it away.

"Are you going over to Danny's?" she asked.

"Thought so," said Tom.

"Tell him Aunt Molly's making dinner for around five-thirty." She took the baby from Tom, and he said, "*Onen'ke-wahi.*"

Ellie said, "Take good care," when he pushed out the screen door. The cat slipped through before the door banged shut. I pushed away the quilt and went to watch my cousin Tom take off. He climbed into a black pickup truck, and when he sped away the two dogs ran and leaped onto the open tail-gate, barking.

Ellie brought the baby over to the door. "The dogs are gone," she said. "Do you want to go outside?"

"Yes."

We sat on the stoop, and the cat played with the laces on my shoes. The sun had come over the house and filled the dirt yard with light. Ellie pointed across the flat landscape. "That brick house a half-mile down is Aunt Molly's. She is your grandfather's sister. Your grandfather died before you were born so you don't know him. He died of the Indian plague."

"What's that?" I asked.

"The tuberculosis. TB. Your mother had TB when she was a girl, but not so bad. She was only two years in the sanatorium. Your Grandfather was in and out for over ten years."

"Will I get a TB?" I asked.

"Maybe. Lots of people do." Then she pointed across the road. "And down there aways," said Ellie, "is your Aunt Bess. She makes quilts, and she's deaf. She can't hear anything except for what's in her head. She's not crazy, but sometimes she talks out loud. In World War One she was a nurse and went to France. All the boys went over to France, but she was the only Mohawk girl. Down at the community center they have the flags they carried, and you can see bullet holes in them. Aunt Bess brought them back. There's a memorial with the names of all the boys who died. If you can write down your questions, Aunt Bess will tell you all about them, but you have to sit still and listen."

"I don't know how to write."

"You can tell me, and I'll write down your questions," said Ellie. Then she pointed on down past Aunt Bess's white farmhouse. "Way far down the line is your cousin Edgar's place. He works with Tom at the mill."

I was thinking about my mother. "When is my mother coming back?" I asked.

"I don't know," said Ellie. "I will tell you when I know. I promise."

"Why did she bring me here?"

"Because you're family, and she wanted you to be safe."

I said, "I don't know my father, but I don't think he would hurt me."

"Sometimes people do crazy things," she said. "One time there was a man over on the third line who got so drunk he knocked over a lantern and the whole log house burned down. His woman and five girls burned up, and all they found in the ashes were their intestines curled up in little balls."

"Is that true?" I asked.

"That is true," she said. "And after that he crashed his car in the river and drowned. He used to make good snow snakes. I think his brother makes them now."

"What's a snow snake?"

"Tom will show you a snow snake," she said. "Now, up

the line in the other direction is your cousin Jake, and our Aunt Ida, and your uncle Lewis. He doesn't talk very well. One time the people were angry, and the Mounties came in a long semi truck and rode their horses down a ramp right into the crowd. They whipped the women with riding crops, and Lewis was there. A whip cut right through his cheek and cut off the tip of his tongue. He talks like he has a mouthful of mush."

"Does he really?"

"He *th*ertainly doe*th*!"

"No!" I said.

Ellie made a face at me. "Ab*th*olutely. I *th*wear!"

"You're *th*illy!" I said, and Ellie caught me up in a big hug with her free arm, drawing me into her and the baby. The baby was at her breast, and I could smell the sweet milk mixed with the odor of Ellie, who was sweaty from the sun and smoky from the woodstove. I reached out and touched her breast and it was very hard and hot, as if there was a fire inside it. "Be careful," she said. "They're very sore." I pulled my hand away, and said, "You mean *th*ore?"

"Ye*th*," she said, and we laughed. Then she pointed to a log house about two hundred yards away. It was covered with white clapboards, but the paint was all chipped and peeling. There were no trees around the house. It sat lonely in a field. "Watch as the sun comes round the back," she said. "In a while you'll see old Jonas follow the shade with his rocking chair. That's what old people do. They follow the shade. Jonas drinks a lot, but he's OK. He makes faces sometimes."

"Like this?" I twisted my mouth into a lopsided smirk.

"No," she laughed. "*Gagohsah!* The masks on the wall."

A fast car raced by the house, honking, and Ellie lifted her arm off my shoulder and waved. "That was Donna. She's a teacher at Six Nations Elementary. She is not Indian, but she looks like one." She paused, looking at me. "You don't look Indian, but I can see your grandfather in you. You're the color of a turtle's belly, though. Pale. Do you get bad sunburns?"

"I never did," I said. "What's a sunburn?"

"Does your nose get all red and peely in the sun?"

"I don't know."

"I understand. I've been in the city a few times. The sun is different there. In big cities everything is all shadows because of the buildings." She tapped my nose. "You're getting red, sitting here in my sun."

"I'm sorry," I said.

She pulled me close again. "It's alright, Turtle Belly. When your nose gets red I'll put spinach on it, and it'll make it cool."

Then she pointed at the lone little house in the field across the road. "Look, here comes old Jonas moving his rocking chair along with the shade."

I saw the old man in blue-jean overalls shuffle around the corner, dragging the rocking chair like a sled through the tall grass. He paused to catch his breath, and then he brought the chair to the far side of the shade. He sat down and leaned back, closing his eyes and smoothing back a tousle of clipped white hair.

I looked up at Ellie. "I have to go to the bathroom," I said.

We stood, Ellie holding the baby against her shoulder, and she took my hand and led the way around the corner of the log house. "We have a double crapper," she said, and we came up to a small building beside a line of trees. Beyond the building was a corral built of poles and planks and, beyond that, a wooden barn of rough-sawn boards. Ellie pushed open the creaky door on leather hinges, and we went inside. There was a long plank with two big holes cut into it. "Do you need any help?" she asked. "No," I said, pulling at my fly. Ellie lowered her jeans with one hand, as she held the baby, and sat down. Her water was strong. It made a hissing sound that echoed in the dark hole. The little house smelled like ammonia. She flipped the lid off a big tin can and pulled out some toilet paper. "Always put the lid on," she said, "or else the porcupines will eat the paper." She dabbed the paper between her legs, rubbing a dark furry place I had never seen before. My mother had been fussy about such things and always kept bathroom and bedroom doors closed. When she stood up, I saw that she didn't have a pisser like mine, and I wondered about her. She saw me looking, and when she pulled up her jeans she sat back down with the baby, and we talked in that dark airless house, smelling the odor rising about the natural ways of life. I didn't understand it all, but I somehow knew that Ellie was right, that Ellie would not lie to me, and when we were finished I no longer felt sad that she didn't have what I did, and I didn't feel proud to have what I had—I felt that the Creator had made us each in his own way and that was the natural way of the world. But she wouldn't show it to me again when I asked, and she said she thought that maybe I was too old to share a double crapper with girls, after all. And then we came out into the sun and the air felt cool and the smell was sweet. I forgot about that talk—not really forgot what we talked about, but how she had said it—and I did not really think about those five minutes until years later, when Ellie was dead, and I thought of everything I could about her so that she would never really be gone.

Ellie asked me if I knew how to run, and I told her yes.

"I mean really run, so that you beat the wind? I don't mean city running, I mean country running!"

She put the baby down beside a bush, and she told me to run in the field. I began to run, but I fell over a stick and Ellie said, "Get up! Run!" And then she ran with me, saying, "Didn't you ever hear about Tom Longboat? He once beat a horse in a forty-mile race, all the way to Hamilton, and when the horse came in he was sitting in a restaurant eating steak and eggs. He was Onondaga, over on the next line. He was in the war with Aunt Bess. He died a long time ago." She said all this running beside me. Then she stopped and picked up a rock and threw it hard toward the tree line, hitting a cat. The cat screeched and ran into the bushes. We walked back, catching our breath. "A cat will lick the smell of milk out of a baby's mouth and suck out all their wind. You always have to watch out for cats when there's a baby," she said.

"Is that true?" I asked.

"There was a woman living on first line road who forgot to throw the cat outside one night, and in the morning her new baby had all the life sucked out of it. Ever since then her man shoots dead every cat he sees. He got bitter, eh."

"If I see that cat go near your baby, I'll throw a rock at it," I said.

"Don't go looking to throw rocks," she said. "Never go looking to throw rocks, or you'll have a bitter heart. You see, there's a way of looking at a cat and thinking 'now there goes a baby sucker,' so you get in the habit of throwing rocks at every cat you see. But the truth is, a cat's only doing what the Creator tells him to do, like catching mice. That's a cat's station in life, and you can't ever change that. Just like every man is born with a certain something inside him that won't ever change, that's how it is with a cat. So don't go throwing stones at a cat, or a man, before you know what he's up to."

Ellie and I came to the baby bush, and she picked up Eddie, who was wide-eyed awake but quiet, and we walked to the house. She pointed behind the kitchen wing at a pile of bare earth heaped up in a crescent by the foundation. "We have a bathroom coming," she said. "The boys drilled a well and set a deep pump last year. They're going to put in a toilet and a bathtub before the cold weather sets in."

"I never saw an outdoor bathroom," I said.

Ellie laughed. "Not most people, even here, I guess. But I'll tell you the truth. Everybody calls that big brick house down the line the family homestead because your great grandfather built it with money he made climbing steel. But this little log house was where he was born. This is the real homestead, built by your great grandfather's grandfather. Seven boys and two girls were born and raised here, that's why there's a two-hole crapper. Otherwise there would be a traffic jam, and that's no good, especially in winter. No one ever got around to putting in a toilet here, I guess because the young ones moved in when they got married and stayed only long enough to build proper houses. Not that this one isn't proper. This house is full of life, and I told Tom, 'I want to stay in this house and I want a bathroom.'"

Ellie took up my hand, and we went to the back door in the kitchen wing. There were split chunks of wood piled up higher than me in long rows. Ellie said, "Our winter wood. It's almost dry enough to burn. The boys cut it out of the bush all summer long." When we went inside, Ellie put the baby in a basket and took a cup of tea while I sat on the sofa. It was so bright with sunshine outside that I could not see much inside the dark house, the log walls chinked with grey plaster and smoke smudged from generations of wood burners. In time my eyes widened to the sights that represented my family's past—faded photographs of ancestors in small brown frames nailed to the walls, mystifying objects with feathers, interlocking trails of small white beads on navy blue wool, the ovoid shell of a large turtle hafted with its own stretched neck and sightless head. I had never seen such things before, including the most important, the Faces, who I would come to know by name—the Great Protector Broken Nose, Laughing Beggar, Spoon Mouth. But at that very moment, despite the magic Ellie had thrown over me with her smoky woman smell and engulfing arms and smile, I kept thinking about my mother with a sinking sadness that made a great quiet panic flutter in my chest. My heart was beating like a bird's. I almost liked being in this place, but how could I enjoy it when I did not know where my mother was or if she would ever come back for me. And if I was concerned that my mother would not come, I was even more concerned that my father *would*. That's what I had been told until it scared me.

I had never known his touch or the sound of his voice, and I had never seen a picture of him. He was always present, though, in my mother's life and in mine, because of her fear that he would find us. It became my fear, although I often wished that he would suddenly appear with gifts, an offer of apology for making us live like animals in dark holes. Until that day when I ran in the open field with Ellie, racing into the wind and seeing her long black ponytail whipping her shoulders, I had never been free. I had never been to a school because my mother knew how easy it would be to snatch me from the playground, and when we played in a city park it was always in the open where she could see strangers coming. I was always left in the company of couples when my mother went to work, most recently with a fingerless war veteran and his wife, living in the basement below our small apartment. The man taught me how he killed Japanese soldiers by thrusting a rifle and bayonet at me as I dodged behind the back of an overstuffed chair that was gashed open with fluffy white wounds. I believed then that if my father came, for good or bad, it would end the fearful waiting, for it was inevitable that he would someday come, and I hoped that every day would be the day of our final peace. I did not know my mother's reasons; if she had told me I would not have understood them. I only understood that all people did not live like we did, afraid.

I sat most of that first afternoon thinking and sorting thoughts, moving from window to window to the screened front door, and staring out across open fields and ragged tree lines and the dark undergrowth of the woods beyond the fields. A cool breeze came up the road, bringing with it the faint distant sound of playing children and the wet earthy scent of the river that lay beyond the woods. It was both ominously strange and exhilarating to be in a house with all the windows and doors thrown wide open to the world. Nothing was locked, and I turned to Ellie and asked, "Can I go outside?"

She said, "Do you want to go outside?"

"No," I said. "But if I want to, can I?"

"Yes," she said.

"Will you come with me?" I asked.

"Are you afraid to go out alone?"

"Yes."

"What are you afraid of?"

"What if my father comes?"

"If he does the dogs will bite him."

"The dogs are gone," I said.

"Then I will bite him. Go outside now, if you want."

"What if the dogs come back?"

"You will say in a loud strong voice, 'SOH-WASS-SA-KWA-TEE,' and they will leave you alone. It means 'Go away dog!'"

Ellie came and pushed open the screen door.

"Go on outside."

I went outside and stood on the stoop, and when the door closed I pressed my back against it. In a minute I came back inside and stood there for a while, and then I went outside again, practicing going in and out on my own but doing nothing else. I became absorbed in the novelty of the game. I did not realize that Tom had pulled in with the truck until the dogs, barking fiercely, leaped off the tailgate, running towards me as I frantically pulled at the door, slipping inside just as they reached the stoop. I yelled "SOWASS SAKWATEE!" and they abruptly turned away and lay down in the sun.

"It worked, Ellie!" I said. "The dogs went away!"

She smiled and nodded at me, and after that I was never again afraid of those dogs because they did what I told them. I went outside and walked among the dogs. I took a deep breath, and Tom, rubbing my head as he came up to the house, said, *"Ioienere rahksah,"* which I somehow knew meant "good boy!"

Blood
and
Rain

Some years later people told me that what happened didn't happen at all because they thought a kid wouldn't know any better. They thought a kid's memory was all washed-out like mist on a lake, obscuring the distance. One thing I learned was that it didn't matter if someone threw the rock or if it fell off a cliff by its own weight . . . the point was that if it hit your head, it hurt. And no one can tell me any different. I know what happened.

I can see it all now, looking back, as if I were standing on a hillside high above my own life. I even wonder at times if it was my own life or that of a stranger, walking by my side like a shadow with movements of its own. I could not shake loose my shadows no matter how hard I tried, but there was one thing I also knew to be the truth. . . . When you live in shadows your eyes get used to the darkness.

Tom and I, with Ellie carrying the baby, followed by the dogs, walked down the line to the big brick house for supper at Aunt Molly's. Every time a car passed us, speeding and honking, the dogs charged into the road like relay racers. One time a passenger in a red car with a white roof came by and pitched open the door, banging Wiskite onto the gravel shoulder ahead of us. Tom called him "Wiskite the Wonder Dog," because, he said laughing to me, "It's a wonder he's still alive."

When we came up near Aunt Molly's house we cut across a stubble field gone brown in the hot August sun, and we came around a large weathered barn with no paint. I never saw a barn so large, looming above us with the sunlight poking through all the cracks.

Tom said, "One time Uncle William came home to visit and he stayed with Aunt Molly and Uncle Osborn. The night before he was supposed to leave, he polished his boots and Aunt Molly starched his shirt and pressed his tie. In the morning Uncle Osborn found him hanging in this very barn, his hair combed and his fingernails clipped short. They say he measured the rope exact, so that when he jumped off the beam his toes were only an inch from the floor. Uncle Osborn never cursed, but that day, when he saw his brother hanging there, he said, 'God damn you!' and he cut him down and dragged his body to the manure pile and said, 'Good enough for the likes of you.' Uncle Osborn died a year after that. They were your grandfather's brothers."

I walked so that Tom and Ellie were between me and the barn. When we came around it to the backside of the big brick house I looked back at the darkness of the barn, the wide doors yawning blackness and loss. Tom said, "You watch, no dog will ever go inside that barn. Dogs sense things."

We walked through the corn in Aunt Molly's garden. It was way over my head, and the leaves on the stalks were deep green and sharp like the edges of paper. I got a leaf cut on my neck below my ear, and I wiped at it, getting blood on the palm of my hand. When we came out of the corn I saw the figure of Aunt Molly behind the house by a tall weeping willow tree. She was an emaciated little woman, wearing a baggy pair of coveralls. She was slowly chopping a limb from the willow tree that had blown down. She put the axe down when we came up to her. I had never seen someone so old. Her face was all bone and parchment skin, and her hair was like snow, pulled back and braided in a long rope. Her eyes were sunken and dark, and when she smiled at me her lips pulled back and she looked like a skull. She took Tom's hand, and she stooped down until we were face to face, and she peered all around my face carefully. She was so small she did not have to bend far to look at me, but when she did I remained very still and stared back at her.

She said, "I see your grandfather in you." She cast her eyes up at Tom and nodded, and he aided her as she slowly stood up.

"Let me see Eddie again," she said, and Ellie turned the baby towards her, pressing him close until Aunt Molly's and that baby's nose almost touched. It was remarkable to see those two nearly sightless beings—each at opposite ends of life—study each other. It was as if the beginning of a circle came upon its own end at an imaginary and inconstant point. I was walking the circle somewhere between the two of them, and I now recall that one time later Aunt Molly told me, "It's not different circles we're traveling but one great circle. We just enter the race at different times." She was eighty-four years old when I first met her, and it was at least ten years later when she said that, and she still had ten years left in the race. I never knew someone with so many breaths.

Aunt Molly turned from the baby and said, "Come on in and eat." We came onto the wooden porch behind the big brick house, and she paused to strip off her coveralls. She wore a yellow print calico housedress beneath and seemed even smaller without the coveralls, her back not nearly so straight and her walk not so confident. She trembled opening the screen door, but Tom and Ellie left her alone to open her own door and see us inside. We entered a beautiful white kitchen with a pink linoleum floor. The stove and the fridge and the sink were all glistening white porcelain with polished chrome trimmings. The curtains were pink, and the table was covered with a red-and-white checkered cloth. It was such a majestic kitchen, with a ten-foot ceiling, that I was overwhelmed.

The kitchen smelled of cooked herbs, all warmth and sweetness with a breeze coming through the open window over the sink, cooling off the room. When I stood next to Ellie I could smell the woodsmoke in her hair and clothing and the di-apery smell coming off the baby. Tom was all musky with sweat from working the night shift at the mill. Aunt Molly, tak-ing my hand, was a flower with talcum-powder pollen, and she brought me into a living room with trailing-vine wallpaper, white gossamer curtains, and old easy furniture arranged around a fireplace. The hearth of the fireplace sloped down into the room, and an old iron tomahawk was wedged beneath a metal fire screen to keep it from tipping over onto the worn carpet. Aunt Molly showed me to a chair, and I sunk into it and remained quiet, staring past her at the high ceiling and a broad staircase with a dark mahogany banister. Then she ascended the staircase, a tiny figure clutching the polished banister with both hands, mounting one step at a time as a toddling child does. Ellie sat in the living room now, nursing the baby, and she told me Tom went outside to finish cutting up the willow limb in the yard for Aunt Molly. I could hear the ringing bite of the axe in even strokes as he worked before supper. Aunt Molly de-scended the stairs, now with a pale yellow sweater draped around her shoulders, and Ellie, putting the baby down on a sofa cushion and buttoning her shirt, joined our aunt in the kitchen to work on supper.

Other people came to the back door of the house, bringing with them dishes of food. They talked in the kitchen and peered through the doorway at me, smiling or nodding in quiet greeting. Aunt Bess, who was Aunt Molly's younger sister, though almost as old in appearance, walked into the living room with her cane and sat across from me, beside the baby on the couch. She said very loudly, "I can see your grandfather in you." When I answered, "Yes," she remained silent in her soundless world, nodding at me with uncanny precision each time my thoughts drifted to her. But when my thoughts drifted to another place, the unknown place I imagined my mother inhabited, Aunt Bess startled me with a loud outburst, "Doughnuts? Yes, the boys in the trenches looked forward to doughnuts, even if they had mud on them."

I remember her saying that, because I nodded at her and she continued, looking straight into me and smiling like a skull, saying, "But I would never give you a muddy one. You are a good boy." Then she gestured, waving me over to her, and I came beside my old Aunt Bess and took a place against her side, with the baby on her other side, and she said, "I have a little quilt with red crosses on it—I worked for the Red Cross during the war—I'll give you the quilt if you want it." I did not know if I wanted it or not at that unsure moment, but years later the handsewn red-and-white cross quilt had grown so thin and tattered on my bed that I folded it carefully, feeling Aunt Bess's half-moon pattern stitches, and placed it in a wooden chest with woolen blankets and mothballs tied up in a linen handkerchief. The quilt came to signify my delivery into another world. That first night at Aunt Molly's, when I could not keep all the names and faces in order, I fell asleep after a dinner of ham and grinding stones and succotash and squash. The grinding stones, round grey corn bread made with red beans, were the best! Aunt Bess had sent her daughter across the road for the quilt so that Tom could wrap me up and carry my sleeping form back to the old log house. That is what I have been told, that I was wrapped up like a newborn baby entering a new world and brought home.

I learned to laugh inside over her sudden outbursts. I reasoned that she might have seen me come in on a snowy day and seen how cold I was, and it would set her to thinking about how cold it was in, for instance, 1928, and then in thinking about the coldness of 1928, she would recall that was the year

a hog froze before slaughter and her father had to butcher the
frozen parts with an axe, which glanced off the pig and cut off
his toes through his boot. Then out of nowhere, Aunt Bess
would suddenly and loudly address me, "Do you have all your
toes? Well, my father didn't. That's how cold it was in 1928."
Later, someone would explain the story to me. That's how I
began to figure out how the mind of a stone-deaf eighty-two-
year-old woman worked, and it surprised me to find my own
mind working that way, daydreaming long, connected streams
of facts and feelings until the ending thought had no connec-
tion with the beginning thought. That, of course, was what us
young people had in common with the old-timers—we both
worked our thoughts so hard we were all crazy. But it was a joy-
ful insanity before, and after, those middling years of rational,
worrisome thinking. As children, and as the very old, we were
so close to the Creator that we were filled with hope. And I always felt close to my Aunt Bess, not so much for the way of her
silent world, but because when I awakened the next morning in
the small room under the eaves of the log house, I was wrapped
up in that red-and-white cross quilt. I knew it was the quilt she
had spoken about to me, and she had kept her promise. She
was not crazy, just old.

When I woke up Sunday morning under the red cross
quilt, my first thoughts were of my mother. So much had happened in those first twenty-four hours that I felt as if my
mother had been gone forever, and I wondered that Sunday if
this was the day my mother would come for me. I hoped that
my mother had cured her troubles, and if not, I wondered if
they had gotten worse. I cried some more, lying under the dark
eaves, and when somehow the crying stopped I heard the
sound of hammers and saws and the wrenching and splintering of lumber. I climbed down the ladder and saw that all the

men were working together, tearing out the side of the kitchen beside the new deep well and foundations. Sunlight poured into the room. Ellie said, "I want a window there, Tom," and then she saw me, standing, red-eyed, in only my underpants, holding the red cross quilt around my shoulders. She wrapped me up tighter and put me on a chair near the woodstove so that I could watch the men working. She gave me a bowl of corn-flakes with milk and a cup of tea. Nearby was a wicker basket of laundry, and sleeping on top was her baby, mindless of the construction.

Ellie opened up my suitcase on the floor. "You were so dead last night we didn't bother to—Here are your pajamas," she said. "After you eat you can take your pajamas upstairs and hang them on the bedpost." Tom left the workers and stood near me, the hammer swaying below his hand like a clock's pendulum. Ellie said, "Tom, drive over to Donna's and get some real clothes for this boy . . . and a pair of boots if she has them." Tom left through the hole in the kitchen, and I heard the truck start and the dogs bark. Ellie said to me, "You remember Donna? She honked at us yesterday. Whenever a kid dies, parents give her their dead kid's clothes and shoes, and she gives them to the kids in the school. She'll have clothes for you." Later Tom came back with a paper bag, and Ellie dressed me in a plaid shirt and a pair of blue jeans with a patch on one knee, and when I sat on the couch so she could lace up my boots, she turned one of them over in her hand, then looked inside. "I remember these. Jackson Hill. He drowned in the river this summer." Then she tied up the scuffed boots and said, "Go to work with the men."

Tom made me the nail boy, tying around my waist a canvas apron with a large pocket full of nails. Whenever someone called out "NAILS," I ran through the construction and let him grab a handful, which he arranged in the corners of his mouth. There was Tom, Tom's brother Marcus, Jimmy Sky and Buddy Sky, and others I didn't know. There were about ten all together, and there were some women, and there were some children, though none my age. I watched the men carefully, saw them laying the sills and the joists and raising a framework of rough-sawn two-by-fours. Buddy Sky had a van full of wires and clips and fuse boxes. Marcus's truck had a water heater loaded on it. Tom, early that morning, had picked up a used toilet—it was blue—and a bathtub and a sink—both white. Jimmy Sky gave them to Tom. They had come out of an old house that had mostly burned down, and the sink had a scorched crack that Jimmy patched with auto-body putty. Years later nobody believed me, but I saw an entire bathroom built in one day, sunup to sundown: walls, floor, roof and shingles, insulation and tar paper, water and wires, medicine cabinet and mirror, light switch, and a bright green AstroTurf carpet, tucked neatly into the corners and cut around the toilet and the vanity cupboard below the sink. When it was all finished—though the joints on the Sheetrock had not been taped and the outside was rough-stapled tarpaper with no clapboards—Tom said to everyone in the kitchen, "I have to shit," and then he closed the bathroom door as everybody laughed. Something was wrong with the water heater though, and there was no hot water, and Buddy Sky said he would come over on Monday to fix it. It was in a little closet with shelves beside it. And when Tom came out of the bathroom, the women went in and arranged towels and soap and hung a pair of curtains Aunt Bess had sewn for over the little window.

Old Jonas from across the road was there, and he started singing a prayer. He gave Ellie some tobacco. He was moving in a circle, and he was very serious. He took from his pocket a dried braid of sweet grass, and he lit the end of it with a match. He took it in the new bathroom and waved it around, passing the smoke into all the corners. Some of the men, and Tom and Ellie, went into the bathroom and rubbed the smoke over their bodies. They waved the smoke into their faces, as if splashing themselves with water. They were silent and solemn. When they came out we ate lots of food—fried bread and corn, smoked birds called *chukkars*, and smoked salmon that Jimmy had caught up north.

It was dark when everybody left. I was laying on the couch watching the *Ed Sullivan Show* on a little black-and-white television. Tom took off his boots and got a cigarette from a pack on the shelf. He sat on a wooden chair with his elbows on his knees, bent over like a tired man. The baby was sleeping, and Ellie hauled out a galvanized-metal tub and put it in the middle of the kitchen floor.

Tom said, "Why're you doing that?"

Ellie answered, "I'm dirty and I need a bath."

"Can't you wait till tomorrow?" Tom said. "We'll have hot water then. Or you can at least use the new bathtub."

Ellie poured hot water from a kettle on the stove into the tin tub. "I've been doing this since we moved here, and I can wait until everything's fixed up right."

I looked down the length of the couch and saw her in the kitchen undressed, on her knees, with her long hair tossed into the tub. She scrubbed her head with a bar of soap and rinsed it with a pitcher of cold water. She stood up and let all the water in her hair run down her body, and she stepped into the tub. The only light came from the television. Her back was turned to me, and her dark skin glistened. Tom, leaning between his knees, had closed his eyes. He jerked up his head, trying to stay awake. I looked at Ellie and watched as she scrubbed herself with the soap and a white washcloth. One time my mother had taken me to a museum in Toronto, and there I saw a painting of a woman with no clothes on. She was washing herself. Ellie, from the back, looked like that woman. She had wide hips and thighs and the muscles in her back were strong. When she twisted to wash behind her knees, her breast was fat. I thought that she was the woman in the painting.

When she was finished, she dried herself with a towel and then wrapped up in the bright star quilt. She came and sat on the couch by my feet and began to brush out the tangles in her hair. She said, "Tom, wake up. That little Italian mouse is on TV."

Tom snapped up his head. We watched TV and laughed. The dogs outside began to bark. Tom said, "I hear thunder."

Ellie said, "It's raining."

The dogs kept barking. One of them yelped, and Tom looked towards the door.

There was a crash against the door, and Tom jumped up.

Someone pounded on the door. "Is my boy in there! I come for my boy!"

Suddenly I was smothered by Ellie, who threw herself and the quilt across the full length of the couch, burying me beneath her. Her wet hair was in my face. Her weight pressed down on me and I could not move. With one eye, I could see through her hair along her neck. The door burst open and there was an angry man. Tom moved in front of me, and I could not see anymore.

"Where's my boy?" said the man.

Tom said, "I don't know what you're talking about. Get out of my house." He stepped towards the man, moving slightly so that I could see past him. The bottom hinge of the door was broken, and the door leaned inside the room at a crazy angle. The man was wet from walking in the rain. He was a big man whose head almost touched the top of the door-frame. He reached outside and grabbed a woman, pulling her into view.

She was wearing a raincoat and dark glasses. She had a kerchief on her head, tied under her chin. Her face was puffy, and the side of her mouth was dark and swollen. I did not im-mediately recognize her as my mother, but when she spoke I moved against Ellie, and Ellie pressed me down tighter until I could barely breath.

My mother said, "I'm so sorry. I had no choice."

My father said, "Where's my boy?"

"He's not here," said Tom.

"Where is he?" asked my father. He gripped my mother's arm and gave her a shake in front of Tom.

Tom said, "Let go of that woman."

"Not till I know where my boy is."

Tom said, "I don't know where he is. He went off today, with some friends." Tom was standing with his legs apart and his hands, clenched, by his sides.

My father looked past Tom at Ellie, wrapped up in the quilt. "You there. You tell me where's my boy."

Ellie said, "Go fuck off, White Man! Don't come messing around here!"

My father stepped forward with my mother, and Tom stepped up to him. My father pulled a knife out of his pocket and stuck Tom in the belly. Tom grunted as he fell back, but he didn't lose his balance. My mother screamed and pulled away. "You promised you wouldn't hurt anyone! You son of a bitch!" She grabbed his face and dug her fingernails into him as Ellie rose off me. My father stabbed my mother with the knife, and she crumpled to the floor. She gasped, and I saw her body shaking like someone shivering in the cold. Her fingers twitched. Ellie screamed, and she came at my father with the quilt, pushing it in his face. I did not move. I was terrified. My father had come to kill me. He had a knife and was killing everyone. Tom was holding his belly with one hand, and he began to throw up on the floor. Ellie's black eyes had narrowed and she kept screaming, pushing at my father who was swinging the knife in the air. My father yelled "You fucking red-nigger bitch!" trying to pull the quilt off his head. Ellie looked around quickly and saw Tom's shotgun in a corner. She suddenly jumped back and ran for the gun, and my father pulled at the quilt and uncovered his face and he saw me pressed into the couch and yelled "SAMUEL!" and his hands were raised, and then the room exploded with the thunder of the shotgun and I saw the hand with the knife blown into bloody pieces. My father flew backwards, a deep sickening roar rising out of his chest as he stumbled out of the door into the darkness and the rain. Outside the rain pounded and the thunder rolled and lightning streaked as the dogs tore into my father. Ellie came into the dark doorway and, holding the shotgun at her side, pointed it and pulled the trigger, jerking when it exploded again. The baby, who was sleeping in the basket of laundry, was crying. I was shaking and gasping for breath, and the rain was blowing through the broken door. The wind was whipping Ellie's black hair around her naked body. Outside the dogs were snarling, and a man was screaming.

There
Lies
My
Mother

I stared at the television, the only light in the room. On the floor in front of the television lay a woman. I refused to recognize her. Her head kerchief was in disarray and hair trailed on the floor. Her sunglasses were knocked upwards on one side and a dead eye stared unblinking at the ceiling. The front of the woman's coat was soaked in blood that looked black, like wet paint shining on a canvas. Her mouth was open as though she was singing, and there *was* a woman singing on the television. I did not move at all. I was aware that Ellie was crawling on the floor beside Tom. I didn't look at them. The next thing I remember was Tom's brother, Marcus, and Jimmy Sky. They were in the house. Marcus knelt down in front of me and said, "Samuel, are you alright?" Jimmy Sky stripped off his big flannel shirt and carefully put it on Ellie because she was naked and cold. I don't know why I did what I did next, but something came over me. I moved my hand and touched a splatter of blood with my finger. I looked at it, and then made a figure of a stick man with blood on the arm of the couch.

The yard was full of whirling lights. A policeman in a dark uniform asked me to tell him what happened, and I said, "I don't remember."

He asked me if the woman being lifted onto a stretcher by two cops was my mother, and I told him, "Yes."

"Who did this to your mother?"

"A man," I said.

"What man?"

"I don't know."

"What happened to the man?"

"The dogs ate him up."

Marcus and his woman, Lucy, stayed that night. Ellie was at the hospital with Tom, who had his stomach operated on. Marcus let the dogs stay inside. They were wet and bloody, and they stayed alongside the couch where Marcus and I slept. Lucy stayed up, with a bucket and a scrub brush, and washed the floor and the walls. Jimmy Sky fixed the broken door. I woke up crying, because I wanted my mother. Marcus said, "Your mother is gone now."

"Where did she go?"

Marcus said, "The Creator took away her breath."

"Is she dead?"

"It was her time to go," said Marcus.

"My mother says a soul is a star inside you."

Marcus thought for a moment and nodded. "Yes," he said. "Your mother was right. But the Creator gives you just so many breaths, and when you use them up you go back where you came from."

Then he covered me again with the red cross quilt and told me to sleep. I liked Marcus, I trusted him, and it was comforting to have him protect me that night. As I drifted back to sleep the only thing I knew was that the long wait was over.

In the time that followed, I would slowly come to understand the events of the night my mother had been killed: How Aunt Molly had called Marcus on the telephone after my mother had first stopped there with my father—buying time— and how the dogs had not eaten up my father, nor had Ellie's shotgun blasts killed him. He had survived the gun and the dogs and was taken away in an ambulance beside the body of my mother and my cousin Tom, who was writhing from the wound in his stomach. Tom would be gone for a long time, but when he came home he would be smiling again, ready to begin the long healing.

At night, standing in the yard with the dogs when the sky was full of stars, more than usual and twice as bright, I knew then many people had died that day. On other nights, when the stars were few, their glow dim, I knew that many people had been born to rob the sky of all that energy. I believed it.

After my mother was buried in the yard of His Majesty's Chapel to the Mohawks, among a company of dead that included statesmen and paupers, my Aunt Molly gave me an old silver brooch in the heart-shaped effigy of an owl, the guardian of the night.

The day was bright and warm, and we walked among the many tombstones, tipped over from time, and my nearly sightless Aunt Molly pointed out from memory the places of my ancestors—my grandfather and grandmother side by side, their parents side by side, uncles and aunts and cousins spanning three centuries. We weaved among the pitted grey stones, Aunt Molly saying, *"Daho. . . Daho,"* excuse me, whenever we stepped on someone below the earth. She worried about our bad manners and apologized to the dead. "When I was a girl," she said, "we used to put moccasins on the dead with holes cut in the soles and pebbles between their toes, so the spirit path back to haunt the living would be too rough. I guess it works. I've never been haunted by an old-timer."

Aunt Bess joined us on our walk among the shade trees and the tombstones. I led them at a slow pace, one deaf and one blind, both of them talking away like crazy people. I learned then that old people love graveyards. They found comfort in renewing memories of old friends and family, and they read aloud the names on the tombstones, talking about the people as though they were not dead but away on a celestial holiday.

When we paused before the grave of Mary Sawyer, Aunt Bess said, "When I was a girl I was up here with your grandfather, and he was an old man. He pointed down at that place and said, 'There lies my mother.' No one ever knew who Uncle Samuel's mother was before that because he never talked about her, but then we knew. Mary Sawyer was the granddaughter of a chief who led the people to this place in 1784. He's buried up beside the chapel, but he's all in pieces. About a hundred years ago some white medical students stole his body and dissected it. I think they got all the parts back. I wonder how those whites would feel if we dug up their grandpas?"

Ellie called out to me then, and I turned my two old aunts around and brought them back to the little white chapel. Ellie took my hand and we went into the chapel alone. We walked up the yellow carpeted aisle and we sat right on the first bench. As she talked to me I stared at the stained glass windows. They showed the twelve stations of the Holy Cross, but the people were all Indians carrying that heavy burden. Ellie said to me, "Do you want to stay with me? If you want to stay you can."

I told her I would stay until my mother came back.

Ellie put her arms around me and hugged me hard against her breasts, and she said, "Samuel, your mother is not coming back. We buried your mother today. She is in the earth outside."

I said, "Aunt Molly told me she would come back."

Ellie looked at me strangely. "How can that be?" she asked.

"There are no holes or pebbles in her moccasins," I said, "and she will come back." I was scared though. The woman we had buried was my mother, but when we had come into the chapel and I was brought before all those people to honor her, lying in the coffin, she did not look like my mother. There was a resemblance, but death had changed her into another person with shrunken features. I believed that my old mother would come back.

Ellie told me I would one day see my mother again, but it

would be among the stars. The stars again. Everything darkness and night, the stars above me, and me below, insignificant and alone. I began to cry, and Ellie held onto me until the minister told her to go home.

August evolved into September, the dark green of late summer faded as corn in the fields and squash on the vines matured for harvest. The days were growing shorter. Tom went back to work in the mill on the second shift after awhile. When he first came home he mostly lay on the couch, and when he needed to get up Ellie hooked her arm in his and pulled him to a sitting position. He didn't eat a lot of food, and he lost weight. Ellie said he looked like an old man with hollow cheeks. After Tom got better he was hungry all the time, and he took two lunch pails to work.

In the evenings, when Tom was gone, Ellie and I worked together. One time we got a bag of horsetails. Ellie skinned the bone out of them and gave them to me. I used a curved knife and scraped the meat and fat off the inside of the skin. Then I salted them and strung them on a cord to hang above the stove. Sometimes a person would come to the door and my dogs would bark, but it was only an old man, a mask carver, coming to buy a horsetail. Ellie gave me a quarter from each tail we sold. Ellie knew all the old men who came to the door. They always stood just outside and never came inside. They stared at me and I stared at them, dark in the shadow of night beyond the light inside. One time a man came back after a week and bought another tail. When he paid Ellie, he gave her a miniature face with a broken nose. It was about the size of her palm, painted black with a red mouth and white hair. She said, "Nia:wen," thanking him, and when he left she gave it to me, saying, "Put him by your bed, covered with a handkerchief. He'll watch over you."

"Is it true?" I asked, and Ellie told me that Broken Nose was the Great Protector, second only to the Creator, who had won a challenge against him. Each of them claimed the power to move a mountain, and each of them did, but the Creator moved the mountain farther and won. The loser fell down against the earth, dishonored, and broke his nose, rising up with a grimace of pain and a disfigured face. The Creator recognized his efforts and gave him the power to cure and to protect. That is what Ellie told me, and she said it was true. "But these little miniature masks are very powerful, too strong for a little one like you. So what you do is put it by your bed where no one can see it."

"How can I do that?"

"Hang it on a nail and cover it with a white cloth, maybe one of Tom's handkerchiefs. That way the power will be there, but not too strong. You don't want to have bad dreams about Haduii." She almost whispered his name. She told me not to talk about such things, saying that it was a secret and sacred society of members who cured the longhouse people. We weren't members so we had to respect their privacy. She said it was OK for us to hang masks on the wall because they weren't alive; they had no openings in their mouths to feed them sacred foods. They were gifts from old-timers, so she figured it was alright to have them. But she still sort of acted like something unseen was sneaking up behind when she talked about it.

I put Broken Nose on a nail above my bed, and every night I asked him to watch out for me.

Ellie and Tom had some horses in the barn, and a pig. In

the mornings I went out with Tom and turned out the horses and fed the pig. There was a young Appaloosa stallion called Star Blanket because he had a black rump flecked with white. He was a special horse, and he belonged to Ellie. Tom bought him as a gift, and Ellie said he was sacred because she had a dream. Star Blanket was prancing across the sky, walking on the backs of birds that flew out of a tunnel of wind. In this dream the white flecks on his dark rump twinkled like stars, and Ellie told me that when she rode Star Blanket she felt as if they were flying together. When I rode with them, sitting tight behind Ellie with my arms wrapped around her ribs, Ellie's hair, smelling fresh from brown soap, covered my face, and I felt like I was thrown against a black sky, riding through stars on Ellie's sacred horse. All time vanished. The sound of the horse's hooves became thunder. When Ellie brought the horse back to the barn and lowered me to the ground, it took a long time for my balance to return. Although I knew I was standing still, it seemed as if the world rocked back and forth. Tom said I better not ever climb steel with such a bad sense of balance, and he knew about that, having once been a connector on a construction crew.

Shoe
Laces

Tom decided that it was time to kill the pig. Many people came to help. There was Aunt Molly and Aunt Bess, Uncle Lewis and Jimmy Sky, and a flock of neighbors and kids. Tom pulled down some fence rails from around the big corn patch and everyone worked, row after row, filling bags or baskets with dry brown ears of corn. All the ears of corn were piled high in the big yard behind the house. The men built a big fire. In the middle of the fire they put a fifty-five-gallon oil drum and filled it with water. I thought we were going to cook all that corn.

The women sat around the pile of corn and stripped back the husks, braiding the husks into ropes with the corn hanging off, twenty-four ears to a rope. They were beautiful to look at. Some of the braids of corn were made up of plain white corn with short cobs, some were white corn on long cobs, and the rest were stubby little ears made up like ragged rainbows, all the colored kernels glinting in the sunlight, red and blue and green and yellow, just like the autumn leaves. Aunt Molly brought me an ear of corn and asked me if I could count. When I shook my head no, she counted off the rows of kernels for me. "See, there are only eight rows. That's *Indian* corn. White man's corn has twelve or more rows, but they call it Indian corn 'cause it's colored. But that isn't right. We have been growing this same corn long before the white man came here, but they had to change it, name it after us, and take all the credit."

While the women were making up the corn braids, the men got a tall tripod of iron pipes and set it up over the drum of water. They hung a pulley from the top of the tripod. Then Tom and some other men got the pig out of the pen and pushed it along—it was so round and fat that it jiggled as it walked toward the field of empty cornstalks. When they got it inside the corn patch they put all the fence rails back in place, and a bunch of kids climbed up to sit along the top rails, excited to watch. I was sitting at the corner when Tom got down on his knees in front of the pig. Some of the men were holding onto the pig, bracing their shoulders up against it, while one of them held its head up by the snout. Tom slipped a long butcher's knife out of a sheath and tapped the pig's throat and neck with two fingers. Then he put the point of the knife under the pig's jaw, sticking it in very fast, cutting down and deep. I didn't know what to think because I didn't know that was going to happen. The pig's eyes widened, and a horrible, loud cry like the screech of braking car tires filled the air as the pig lunged right over Tom, knocking him flat on his back. The pig trampled Tom right into the corn patch. The men holding the pig jumped away and laughed at Tom. It was a big joke to see Tom get stomped on. The pig ran like crazy, smashing down the cornstalks, gushing blood all over. All the time the pig kept screaming, and I wanted the awful sound to stop. The men hooted when Tom stood up. He had blood all over him, and when I saw him like that I became very scared. I thought that maybe he had been stabbed again when the pig trampled him, and the sight of all that blood brought back the night when my mother had died. I closed my eyes, but I could still hear the pig's high bellowing. I leaned my head against my knees and squeezed my eyelids as hard as I could, but it did not keep out the sound of the dying pig. The feeling of being sick came over me, and then suddenly I was transported. I was weightless; I couldn't feel my body. My stomach rose up through my throat and flooded my mouth.

Uncle Lewis found me lying on the ground. He shook me by my shoulders, and I woke up among the corn. I had fainted and toppled off the split-rail fence. The back of my head pounded. Uncle Lewis said, with his halting lisp, "*Th*am, come and *th*crape . . . the hog." The men had dragged the pig out of the corn patch on ropes attached to steel hooks fixed through the tendons on its hind legs. It left a dark wet trail in the yard, right up to the drum of boiling water. They hauled the pig on the pulley and dunked it head down into the rolling water. It must have been really dead after that. Anyway, it didn't make a sound. They pulled it out and rolled it on the ground, and they went to work scraping off the bristles with curved knives. It was like they were shaving the beard of a big fat white man with pink skin. All those long hairs blew around the yard. Some women had another kettle set in the coals beside the drum, and they chopped up onions and carrots into a boiling batch of dried yellow peas. Uncle Lewis put a knife in my hand and guided it. We leaned over the rump of the pig, and the knife made a rasping sound as we scraped bristles. Jimmy Sky pushed us out of the way and ran a knife up the pig's belly. The insides of the pig tumbled out on the ground. Its guts were shiny, blue and grey and dark, and they smelled like seaweed rotting in the sun. One of the older kids jumped in with a pocket knife and grabbed something, cutting fast.

Tom laughed, "Kickball!" when the boy ran away. The boy acted like a thief, but they let him get away with the bladder. Some of the other boys cheered when he waved it at them. They called him a warrior.

People, men and women, descended on the pig and they cut it apart. Jimmy Sky chopped the backbone with a hatchet until the pig fell in two halves. The women took away the head and cooked it in another pot. Tom sawed up the ribs, and someone else twisted a knife through the joints until the hams lay on the ground. Jimmy sliced the bacons out, and Uncle Lewis sawed off the hocks. Peter Killdeer backed up his truck and mounted a sausage grinder on the tailgate. Ellie brought him a big plastic bucket and all the scraps went through the grinder.

Aunt Bess, with thin old fingers, massaged the greasy sausage and dumped handfuls of sage, thyme, and other herbs into the bucket. Dogs were running into the corn patch, licking blood off the brown stalks. It was a feast of blood. I couldn't help but notice the designs left on the earth by footprints, and it seemed as though we had painted the earth with blood, vibrant and alive. It would not last after the next rain, but it would remain in my memory for many years.

At noontime we had pea soup with pig-head meat and round pulls of fry bread, hot from a skillet of grease. Ellie and I ate out of bowls, and we drank cider from paper cups. Some people brought tin cups and drank their soup from them. Aunt Molly and Aunt Bess sat together on the grass, sharing one piece of fry bread that had been dipped in the soup. They didn't eat too much, those old ladies; they shared a lot. The warrior boy came up to Tom. He had the pig's bladder, and he handed it to Tom, who tied off one end with a string the boy gave him and then stuck a paper soda straw in the other end and inflated the bladder until it was stretched pretty big and tight. Tom tied the other end with the remaining string, and the warrior boy went off to play a game of kickball with his friends.

Ellie said, "Why don't you go and play with them?"

I said, "I ate too much soup and fry bread." I really didn't want to tell Ellie that the warrior boy with the knife scared me, but Ellie said, "It might be a good idea for you to play with Carver. If you be his friend he'll look out for you someday. And someday you'll look out for someone smaller than you. It works that way."

"Is that true?" I asked.

Ellie said, "Go and play with Carver and the other boys. Play hard . . . and don't cry if you get hurt."

So I put down my bowl and spoon and got to my feet and

slowly walked up to the field of play. I stood there for a long time watching the guys wrestle over the ball, and when it was kicked near me I ran over to grab it, but Carver beat me to it and he swung his elbow at me, hitting me in the face. I fell out of the way and rolled over in the grass, putting my hands over my face. When I looked up I saw Ellie, and she was saying, "Go on, get him!" I felt my right eye swell up and it hurt a lot, but I got up and ran into the game.

Carver was pushing people around and he was kicking the ball. I came up behind him. When he turned around I hit him as hard as I could, and he grabbed his nose and fell down. I picked up the bladder ball with both hands and started to run. But I didn't know where I was running, and with all those guys chasing me I just ran, the way Ellie and I had run in the field, around and around, dodging and ducking, until finally they all caught up with me, including Carver, and buried me beneath their weight. They were all hard elbows, knees, and hot breath.

Carver was especially rough on me, but I tried to watch out for him. He wanted the ball more than he wanted me, and I pretended to drop it just before Carver got me, so that he beat up someone else.

There weren't any teams, and there wasn't a goal. The only object seemed to be to get hold of the ball and run with it for as long as you could. One boy busted his arm under the pile, and his mother carried him to their truck. Another guy got a busted mouth and stood off to the side bent over, his hands on his knees, spitting blood between his bare feet. His name was Raymond, and he had a curved backbone.

Slowly the game got smaller. One by one, the work ended for the day, and the people grabbed their kids and left, until there were only a couple of us, hot and worn out.

Turtle Belly

Jimmy Sky took all the ham and hocks and bacon to soak them in brine and smoke them with wood chips. He would bring them back in a couple of weeks. Aunt Molly took all the sausage, wrapped and tied in wax paper, to her freezer. We kept the roasts and chops. Tom and I carried all the braids of corn to the barn and hung over a hundred braids from the rafters. Tom said we would eat that corn all winter in soup and stew. It was after dark when we were finished, and we came inside to a warm house. I didn't realize how cold it was outside, but already the frost was beginning to sparkle. Ellie was nursing her baby, lying back on the sofa, both of them half asleep. Tom loosened the ties on his boots and sank deep in his soft chair. I sat on the floor between Tom's legs and leaned back against his thigh. He gave me a hug with his knees, and we sat in the dark watching the TV. I thought about the big slow pig, how for the past couple of months I had carried out the table scraps in a slop bucket every day, how the people had chopped up that pig into little pieces, wrapped up neatly. In the morning there would be no trace of the pig. No blood in the fields or hair blowing in the yard. Tom said, "Look out the window. It's snowing."

We watched the snow brush against the window. The flakes were fat and weightless, the kind of wide lazy snow that does not rush toward the ground but suddenly lifts upwards on a draft. The snow was playing in the sky, and we just watched it. After a while Tom began to snore, and Ellie was asleep on the couch with the baby lying on her belly. I got up for my red cross quilt, and I came back with it, wrapped up, and lay down on the floor, leaning against Tom's legs. Besides Ellie, Tom was my best friend, and I loved him. Tom had said to me, "You don't have to worry about your dad, he won't get you. They locked him up for a long time." Tom said I would be a man and

50

my father would be old when he came out. Tom said my father might not live that long, so I shouldn't even think about it. Tom said my father was a crazy man to kill my mother.

My right eye was closed up from when Carver elbowed me during the game of bladder ball, and my face hurt. I was so tired now, and everyone was sleeping. I looked past the window at the snow coming down. Some of the flakes landed on the glass and melted. The water seeped down the panes like tears on a shiny blackboard. I missed my mother so much. I thought about her all the time. I tried to think about her. I forced up memories. She was so tall and skinny, wearing a brown skirt and jacket that was tight in the waist; her hair was pulled back and knotted above her collar. She had high bony cheeks and a wide mouth that was always smiling when she was with me. She looked a little bit like her cousin, Ellie, but Ellie wasn't so lean or tall. Ellie was made up of muscle and strength. My mother was softer, more quiet, and when she held me she whispered with warm breath in my ear, "I love you." Now, here I was, warm against Tom's legs, everyone but me sleeping, and the first snow of the year coming down like a cold blanket to cover the ground where my mother lay.

I rose up from the floor, still wrapped up in the red cross quilt, and went to the window. I looked north, towards the chapel, with so much longing for my mother. She must have been so cold out there. I didn't know any better then, but later I learned that the earth only freezes to about four feet in winter. That's the reason why people are always buried six feet down, so they stay warm inside their mother forever and ever.

Then I saw right under the window the curled forms of the two dogs. The snow was falling on them, and they were still sleeping. After awhile one of them, the black one, raised his head and looked right at me. And then, as if he sensed nothing mattered, he fell over asleep again. I felt cold then, an emptiness that froze me all over, and I shivered past the sleeping people and rolled up in my quilt on the floor beside the hissing woodstove. The heat blasted me; I felt my hair on fire; but I could not get enough of it to warm all the coldness inside me.

I'm not sure who, but someone carried me to bed after I was asleep, because I woke up the next morning, warm and happy, with a sore eye, to a glistening white-diamond world spotted with snowy dog tracks. It was early, and when I looked out the window under the eaves I saw Ellie riding Star Blanket out in the field, her long black hair whipping the air as she galloped in wide circles. The horse snorted steam, and Ellie urged him faster and faster. I liked watching Ellie ride. She had wide hips that rose up and down and a round behind. Her breasts bounced against an old brown canvas coat and her nostrils flared, her jaws set tight, her eyes dark and serious. I had never seen a woman on a horse, and I was fascinated by all that movement and speed. I had never seen a woman nurse an infant, or pull her pants down in an old wooden outhouse, or take a bath in a tin washtub by a woodstove, until I came to live with Ellie. I liked it, but I wasn't sure why. I just did. Perhaps, it was that she was so unlike my mother, despite them being close cousins, and Ellie was alive. My mother was dead, and I needed to be with this living woman so much that I could not take my eyes off her. I stared at her all the time, as if I was now fixing my love upon her. And then, that morning, as I watched Ellie so intently, something happened that scared me. I didn't know how to understand what had happened, and what had happened was that I had not thought of my mother as I had every waking morning for the past three months. Getting out of bed, warm and rested, seeing Ellie riding across the frozen pasture, wishing Ellie would come in soon and greet me with her wide bright smile and hug me up to her—I had not thought of my dead mother. Why didn't I think of my mother? How could such a thing happen? Maybe my memory was dying, too.

I watched Ellie bring Star Blanket back to the barn, and I dressed really fast in old jeans and a red flannel shirt. Pulling on my socks and black canvas sneakers, I quickly climbed down the ladder-like staircase and beat her to the kitchen. When she came in, all frosted up and red cheeked, I stood there angry because she had made me forget my mother.

"Tie my shoes," I said, kicking up my feet.

Ellie looked down at me as she unwrapped her coat and hung it on a peg. "No," she said, turning her back to me.

"Tie my shoes!"

Ellie did not even bother to look over at me. She rubbed her hands together over the hot woodstove, then walked to the wooden countertop.

I pulled myself up on a stool beside the woodstove, swinging my feet back and forth, waiting for her to change her mind and tie my shoes. When Ellie did turn around she thrust out a bowl of cornflakes and milk with a spoon perched on it. I took it on my lap and held it tightly with both hands. Ellie carried a cup of coffee past me into the big room, turned on the television, and sat down on the sofa. I very slowly spread my fingers on the bowl, trying to see how lightly I could hold it. I watched the back of Ellie. The bowl was slipping. Ellie was sipping coffee and watching a game show. The bowl was weightless. I just let it fall. The bowl shattered and the floor was a mess, but Ellie did not even look up.

I sat on the stool all morning, waiting.

Once Ellie got up and brought the baby downstairs to eat at her breast. When the baby fell asleep, she put it on the couch beside her. She got up and walked past the mess on the floor, poured herself another cup of coffee, and went back to the couch.

I said very loudly, "I want some lunch!" But Ellie did not care about me. She didn't like me at all. Ellie talked to the baby, saying, "Ionienere rahksah," Good boy! She held him high in the air and brought him down on her shoulder, saying, "sack of potatoes!" When the baby slept she went to her chores, sweeping the wide plank floor in the big room, scrubbing out some diapers in the old chipped sink in the corner of the kitchen, hanging them on a line above the woodstove.

I watched her with narrow eyes. She washed and rinsed her hair in the sink, too, and then rubbed it with a towel while leaning backwards over the woodstove. The tips of her long hair swept across the black-iron stove top with a steamy hissing sound. She walked around the house with her hair hanging in damp strings that stuck to her cheeks.

After awhile I just stared at my untied shoes. My mother would have tied my shoes. My mother would have done everything for me. When I looked up, Ellie was standing on the other side of the big mess of broken bowl and cereal.

"You're not my mother!" I said.

She just kept staring at me.

"I want my mother!"

Ellie sidestepped the mess on the floor, avoiding the broken bowl with her bare feet. She kneeled down in front of me and slowly tied my shoes, and then she reached up and put her arms around me. I found myself holding her so tightly as she carried me around the big room, and I was crying against her shoulder with my face pressed into her wet hair. I was blind and crying, and Ellie rocked me from side to side, her voice a soft hum. "I know, Baby. . . . I know," she whispered, pressing all her heat against me, smelling like woodsmoke and talcum powder, her heart beating as fast as mine. I could feel her heart quick as a bird, and she squeezed me so that I could hardly breathe, until it all poured out of me, "I hate my mother. My mother died and I hate her. Why did my mother leave me alone . . .?"

Ellie kept kissing my ear, my cheek, and she said, "It's alright, Baby. Everything's going to be alright. Ellie loves you."

We rocked together until I lay limp against her shoulder, and then she sat us down on the floor in the big room. She untied my laces, smiling, wiping tears off her face, and she said, "Let me teach you how to tie your shoes."

Earth
Paints

I sat right up front, and I didn't ever look back because when I did everyone stared at me. I kept my head low and didn't talk too much. Sometimes I'd say, "Yes," or "No," if I had to, but mostly I tried to make myself as small as possible. The teacher was white, but she knew some Mohawk words, more than I did. She said *yes* was *henh* and *no* was *iah*. Everyone called her *Wenhniserahawi*—Teacher. I didn't want to sit right up front, but Donna made everyone change desks so I could sit in the first seat in the middle row. There were five rows, all grumbling and dark eyed because it was my fault they all lost their seats.

It was November, and Ellie told me I had to go to the school. She said I couldn't just stay home all the time. I promised to work more—help her with the horses and the baby. "I have an idea," I said. "You could be my teacher!" But Ellie said everyone had to go to school or else they'd be like wild animals.

The first day Donna told everyone to work while she got some bags of clothes out of the cloakroom. I was standing by her big wooden desk, and she held clothes against me to see if they would fit.

She asked the class to bring in extra clothes for me, and a girl named Anne said, "I have a dress I don't wear no more." Everybody laughed.

I hated it there, and I hated all the people. I hated the classroom, because it had big windows so I could see outside, watch the snow falling, see the wind shake the branches. I hated the desks, bolted to the floor in a line, with wooden lids that lifted up and a hole in the right corner with a bottle of blue ink stuck in it. The blackboard covered the entire front wall, except for where the door led to the cloakroom. The only thing I didn't hate were all the paintings tacked to the walls. I never saw so many colors—orange and green stick people, swirling lemon dogs, purple chimneys, and blue trees. Some of the colors were so bright they were like acid—copper green and raspberry—and they leaped off the paper at me. That's the only thing I liked in first grade—paint.

At Christmastime Tom bought me a new pair of boots, and Ellie gave me a knife. Aunt Molly made me a pair of socks. I liked the boots best because they didn't belong to a dead kid. It's hard to walk in ghost boots.

My teacher, Donna, drove up to the house on Christmas Day, and she pushed past the dogs to bring me a present.

Ellie said, "You didn't need to do that. We gave Sam some presents."

Donna said, "I got a little something for all my kids. You don't want him to be the only one in school without a present from his teacher, do you?"

Tom said, "That's real nice of you. Nia:wen."

I showed her my knife. "Tom said he was goin' to get a whole truckload of horsetails from the slaughterhouse, and I can skin them and sell them."

Donna kneeled down and held out a present wrapped in red and green paper. There was a golden bow on it. "If I give you this," she said, "Will you promise to work harder and use a pencil?"

"What's in it?"

"Something you'll like—but you have to promise."

After I promised she let me open it up, and it was a pad of paper and a set of watercolor paints with brushes.

Ellie told me to say thank you, and I did. It wasn't that I didn't want to say thank you, it was that I was thinking about having to keep my promise. If Donna had given me something like a book or a hat, I might have been able to figure out a way to break my promise. But *paints?* I was trapped, and we all knew it.

It wasn't long before I was at the little table in the kitchen with a tin cup of water, making pictures.

I heard Donna say, when she thought I wasn't listening, "The only thing he does is paint. He won't talk or play or even try to write his alphabet."

Tom said, "I'll talk to him."

I didn't care. I was making a perfect picture. It was a big pig with a knife stuck in it, running around with bright red blood everywhere. The blood was like a river, and I made long, flowing scarlet brushstrokes across the paper. Then I carefully tore the sheet off the pad and set it aside to dry as I made another picture. It was a big man picture, and my dogs were all around him, not just two dogs, but a dozen. He was afraid of my dogs. It was a great picture of my dogs eating him.

Sometimes, when I didn't feel like talking to anyone, I would paint pictures. Sometimes, when I remembered things, I'd paint pictures. I worked at my alphabet; I kept my promise, but I was better making paintings. I couldn't write all the words I felt, but I could make a picture that showed everything I wanted to say. One black cloud on a piece of paper, all the blue raindrops, said more than my alphabet could. I painted all the time. I still have stacks of paintings from back then, somewhere.

In the spring, when the snows melted and the water ran down the dirt driveway in swift rivulets, I noticed colors in the waters. I bent down and stared at the colors—a muddy yellow and a rusty red. I slowly walked along the cold channels, won-

Turtle Belly

dering where these colors came from, and then I saw them. In two layers, near the road, where the wash had undercut a bank and was flowing past the raw, open earth. Wiping my finger through the layer of red, then rubbing the color against my thumb, I saw a color that excited me. I never knew *where* color came from, and in that moment, without anyone having to tell me, I knew that color came from the earth. I could not have been more elated—I streaked my fingers and hands with yellow and red. I rubbed my face with colors, cold spring colors, red and yellow and black, while looking at my reflection in the moving water. I was staring into the water flowing across the earth, but I could see the sky reflected past my own mirrored image. I could not imagine a more wonderful thing than seeing the sky, the earth, the silvery water, and myself painted like a warrior, all coming together. That was the closest I ever felt to myself, and it would always be that way. When I painted, it was only me, and the aloneness was me being my best friend. If most people are really honest, there isn't much to like about yourself. Mostly, we are all just big liars and no different than dogs running in packs. But if you find something you can really do alone and don't care what anyone thinks, then you have yourself as a friend. No one can take that from you. Most people don't have that. I found that out. Most people think they got it big time when people stare at their shiny car or give them a ribbon for growing a fat hog. That's nothing. I knew that art was the only thing. It's like you want something today, and it's gone tomorrow. But art was something only you did, and no one else could be inside you then. That's when I guess I realized that there was something in me, but I didn't know exactly what it was. I didn't even know it was called *art*. I just knew that color was infinite and it seemed to soak into my fingers and hands like a disease. The fluidity of the water and the glinting sun distorted my projected self. Clouds, like handfuls of white goose down, drifted in the water, and so did tree limbs in full bud. Birds were flying in the water, and the gravel rolled against the sky.

When Ellie called me for supper I ran inside. She looked at me and said, "Go wash up."

When I looked in the bathroom mirror all the earth paint had dried, caked and cracked. The life of the color had died, and I was just a grimy little boy. There were no clouds or birds in the mirror, no sunlight, no movement. Just me, covered in dry mud.

Ellie said the old-timers called red ochre "Holy Paint."

I looked at the bits of earth color under my nails, and I didn't feel so dirty.

Corn
Soup

The first time I rode Star Blanket alone I busted my ten-year-old head against a tree.

I was knocked out, senseless, and I dreamed that I saw a small man who came from underneath a fern and knelt down with cupped hands to drink from the runoff of a spring.

He was small enough to hide behind a skunk cabbage or roll into the shadow of a boot print. He was dark like the old-timers, brown and leathery, but he wasn't old. He was not young either—he seemed to be no age or all ages. He wore a piece of hide around his waist like a skirt.

When he finished drinking he splashed water on his face and combed his fingers through long black hair. He looked up at me, startled, and then spoke to me in a strange *hyo-hyo-hyo* chanting language, saying that if I ever told anyone I had seen him, or where, I would never see a little person again. Then he said he was hungry for corn mush. He also wanted tobacco. All the while I knew that he spoke a strange language, an old language, and I knew that if I could understand all this then I too was part of the old language, the old ways. He said to me, "Turtle Belly, come here often and bring *oien:kwe'onwe*, tobacco, and you will make me happy."

I said, "How do you know my name?"

He answered, "Because it is my name also."

I asked him, "Is that true?"

And he answered, saying, "I am that small part of you that holds onto the past, that knows all about the earth."

Then he danced in a circle, singing a hyo-hyo-hyo song that reminded me of my dead mother, and it made me love the earth and the things that came from the earth and the sky dome above the earth with its morning sun and its night stars and moon. He stomped his little feet and shook his shoulders as if trying to throw a burden off his back, and his voice made a guttural *glunk-glunk-glunk* sound, like the rhythm of a water drum. His eyes were as dark as the night, but they had the sparkle of stars, and when he looked at me I thought of my mother among the stars. Then he told me that we all must go back to earth. I wasn't confused.

I told the little Turtle Belly dancer that I would bring him tobacco and corn mush, because I felt then that feeding him was really another way of feeding myself, because we were the same. We came from the same Creator and would return. That is how I really felt, and I knew that he understood.

He said, "Ioienere." Good!

It was as if, as he danced, the days and nights whirled around me. And then an ancient snapping turtle with moss growing on the rim of his back came out of the undergrowth, and the little man sat down upon its back and was carried away.

Tom picked me up and carried me home.

I think I was a little crazy.

Later Tom told me that when the horse came home without a rider, he came looking for me after a while. When he could not find me, he called his brother and Jimmy Sky, and they called others, and they searched through the woods all night long. They found me at dawn, with a busted head, dancing in a circle. Tom said I was singing hyo-hyo-hyo quietly to myself.

When I came home from the clinic, I asked Tom if he ever saw little people in the woods.

He said, "My dad told me that sometimes folks leave little bows and arrows, or bags of corn, or miniature canoes in the woods for the little people, and he said that if I ever told someone I saw a little person, I would never see another one."

"Did *you* ever see one?" I asked.

Tom said, "I don't remember," and then he changed the subject. "How does your head feel?"

But I persisted. "Do you believe in little people?"

"The old-timers believe. They believe the whole forest is inhabited by spirits—good and bad—and even a parallel world made up of tiny people."

"What's a parallel?"

"Looking in a mirror is a parallel. The forest, if you look at it right, is a sort of mirror for what we do." Then Tom stared at me, kind of crooked, worried. "You bumped your head pretty hard, lay out there all night, had a long time to think. Sometimes when you're all alone your mind gets to believe in things, sometimes you just sort of overhear things the old guys talk about, like Jimmy Sky talking about the old ways, say while you're hanging around the barn. Sometimes you don't even know you're hearing things until one day, say when you've bumped your brain, your head gets filled with a dream that seems to make sense. Then maybe you might think it wasn't a dream at all." Tom questioned me with his eyes.

I said, "Like maybe I might have dreamed that a little person asked me for tobacco and corn mush 'cause maybe I heard it somewhere before?"

Tom said, "I suppose it could work that way, yes."

I said, "But if I never heard it before, thinking real hard so that I know I never heard it before, then it would be a pretty funny dream, eh?"

"A pretty funny one, alright," said Tom. "I suppose that would be a dream that would seem almost real."

"It sure would," I said. "It would make you almost want to take one of your smokes and leave it out in the woods . . . and some mush, too."

Tom smiled. "Well, if it was a dream that seemed real, you

might want to use Indian tobacco. The kind Jonas grows, not the store-bought kind like a smoke. A person would have to get some Indian tobacco from Jonas."

"What about mush?" I asked.

"Well, I suppose you'd have to cook up a kettle and give the first spoonful, if you were generous. You could put it on a little piece of birch bark curled up like a bowl."

"It would be the right thing to do, if you believed a dream was real," I said.

Tom said, "I guess everything's real, if you believe it hard enough."

"Of course," I said, "I never actually told anyone I *saw* a little person, but I might have dreamed it. You don't get in trouble talking about a dream."

Tom answered me, saying, "No, not likely anyone would blame a fellow who cracked his head on a tree for having a dream. But dreams are very important."

Then I narrowed my eyes and asked Tom, "I kind of have a taste for corn mush. Maybe you could ask Ellie to cook up a kettle?"

Tom said, "And some fry bread."

I asked Tom, "Would a person have to have a reason to ask Jonas for tobacco?"

"Well, I guess so!" he said. "A person would have to have a pretty good reason to ask anybody just to give them something. I suppose if a person were to trade for something, his reason would be his own, though. Yes, I think that's how it works, most often."

"I wonder what a good trade would be for tobacco?"

"Could be almost anything, even corn mush," said Tom.

"What are you two talking about?" We both looked up as Ellie came downstairs with Eddie saddled on her hip. She put

Eddie on the floor, and he ran barefooted and jumped on me, lying on the sofa.

Tom said, as I wrestled with Eddie, "Seeing as Sam here is a wounded warrior, maybe some corn mush and fry bread for dinner would give back his strength."

Ellie said, "He looks pretty strong to me."

"Nothing like corn soup," said Tom, "to heal a boy."

How I loved Tom at that moment, but it instantly came to me that I had to give Turtle Belly Dancer Man corn mush *and* tobacco, and I'd better visit Jonas right away.

Ellie said, "I'm cooking up chicken and squash."

Tom said, "It'd only have to be a small pot. I guess a corn soup would get a boy back to his chores real fast."

Ellie said, "Then you'd better run over to my mother's for some lyed corn."

Tom began to tie up his boots; Ellie went into the kitchen and set water on to boil. Tom whispered as he stood up from his chair, "Don't you eat all that corn mush after Ellie makes it. You leave room for chicken and squash, too."

"I will, Tom," I said, and then he picked up the truck keys, playfully yanked Eddie's ears, and left the house.

I got off the sofa, leaving Eddie alone to watch the door for his father, and I went up to Ellie. I said, "Ellie, it came to me that I should ask Jonas to come and have some corn mush."

Ellie said, "If it came to you then I guess it's alright."

"Then I'm going over to ask him," I said.

"Hold up that head," Ellie said. "Keep it high up so the Creator sees you're wounded, then it will heal fast."

"I will," I said, running to get tobacco from Jonas.

My head still ached, and the afternoon sun was so bright and hot it seemed to wrap around the world and swallow me up.

When I crossed the shimmery black highway I came into

the high grass of Jonas's front yard, a wild yard defined only by two dirt ruts where cars sometimes parked—family calling on the old man—and the skid marks of the rocking chair the old man dragged around the little tar-paper building as he followed the shade. In the four years since my mother died and I had come to live with Tom and Ellie on the Reserve, I had only once come into this yard. It was to bring him a horsetail that Ellie had skinned, salted, and dried, and then I only left it by the front door for him to find because I was late for school. Plenty of other times, though, Jonas had waved at me from his rocking chair when I was walking on his side of the highway. I don't think he could see much beyond his own yard because he never waved very far away. Ellie told me his old woman was dead, and his kids had grown up and moved away, and he followed the old ways.

I knocked on the screen door, and he came up, pushing the rocking chair in front of him. The wooden floor was scuffed up and worn, and he came around the chair and sat down in it and stared at me. I said, "She:kon, how're you doing?"

"Good," he said. Even with one word I could hear the old-timer's accent, as though English was still a foreign language to him.

"I came over from across the road," I said. "I want to know if you have some tobacco you'll trade me."

Jonas stood up and turned his back on me, and I thought I had made him cross, but then he backed out the door, pulling the chair near the corner of the house. He sat down and looked at me. He was dark, like the little man in the forest, with old watery eyes and clipped white hair. "What does a little guy like you want with tobacco?" His voice was slow and heavy, but friendly, like he was joking with me.

"I can't really say. I just need some tobacco."

"You're not gonna wrap it up in a leaf and smoke it in the outhouse, are you?"

"No," I said. "It's a gift for a friend."

"That's good," he said. "How much do you need?"

"Well, I don't suppose he needs too much. Maybe just a pinch or two."

"A pinch or two?" He smiled, showing a couple of spaces where his teeth were missing. "A pinch or two won't go very far unless your needs are small."

"You could say that," I said.

"What do you have to trade?"

"Ellie's making some corn soup. Tom said a bowl of corn soup would be a good trade."

"Good enough," he said.

Jonas pointed off in the distance, down the line of the highway, past the faraway houses where my old aunts lived.

"Down there, where the railroad goes through, used to be a little station house. It was painted green and white, and a train stopped there two times a day, one from each direction. When I was just a little guy my father brought me down on a horse to see the train station, and he said to me, 'That train station will take you anywhere in the world.' I never forgot that. Anywhere in the world. Just name a place—Chicago, Texas, China—that train station will get you there."

"What's that got to do with corn soup?" I asked.

"I guess it's like losing something that don't ever come back. Not everyone knows how to make the old corn soup. Pretty soon, no one will. There was a kind of hope in that old train station, knowing you could go anywhere you wanted, just like there's a kind of hope in the old corn soup, knowing

Turtle Belly

that the people will keep on going. I suppose if you learned how to make the old corn soup from Ellie, I'd figure it fair all around."

I said, "It don't really seem like much."

"There's a lot to corn soup. Carry you all through life when you understand corn soup. Besides tobacco, I guess there isn't anything more sacred than corn soup. I guess a person becomes kind of sacred himself when he makes corn soup."

I thought about what Jonas said, and I knew that sacred things dealt with our Creator, but I could not see how a pot of corn soup bubbling in an old black-iron kettle made any difference to the Creator. Jonas smiled at me and shook his head. "Did you ever hear about the three sisters?" he asked, and I shook my head no. "Corn is one of the three sisters, our sustainers. Corn, beans, and squash. Shon'kwaiatison, the Creator, gave these gifts to us to sustain life. Nowadays people forget that these are gifts, like tobacco, whose smoke carries our prayers upwards. People get all crazy and forget the days when corn carried the people through hard times, when corn was sacred because it was all they had to eat. People forget that all the forest dwellers and the Great Rim Dweller, who lives on the rim of the world, and even the little people go hungry without corn, and they cry out also for tobacco. People forget that everything we have, even clothing and our automobiles and our lightbulbs, comes from the earth. People forget to look after the ones on the other side, to give back gifts. All the time we are visited in our dreams, and we ignore it," he said.

"Some dreams seem real," I said.

"Just remember one thing," he said. "We're not alone, no matter what you call it. From the stars in the sky to the roots in the earth, things are moving around us, even when we sleep. It's a busy universe."

70

"It's awful hard," I said, "to keep it all sorted out."

Jonas struggled up from his rocking chair. "Come on around the side, and I'll get your tobacco," he said. He began dragging his chair for support, and I trailed beside him.

Alongside the house was a row of small wooden boxes arranged to catch the sun's full southern brilliance, and each box contained a carefully cultivated tobacco plant, with pale green leaves about the size of my hand and yellow flowers on top supporting bell-like seedpods. Jonas bent down to pick a few leaves, and he spoke quietly. "You grow them in boxes to control them, so they don't grow everywhere," he said. "It's too sacred to go wild. You'd be walking on it otherwise. That would be a bad thing."

He smoothed a few leaves together on his left hand, arranging the stems in uniform lengths, and then he reached up for a small ball of red yarn stuck on a finishing nail in the side of the house. He broke off a piece of yarn and tied the stems tightly, saying, "Hang these up to dry overnight by your stove and in the morning crumble off whatever you need. You can burn it in a little dish on top of the stove when you pray." He handed it to me, and I looped the yarn off my finger, and the leaves seemed already wilted, slowly spinning on the end of the yarn.

I knew a few Mohawk words, and I thanked Jonas, "Nia:wen!"

He said, "Yo!" and told me to run home.

I protected my tobacco and hung it very carefully above the stove on a nail set in the log wall. A big iron kettle of water steamed away, and Ellie had opened all the windows to let the muddy river breeze drift through the house.

"What's in the pot?" I asked.

"A pork hock," said Ellie, wiping hair off her face.

"What else?" I asked.

"Just water."

"You just boil a pork hock, that's all?" I asked.

"Until you put in the corn," she answered.

"When do you do that?"

"When Tom gets back with it."

"Then what?" I pulled up a stool, climbed up, and leaned over the kettle, breathing in the steam.

"Then I put in a can of red kidney beans."

"What next?" I asked.

Ellie stepped back from the pot and stared at me. "Why are you asking so many questions about corn soup?"

I leaned away from the pot and shrugged. "Do you think Jonas likes it this way?"

"Yes, Jonas will like it. This is the old way."

"Are there other ways?"

"Some people put in wild onions; that's an old way. Some people put in pepper and salt, but mostly it's just lyed corn and red beans cooked up with a pork hock. If it's for ceremony you never put in salt, though, 'cause the spirits don't like that."

I climbed off the stool. I remembered seeing Aunt Bess lye corn, boiling it in wood ashes until the hulls fell off, sifting it through a basket, and washing it over and over again in cold water to get off all the lye.

When Tom came home I grabbed the lyed corn from him and ran to dump it in the kettle. I opened the can of red beans and put them in too and stirred it all up. The broth was kind of grey looking, and it smelled woodsy from the smoked pork hock. It made me hungry, and then Ellie melted lard in a skillet and kneaded dough for fry bread. Eddie, who was just four years old, waited near his mother, real quiet, and scooped up little pieces of raw dough that fell on the floor, eating them fast. I think Ellie let bits of dough fall on purpose, but Eddie didn't know, and Ellie pretended to scold him when she caught him eating off the floor. "You should let those hungry ants come and get that dough," she said, "instead of having it all to yourself." Then she'd turn her back and drop another piece.

The dough, pulled wide and thin, floated in the grease and turned brown like an autumn leaf lying on the surface of a dark pond. It smelled sweet and hissed in the bubbling oil. Ellie picked up each piece with a long wire fork, dropping them into a brown paper bag on the floor. We still had the old grey cat, the one whose ears had frozen off, and he licked the paper bag for the grease that soaked through. He purred, rumbling inside, and his tail stood straight up and quivered.

Ellie boiled a small chicken in another pot, and its feet, all bony and yellow, stuck out of the pot. Ellie called them the chicken's handles, and when it was cooked through she lifted it out by its handles and put it on a big plate. Then she put chunks of bright orange squash in the pot with the chicken broth and boiled it. After a while I was going crazy I was so hungry, and when Ellie got out a mason jar of maple syrup for the fry bread I said, "Maybe we should tell Jonas to come over now." Tom went across the road and helped Jonas walk over, and he came inside the log house carrying his own wooden bowl and a tin spoon. He nodded at me and came up to the stove, and Ellie filled his bowl with corn soup, putting a piece of squash and a piece of chicken on top. He took one piece of bread and slowly sat down on a hard-backed chair and began to eat. We waited while he ate, everything silent except for the sound of him eating and the cat's rough tongue, scraping the greasy paper bag. I don't think I was ever so hungry, waiting for a guest to eat his fill, before we would eat what was left. Jonas didn't eat slowly, or too much, but I was glad when he stood up and said, "That was good soup. Nia:wen." He nodded at me again, and Ellie began to fill my bowl.

Tom walked Jonas home, and I sat on the floor eating fast, dipping my fry bread in the jar lid of maple syrup, pushing the cat away all the time. Ellie said, "Slow down," and when I slowed down I remembered that I had not saved the first spoonful for the Little One in the forest. I decided that it would be alright if I saved the last spoonful.

The next morning I was awake and dressed before anyone. I ate a piece of fry bread, and I ran through the fields, my pant legs soaked with dew and stained with pollen and milkweed down. I had a little bit of corn soup in a jar and a whole leaf of tobacco wadded up in my pocket. I had some string and a pocket knife and a big spoon.

It seemed to me that any place in the forest would be alright, because I didn't remember where I had been that night alone after falling off the horse. When I came to the forest I cried out, "I'm here! I brought some gifts!" Then I waited a minute, and it was very quiet. It was not quite morning yet in the forest, not like the fields that were sparkling with a hint of sun. The forest was layered with mist and ground fog . . . and perfectly still. I looked around for a while and found a few ferns and some skunk cabbage. I was satisfied that no little people were around, and I went to work, digging a wide deep hole with the spoon. I had it all worked out, because I had figured it while lying in bed. That little guy was greedy. He didn't have any manners—just asking for things and not offering to trade. So I figured out that I could catch him, maybe show him around to everybody.

So I dug the hole, and then I bent down a branch and made a snare in the hole. I covered it over with pine needles and dry grasses, smoothing it all out so it looked normal. When

I was finished, I put the tobacco and corn soup in the middle. That little guy would fall right in, and the snare would snap him up, and I'd find him dangling in the air. Or else the little guy had just been a dream when I knocked myself out. It didn't really matter one way or the other, but I wanted to find out.

Suddenly I felt very strange, like I wasn't alone, kind of scary, and I slowly rose up. I turned and abruptly ran all the way home without stopping, even when it felt like my chest would explode.

I suppose I thought it might actually be possible to catch a little person in the forest—everybody seemed to think there was something to them, and it was kind of scary, but also exciting, to be the very first person to try to catch one. I don't know why nobody ever tried before. It didn't make sense. Everybody talked about this stuff, but no one had any proof. I figured I might be kind of famous if I got the proof, but I was worried. If I didn't catch a little person, everyone would still believe in them. There had to be a way to prove that they didn't exist, but I couldn't think of it. The only thing I could do—by catching one—was prove that they *did* exist.

I sipped a cup of tea, dipping a piece of fry bread in it, watching Tom tie his boots at the kitchen table. I said, "Remember we were talking about little people?"

Tom didn't look up. "I remember."

"I was wondering, if the old guys believe in them, how come no one ever tried to catch one?"

Tom looked up at me. "I heard about a young guy who tried once, and he died."

"He died?" I asked.

Tom said, "It was awful. He waited under a bush with a blanket. He was going to throw the blanket over a little guy and catch him. He waited all day, and when night came he got a little sleep. In the morning his people found him suffocated by his own blanket, all wrapped around his head. I don't know if it's true, but the old-timers believe you'll die if you try to catch a little person. You'll die the same way you try to catch them." Tom finished tying his boots. "Let's get to work," he said.

I was seized by panic. "The little people wouldn't kill a kid, would they?"

"They don't have a very good sense of humor," said Tom. "That guy I told you about was only twelve, so they say."

I began thinking that if a little person fell into my trap, the snare might not catch his waist but, instead, his neck. I couldn't imagine how *I* could be hanged. It just didn't seem possible.

I went out to the barn with Tom, and we fed the horses. Tom said, "Take Star Blanket to the corral and turn him loose. He needs a workout."

I snapped a line on his halter and led him out the door into the corral. We walked about a dozen yards, and I turned around to unsnap the line. His eyes rolled back, and I looked over my shoulder. The shadows of three crows passed over the earth, and Star Blanket lunged past me, the line going slack over my shoulder. Then he sidestepped back, and somehow the line crossed over me so that I had to twist out of it. But it caught up on my collar, and the horse began to pull away so the line tightened.

Tom came up fast and settled the horse. I pulled the line over my head. Tom said, "Be more careful!"

I said, "I gotta go do something."

Then I ran like my life depended on it to the forest and searched out my trap. I was shaking, like I'd just stepped out of the bathtub on a winter morning. That's just how I felt, all naked and shivery. When I found the trap, I froze, staring at the scene. Everything was all ripped apart, the corn soup and tobacco scattered and the hole revealed. The string waved gently in the air, the noose shredded. I slowly looked all around. I didn't even breathe. Then I backed away, sure now that the little people were out to get me.

I fled to Jonas's tar-paper shack. I banged on the door, and he came outside.

"I did a terrible thing!" I said. "I tried to catch a little person, and now they're going to get me! I don't know what to do!"

Jonas said, "This is serious. I'll have to think about this. Come back in about a week."

"A week! I'll be dead in a week! You have to do something now! You know about these things!"

"Tell me what happened," he said. Then we talked for a long time.

Jonas grew real silent, and I waited. After a while that seemed forever, he said, "I guess you're even. The little person escaped, and you escaped. Just the same, I'll give you some tobacco. You better leave some gifts."

"I'll do that!" I said, relieved that I wasn't going to die.

"Just don't ever go trying to catch things you don't know nothing about. That's what always gets people in trouble, especially you young guys. You think you know everything!"

"I'll remember that," I said.

Jonas rubbed his stomach. "You bring some corn soup next time Ellie makes a pot."

The
Wash
Rack

The Wash Rack

His name was Duane, and he looked me straight in the eye and said, "Don't bullshit me, kid. How old are you?"

I hesitated, shifting my weight around, scraping the toe of my sneaker across the bloody concrete floor. Duane was a big guy, a real big red-haired white man with a beard. He was wearing a yellow hard hat and a bloody apron.

I said, "I'm old enough."

"You gotta be sixteen, kid. You don't look more than eleven. What grade you in?"

I was thirteen and in grade eight, but my arithmetic wasn't very fast. I said, "I got held back."

He swung his head around, staring at the concrete walls when he sighed. "I ain't got time for this bullshit. I know who you are; you're Tom's kid, with the horsetails. You got a nerve," he said.

"I can do the job. I'm a good worker."

He lowered his head and rubbed his hands on his knees. His fingers were thick and scarred. He looked up at me, and I didn't flinch.

"I'll give you ninety cents an hour on the wash rack. In between sides, you'll be the guts boy. If there's a calf, you'll bleed it. Two ten-minute breaks; a half hour for lunch. Shift starts at 6:30. Time clock's by the ramp. Think you can handle it?"

"I can do it," I said. "But minimum wage is a buck twenty-three. I know that much!"

"Sue me, kid, then take a fucking hike."

"I'll take it," I said, hating his pig eyes.

"Don't jack me off. I'm tired of you kids quitting," he said.

"No shit, I can handle it," I said.

Duane stood up and grabbed the shoulder of my shirt, dragging me to a locker room with a grey concrete floor and

79

yellow cinder-block walls. I got a wide metal sheath like an envelope that fastened around my waist with a clip on a chain. He picked a bunch of knives out of a bin and stuck them in the sheath. He gave me a long tapered "steel" to sharpen my knives. Then we went out to the wash rack.

It was a steel cage with a mesh floor and an up/down control connected to a hydraulic lift platform.

"In case you can't read, green is *up* and red is *down*," he said, and then we went up. Duane yelled out, "Move 'em along!"

I looked down the line from my perch, and far in the distance I could see cattle, brown with white faces, herded in close to a gate, their eyes like jewels, their nostrils flaring with the scent of their own blood. Up the line I saw the skinners, the gut bins, piles of steaming hides, and heads, a chain winch, electric saws, bloody floors, and drainage grates.

Above me was a steel track that conveyed sides of beef on sharp steel hooks hanging from rollers.

Duane said, "You go up and down; you turn the meat around." He looked down the line. "I need some meat!" A side of beef rolled into place. "This is a good one. Look, here on the flank, you got some bruises. Cut it out with your knife. Sometimes you get an abcess or a cancer in the muscle. Cut it out. Then you grab this hose and spray it down—get inside the cancer and wash it out. Top to bottom, make it look good for the inspectors. Wash off all the hair and shit, then send it along. You got that? If it looks bad, use your knife."

"How do I know if it's bad?"

"Green is bad. Good meat don't look green. Yellow's not so bad. You'll learn."

He turned the side of beef around, paused, then grabbed one of my knives and sliced a circle of muscle out of a flank. He tossed it off the rack, and when I looked down I saw that the concrete floor was strewn with chunks of meat coagulated black and green. "You got it?" he asked.

"I got it."

"Roll the line!" he called out, and I flinched at the sound of a gunshot. He lowered the rack and stepped off, and I waited for the next side to come along, before I played with the up/down switch.

It was alright, going up and down, with a waistful of knives and a pressure hose. The next side of beef came along, and I turned it around on the swivel hook hanging from the track. I sprayed it with the nozzle, and the cold water steamed. I rubbed the side, and the carcass was warm. There was a big black bubbly mass on the shoulder, and I whipped out a knife, trimming it away. It felt like a handful of hot Jello.

I heard another gunshot. Looking down the line from my high perch, I could see a cow dropped on her knees. It smelled like manure and blood, mixed into a big stew. Men and machines were piercing her with steel hooks and bars and spreading her so the skinners could undress her, split her, tumble out her guts into a bin, like an ore cart on a rail line. A man with an electric saw sliced off her horns, then her head, then traveled with such precision through her spine, as the body was lifted up on the chain winch, that it parted in two and was sent reeling along the line. Another gunshot split the air, and I pushed off the first carcass and hauled in the next one.

It wasn't that the work was so hard, although I did put all my energy into spinning those sides of meat around and pushing them on down the line; it was that they came so fast and began to pile up. It took a lot to keep up, they were killing so many cows, and when a loud bell rang out for the break and the men stood up from their bloody work, I leaned back and took a deep salty breath. I was soaked through with blood, and so was everybody else walking beneath me to the lunch-room, like scarlet coal miners with bright eyes beneath a glistening red mask.

In the lunchroom, I sat on a black bench at a table with scattered ashtrays. You would have thought it was a woman's party, because all the butts in the ashtray were stained red, like lipstick, but it was blood. And the floor was wet with red rubber-boot footprints. I smoked two fags fast.

When I went back to the wash rack someone called out "CALF!"

Duane came below me and said, "Move your ass, kid."

We hurried down the line, and a little white man with a long knife was slicing through the umbilical cord of an unborn calf, which had tumbled out of its slaughtered mother.

Duane said, "Pick it up and come with me."

It was a fully formed Black Angus calf with gelatinous white hooves, delicate and transparent. When I grabbed it up, it was heavy and limp and hard to hold onto, its soft hair coated with slippery fluid. I struggled to carry it as I followed Duane down the line, around a corner, to a work station with a cabinet bolted to the wall, a table with a strange hinged-plastic form, and a steel barrel against the concrete wall.

Duane lifted the handle of the plastic press to reveal the hollow shape of a four-legged creature. "You chuck it in here; lay it out nice." He opened the cabinet doors and took out a widemouthed bottle wrapped in sterile plastic. "Keep it clean," he said. "Then open the bottle, stick in the cord, and pull down on the handle. Pump all the blood out. Up and down, squeeze out all the blood. Then close up the bottle and run it over to the fridge."

"What for?" I asked.

"It's pure blood. They use it for research, like cancer. It's valuable. Anytime you hear someone yell out "calf," you come down and pump out the blood."

I did what he said after he left—I put the unborn calf into the press and pumped the handle so that all the blood drained out the umbilical cord into the bottle. Everytime I squeezed I heard a wet sucking sound. The calf was dead, but when I let up on the handle, it sucked air back into its stilled lungs. When I pressed down, the air came out of its wet nostrils. The blood trickled and filled the bottle. When the blue cord slowed to an intermittent drip, I opened the cavity shell and dragged out the body. I hauled it to the barrel in the corner. The barrel was filled with bodies. Their oversized heads were turned backwards; their legs and hooves were twined and stuck out like translucent twigs smeared with blood. I dumped the calf into the barrel, and I couldn't go on. Something inside me was tossing around in my stomach. I'd slaughtered pigs and butchered deer, but this was different. I was tired, soaked with blood, and sad. Around the corner people were yelling, "Wash rack! You're holding up the line!"

Sometimes you make a promise and end up fucked. That's what I told myself, thinking about this rotten dirty job. I hated it. I really needed the money, though, if I was going to have *any* fun that summer—some bucks to buy smokes and beer when I hung out with the big guys. I didn't realize that work was all this bullshit: guys yelling at you and pushing you around, hot and bloody, no time to even think.

I unsnapped my chain and dropped the knives by the barrel of dead calves. I walked around the corner, then turned back and slipped out of the slaughterhouse through a fire door, so no one would see me leave. I didn't want anyone to see me. I was afraid someone would say, "Can't take it, kid? What are you, a pussy?"

When I got home, all sweet and salty with blood, I didn't talk to Tom—I didn't know if he'd understand—but I did talk to Ellie after I had a bath. Tom was out in the barn, and Ellie was cooking burgers for supper. They both knew I didn't finish out my first shift, but they hadn't said anything.

I said, "I really hated it."

Ellie said, "You have to do it. Sometimes I really hate cooking supper. I have to do it."

"It's different, Ellie," I said. "You didn't get pushed around like I did."

"You don't know what pushing is," she said.

"I saw a barrel full of dead calves, milked of all their blood," I said.

"You haven't even begun to see," she said. "Tomorrow you go back and ask for another chance. Tell 'em you got sick or something. Just act real dumb, and they'll take you back."

That night I lay in bed and smoked a dozen cigarettes thinking about what Ellie had said—acting dumb, going back for another shot at it. I didn't know what I was going to do. I tore the filter off a smoke like the big guys did, and I started thinking about Jonas. He'd been dead a couple of years, but when he was alive he never worked. He only did what he wanted to do. He didn't give a shit about anything except spirits and boogers and all that old-time stuff. I figured there might be something to it after all—it beat the shit out of working and punching the time clock. That was really the life old Jonas led, sitting in the shade in a rocking chair, growing tobacco, shooting flies with a rubber band and a paper clip, and all the time, friends hanging around.

But I also got to thinking how I'd walk away with at least ten bucks a day, more money than I'd ever seen, fifty bucks a week. That was a lotta beer and smokes. It sure would put me in good with the big guys, buying all that beer and all them smokes.

I still didn't know what I was going to do by the time I fell asleep. I don't know what time it was, but it was late.

The sun wasn't even up when Ellie came in and woke me. She shook me for a while and then pulled me up so I was sitting on the edge of the bed. She helped me get dressed and gave me a cup of coffee, and then she shoved me out the front door. I started walking down the line, bleary eyed. The rim of the sun was glowing above the tree line, and there wasn't any wind moving. Already it was feeling hot and humid.

I kept saying to myself that I was going to stop and turn back, but I kept on going down the line, right out to the main highway. I couldn't even feel my legs, like they didn't belong to me and were taking me against my will straight to the slaughter house. I knew what cows felt like then, just marching along all slow and stupid. I felt dumb as a cow.

Ellie was right—they took me back—but Duane was a shit-face about it. He smacked the back of my head a lot, said he was knocking some sense into my half-breed head.

"You're half white man!" he roared. "Don't you got at least *half* a fucking brain?"

"I guess so."

He grabbed the front of my tee shirt and leaned over my face. "Don't fuck with me."

At night I sat on my bed and stared at my watercolors tacked to the wall. They were mostly red. I thought my best one was the image of a red beating heart being brought up and molded into the shape of a clay pot, like the vessels of life that contained our spirits. When you see our old clay pots, you can't help but think of them as hearts, nestled in the coals, warm, and sustaining life. The old pots were like that . . . tapered on the bottom, flaring up to a collar where all the membranes and arteries mingle like junctions of life coming and going. You begin to think that way when you see a heart beating on a cold concrete floor. Alone in its redness. Blue is death.

Maybe that's why we always saw the red sun of morning and the blue sky of night as the opposite ends of life. I knew something, working on that wash rack for a summer. Red was about movement, and blue was about calm. Life and death. Day and night.

The white man only knew about yellow and green.

Dancing
Mares

We traveled in packs like wolves, howling to each other, pissing on fence posts by the side of the road or on the cinderblock wall of the community center, right under the overhead lights where everyone could see us marking our territory. We didn't care who saw us or what they thought. "When you gotta go, you oughtta go!" said Larry Killdeer. He was the oldest, at fifteen, a tall, dark lacrosse player. I was next, just a few months shy of my fifteenth birthday, average for my size and tanned pretty dark, but my hair was bleached by the sun and not nearly as dark as I liked it. Alvin Cloud was a couple of months younger than me, but he was so big, I mean *all* over, and we called him a rude nickname which meant, if you held your hands far apart near your groin, that he was great like a horse or a bear. And he was kind of ugly, flat faced with purple lips. He didn't care. He said, "All cats look grey in the dark. I got alls I need right here." But he had never tested the theory. There were some younger guys about thirteen that we let travel around with us, but we called all the shots, making them jump like rabbits. "Go on now, get me a soda pop and make sure it's cold." Or, "Talk one of them big guys out of a few smokes, and I'll let you have a drag." One time we let one of the smaller guys piss alongside us on the fencerow, only we didn't tell him the wires were hot. We knew where to aim, but, God Almighty, he didn't. When he sprayed right on that hot electric wire, he flew straight out of his new sneakers and fell on his back in the tall grass, his eyes bugged out and spit foaming down his chin. It sounded as though he was gargling, his voice all choked up. I felt pretty bad then, because you never know how someone will take a thing like that. When he came around, Alvin gave him a smoke and said, "You gotta keep your eyes open, kid. What'dya think I am, your guardian angel or something?"

We were awful rough on those younger guys, but the

older guys had been just as rough on us. That's how we learned to stand on our own two feet. The next step was to get even with the older guys, now that we'd come along so far and knew so much. Someday, the young ones coming up would get even with us, too. Tom, who had raised me like his own son, said, "It's a circle, eh? Round and round. You watch a bunch of wolf pups grow up like that, tagging along with the bigger boys, imitating their ways, getting slapped back, earning respect, slowly coming into their own station in life. That's nature's way, you know."

We were growing up fast on this flat reservation, crosshatched with straight highways and tree lines, littered with log houses, tar-paper cabins, and rusted-out trucks. I watched the big guys carefully. It wasn't so long ago that Carver Hill was like us, and now he was sitting on the hood of his own pickup truck in the parking lot of the community center, drinking beer, surrounded by girls. It was the last night of the annual powwow, and Carver had his knees around some girl dressed up in all her dance regalia. He kept pulling her ribbon shawl over her head and bending in to kiss her. Alvin, Larry, and I thought it was great the way Carver had backed his truck under the big light and was doing all that kissing in front of everyone coming in. Old people shook their heads at him, and one of the tribal cops told him to knock it off, but Carver yelled, "There's no law against kissing!" Then the cop told Carver to get rid of his beer, and Carver stood up on the bumper and drank down the whole bottle. "There, it's gone! Satisfied?" The cop just shook his head and walked away, and Carver grinned, nodding at his friends. He hopped off the bumper, tucked his fists into his armpits, and crowed his way into the dance arena like a proud fighting bird.

We were still sitting on the roof of a new black Olds with

New York license plates. We didn't care. Larry said with a tone of respect, "Did you see how Carver put that cop down?"

"Them cops got no power," said Alvin. "What's he gonna do? Bust one of his own? Like shit he would."

"He might," I said, "if Carver drinks too much."

Larry said, "How white would a guy have to be—" He stopped and looked at me. "No offense, brother."

"None taken," I said. "He'd just drive Carver home. He wouldn't arrest him unless he jumped on your old granny, and then your old granny would bail him out for more."

Larry narrowed his eyes at me. "Don't take this personal or nothin', but I'd appreciate it if you'd stay away from me for ten days or so."

"Oh yeah," I said, "and why's that?"

"Well, my bitch dog went into heat today, and I don't want any puppies that look like you."

Alvin burst out laughing, rolling off the roof of the car. "Busted!" he yelled. "Big time!"

I had to think fast. "I can see why," I said. "It'd make you too guilty to eat them."

Larry was wearing down; I could see him straining, and then I waved him silent. I leaned over the car and barked at Alvin, "Shut up! It's Ima Jean!"

Alvin jumped up from the gravel parking lot. "Where?"

I pointed for both of them. "Coming up to the front door with her friends. She's in the light now."

The way she moved reminded me of something Ellie told me when one of our mares came in season. "Look how she dances from side to side. It gives the big boys the jitters." That's how Ima Jean moved, her hips swaying back and forth while the rest of her stayed put, and it gave me the jitters, too, just like

Star Blanket, our stallion. Star Blanket went almost crazy when the mares danced, and now I knew why.

Ima Jean passed under the cool white light, and her black hair, long down her back, glistened iridescent blue, like the wing of a raven. Then she was gone, inside the arena, and we released our breaths in a whistle that mingled like a howl. We were all Wolf Clan and proud of our howling.

I suddenly announced, "I'm going to dance with her tonight."

Larry said, "Even my dog would put up a fight, and she's in heat."

"That's because she misses you," I said.

Alvin pulled me off the roof of the car, and I landed on my feet. "Knock it off," he said. Larry slid down the windshield and the hood. He came around to us. Again Alvin said, "Knock it off! This is serious." Alvin pushed Larry away from me. He stood at arm's length with tight fists. He did that all the time, but he never really hit me. Alvin looked at Larry. "Don't you believe him? He said he was going to dance with Ima Jean! That's what you said, Sam."

"That's what I said."

"People say lots of things. Don't make it true," said Larry.

Alvin looked at me. "Do you speak the truth?"

"Among friends I do."

"Then do what you said you'd do. Dance with Ima Jean."

Suddenly a loud voice barked at us: "What the fuck are you doing on my car!"

We jerked up to see an old guy, maybe forty, with a young woman close at his side. He looked like a white guy, all sunburned and pink and going bald, but the woman he was with was Indian. "Take a fuckin' hike," he said, thumbing down the road.

Larry was ready with those tight fists, and he stepped out as the man approached.

"Larry," I whispered, "we ain't here to fight."

Then as they came up to us, we saw that the woman was all bellied-out pregnant and the man had a metal veteran's flag pinned on his striped shirt. One armless sleeve was tucked into the waist of his jeans.

Larry said, "Sorry about your car. We were just heading inside the arena."

The couple brushed past us, and we meandered through the parking lot toward the entrance. Alvin mumbled, "Like you were going to take on a vet."

"I thought he was going to take me on," said Larry.

"Right," I said. "Everyone's going to take on Larry."

"Don't make no difference right now," he said, "because you're going to take on Ima Jean."

Inside, under bright lights, the arena of the community center was filled with a thousand people. They were in the bleachers, looking down at the big dance circle with the drum in the center of the basketball court, and they were milling about the vendors' tables under the hoops at either end, buying fry bread and bean soup in paper cups. There were a lot of dancers in the circle, men and women, not with each other, all deep in concentration on the sound of the big drumbeats and the voices of the six singers coming over the loudspeakers. Some of the men wore rainbow-colored outfits with fancy ribbon-worked shirts and dazzling feathered bustles and beadwork and painted faces. They spun around as if they were flying. Some of the little girls hopped to the drumbeat, fast and laughing, spreading their fringed shawls like wings on currents of air. I loved to watch the little girls dance—five years old, six, seven—they bounced off each other and their eyes sparkled, they were having so much fun. But I also liked to see the old people dance, because they were slow and dignified, never missing a beat of the drum with their feet and always stopping on the last beat. When the old people danced they acted like they were sacred beings, and they just let the younger ones whirl around them as if we were all related. That was beautiful to see—all the people together, from the very young, who could hardly walk, to the very old, who could hardly walk. We all helped each other by being together, and we all did it at our own speed.

Suddenly, while watching all those people, I heard Ellie's voice behind me. "Where you been?"

I turned back quickly. "Just hanging out. Kind of bored I guess."

Larry said, "He's looking for Ima Jean. He's going to dance with her."

Alvin raised his palm, and Larry slapped it hard.

Ellie looked at us and smiled, her white teeth shining in a round brown face. "Didn't Ima Jean turn sixteen this summer? I'd be careful, you guys. She might dance all over you *erharni-wah*." Her word meant little puppy dogs.

"Come on," I said, grabbing Larry's arm, moving away as Ellie laughed.

When the singers sang a social song for couples, we saw pairs wrapped in blankets doing a slow two-step shuffle. I could see the flash of eyes or teeth inside the dark cave of navy blue blanket pulled over their heads. I could sense the fidgety laughter, the whispers, the promises, and I remember Carver saying, "First you got to get them to dance under the blanket, then you got to lie as if your life depended on it." I wasn't too good at lying, and I figured that if I ever did dance under a blanket with a girl, I would knot up into a ball of honesty.

Larry said, "There she is!" slapping my back and pointing across the arena. Alvin and I craned past the dancers, and Alvin said, "I see her. She's with all her friends by the fry bread booth." I saw her too, in the middle of a dozen girls. She was shifting from one foot to the other and back, her hips moving all lazy in tight new blue jeans.

"Well?" asked Larry.

"I'm thinking about it," I said.

"No time to think," said Alvin. "You promised us."

"Alright," I said, my heart all soft and spongy. I went straight up to Carver, who was sitting on a bench in the arena with his blanket folded beside him. He was talking to some guys, and I said to him, "Give me your blanket."

Carver said, "You're too young."

"Come on, man. Give me a break, just this once," I said. "Whatever you want."

Carver said, "Give me a smoke, little brother," and I gave him a cigarette and lighted it for him. Then he picked up the blanket and blew smoke on it and handed it to me. He said, "Good luck."

I walked around the ring of dancers. My friends were watching me. Some girls were watching me. All of the people were watching me, I imagined. Ima Jean was joking loud to her friends with her back turned. I came up behind her and stood there with the blanket draped over my arm, waiting. I saw the eyes of her friends looking at me, and they glanced toward Ima Jean. She turned around to see me there with the blanket. Her high cheeks were rosy, her eyes mischievous. She said, "I'm not going to dance with you. You're just a crazy kid."

I said, "Do you think I was going to ask you?"

"Who were you going to ask then?" she asked.

I looked at the first girl behind her, her friend Anne, and

I said, "Anne. I was going to ask Anne. . . . ANNE!" I was suddenly very conscious of having to piss. My hands were cold, and my chest was light and airy. Anne came up to me and I took the blanket and put it around our shoulders and pulled it over our heads, and we slowly walked into the center of the arena. But I didn't know what to say to her. I suddenly felt speechlessly in love. Anne whispered, "I know you really wanted to dance with Ima Jean."

I softly said, "No, I wanted to dance with you," lying like Carver had told me. I had gotten under a blanket.

Anne's left shoulder and my right shoulder were pressed together, and I felt her arm come around my back under the blanket. I put my arm around her waist. We slowly danced a round dance, shuffling forward with the hard-soft hard-soft beat of the drum. The song abruptly stopped, just as we had worked ourselves into the rhythm. I said, "Thank you," and began to pull my arm away, but Anne pressed her arm down against my hand, holding it tight against her ribs.

She turned her face into my neck and whispered just below my ear, "Let's dance another one." When the singing started up, we began to move inside the blanket. I lowered my hand and slipped my fingers up under her tee shirt. I tickled her skin. She laughed, and her breath was warm. It smelled like bubble gum. She bit my ear hard, and I squeezed her tight against me. She held my ear with her teeth, and I pinched the skin on her ribs. She still did not let go of my ear, and I moved my hand up to her breast and held it through her bra. She quickly let go of my ear and said coldly, "Don't do that."

I did not let go of her breast. It was the first breast I had ever touched, and I think my hand and brain were paralyzed. I said, "You wouldn't let go of my ear."

"I was only teasing," she said.

"So am I."

"Then let go," she said, bringing up her hand to cover mine. She held her hand, on top of her tee shirt, hard against mine underneath. I could not let go if I wanted to, and my chest was light and quivery. Suddenly the song stopped, and she spun out of the blanket, walking away with a deep scarlet blush on those pretty brown cheeks.

I folded the blanket over my arm and brought it back to Carver Hill. He said, "You look like you got your face slapped hard."

"I got my ear bit," I said, "and it was *sweeeeet*."

Carver said, "You liar. Give me another cigarette."

I gave him the whole pack.

"What's this for?" he asked, his round face wide with surprise. He lighted up a cigarette.

"When I asked you for your blanket, you asked me for a butt. Now you asked me *first*, and I'm asking for your blanket in return. I now own this blanket," I said, and I took it off his arm. He reached out, and his friends began to laugh.

"What's so funny?" he roared.

One of his friends named John—a big guy with long hair—pushed between us and said, "He got you big time, Carver."

Carver threw down the cigarette and crushed it out on the floor of the gym with his boot. "No way. Here's your pack back," he said, but I wouldn't take it.

John said, "You accepted the pack and smoked one."

"Who's side are you on, man?" He spun around, then turned back frustrated, shaking his arms at his sides. The cigarettes were falling out of the pack, and John said, "You're losing all your butts." Carver bent down to grab them, and John gave me a shove. "Take off, man."

As I walked away I heard them laughing about how Carver had been busted big time. Carver yelled, "I'll get one on you." I didn't turn back. I was smiling so hard my face felt hot. Finally, I had scored a big bust on one of the older guys. The wolf pack—my friends—were waiting for me on the other side of the dance circle, and Larry grabbed the blanket and put it around his shoulders. "Who should I dance with?" he asked.

I said, "Don't dance with Anne—she'll bite off your ear." I tipped my head toward him and the other guys.

Larry said, "Christ, those are teeth marks!"

There were a couple of smaller guys with astonished faces and open mouths. I was all fired up. I wanted to use my blanket again. "Hurry up, Larry."

"Alright! Who should I dance with?"

I looked around the gym. I saw Anne and Ima Jean and about seven other girls. One of them was a girl who dances with everybody. Her name was Angie Hill, Carver's sister.

"Go ask Angie Hill!" I said. "It'll kill Carver to see his sister under his own blanket."

"He'll kill me," said Larry. "Bad news."

"If you can't make up your mind, give me back my blanket."

Larry acted like he was looking at the girls, but after a minute he gave me the blanket. "I don't see the girl I want to dance with anyway."

So I took the blanket eagerly, and I walked away from my friends. Carver and his crowd were now standing near the girls, and when I walked past them Carver threatened me, "Big time, little one." I knew what I was going to do. I was going to dance with Carver's baby sister. It was killing me! She was right up front, and I came to her. I nodded down at the blanket and then looked into her face. She wasn't very pretty—she looked a lot like Carver only with softer features and a wider mouth. She glanced past me, at her brother, then said, "Why not?"

We wrapped up in the blanket, and I felt her squirming against me as we entered the dance circle and waited for a song to begin. When the singers started up, they sang a song that was half English words. It went:

Indian girls, Indian girls,
Oh how I love those Indian girls.

Then they changed it to *Mohawk girls,* then *Seneca girls.* It was a joke song they had learned from a Winnebago guy, and it always made people laugh or blush when they sang out their tribe. When they sang *Cayuga girls,* Angie Hill turned in the blanket and began kissing me all over my face. My heart pounded, and I tried to kiss her back, but she was moving too fast. Her kisses were wet, and I felt her tongue licking me. I moved my hands everywhere under the blanket, but she always, somehow, grabbed them away. I was trying to grab anything soft and warm. When the song ended, she abruptly slipped out of the blanket, and I stood there breathing hard, my heart flip-flopping.

When I regained my senses, I folded the blanket over my arm and walked through the people. They were all still laughing at the song, and I laughed with them. I saw Angie standing with Carver, and they were laughing. When I rejoined my friends, they doubled over, holding their bellies. Larry rolled on the floor. He was yelling "Big time!" and tears were running down his face. When I turned back to the dance arena people were looking at me. Carver was pointing at his sister, and she was holding up something shiny. Larry picked himself off the floor, and he grabbed a wooden dance wand from an old-time guy. The board had little round mirrors set in the wood, and he waved it in front of me. My entire face was covered with big red lipstick kisses. When I saw all those people laughing again, my heart caved in, and I could hear Carver still yelling, "You got busted!"

Larry and some of the guys came with me as I hurried away, heading for the locker room. I scrubbed my face with pumice soap, and Larry gave me one of his cigarettes.

I left alone and walked three miles home in the dark, the blanket wrapped around my shoulders against the bitter chill I felt. Dogs rushed out from squat shacks and barked at me and followed me along the cornfields, laughter in their snarls. I came up to our old log house and sat in the shadow of a big elm until Tom and Ellie came home and went to bed. Later, I slipped inside and climbed up the stairs to my bedroom, turning on the light by my bed under the log eaves and throwing back the covers. There, staring up at me with frozen blue eyes, was a naked centerfold from an old *Playboy* magazine. She was a damned blonde, at that, with pasty pink nipples. Ellie cracked open the door. "I didn't want you to be alone," she said. Ellie was giggling in the hall. I grabbed the centerfold and chased her down the stairs, and I said, when I cornered her in the kitchen, "Why don't you just leave me alone!" I tore up the centerfold and threw the pieces at her feet. She just laughed, her eyes flashing in the bright moonlight that shined through the window. She sidestepped me, heading for the bathroom, leaped in, and closed the door between us. "Don't you like blondes, Turtle Belly?"

"Don't ever do that again!" I said.

Ellie cracked open the door and looked at me in the light shining from the bathroom. "You have lipstick on your face," she said, then closed the door fast.

"It's none of your business."

"No need to get so mad," she called out. But I ignored her because someone started pounding hard on the front door. They called out, "Sam, open up. There's someone here to see you!"

"Who is it?"

Ellie came out of the bathroom and followed me to the door.

"Open up and find out."

I recognized the voice. "What do you want, Larry?"

"I told you . . . we came by to visit. Come on out."

Ellie reached past me and opened the door. Larry stepped onto the jamb into Ellie's view. He started backwards.

"Hi, Ellie," he said, weaving slightly. "We come to see Sam." He was holding a bottle of beer.

"Who all is out there?" asked Ellie.

"Just me and some girls."

Ellie leaned out the door. "Get here where I can see who's out there," she said, and I swallowed hard when Ima Jean and Anne came near. They said hello with downcast eyes, their shoulders pulled down, making them look small in the moonlight.

Ellie asked, "Who's old truck is that out on the road?"

I nudged Ellie and said, "It's Carver Hill's truck."

"Is Carver out there?" she called, and when she got no answer Larry said, "I drove up."

"Well, you're walking the rest of the night."

"God, Ellie, it's near five miles."

Ellie looked him stern in the face and said, "That truck just ran out of gas." She put out her hand. "Give me the keys."

Larry reached deep in his pocket and gave them to her.

"So what do I tell Carver?"

"Tell him it's bad luck to loan out a truck on a full moon night. . . . Old Indian legend."

Larry shifted uneasily in place and shrugged. "Well, do you mind if we hang out for awhile? At least you could let us finish the beer."

"How many you got?"

"A couple more," said Larry.

Ellie remained silent for a moment, and then she turned away saying, "Keep it quiet out there."

I went outside, closing the door behind me, and stood with my hands in my pockets. I forgot that I had ever been angry at Ellie as I stood in the yard with Larry and Anne and Ima Jean. In the moonlight Ima Jean's hair was iridescent jet, and her cheeks glistened. Anne looked pretty good, too, but I worried she might bite my other ear if I tried anything.

When they walked up the driveway to the truck, I followed. I looked in the back of the truck.

"Christ, there's a whole case back here," I said.

"That many?" said Larry. "I must have counted wrong. Shit!" Then he laughed his ass off!

"Where's Alvin?" I asked.

"His sister caught him drinking and dragged him home."

"How'd you get Carver's truck?"

"He was fighting with the cops, and it was just sitting there with the keys in it. We'll get it back to him."

"You're nuts," I said, "taking Carver's truck." I grabbed a beer and pried off the cap under the door handle of the truck and drank it down hard. I threw the bottle into the back of the truck, where it broke.

Larry said, "This is Carver's truck, man!"

"I know," I said, grabbing up another beer.

Anne lighted a cigarette and gave it to me. She said, "Carver got you good. You still mad?"

"No," I said. Anne took my beer and shared it with Ima Jean, and I watched Ima Jean pucker her lips and throw back her head to drink, as if she was lying back to be kissed. It was sweet to see her like that. I thought I might try to kiss her later on if we could get off the subject of Carver.

Ima Jean gave the beer back to Anne, and her mouth was all shiny wet with beer. She laughed at me, saying, "Don't you never dance with Angie Hill again. She got you good."

"I know that trick now," I said.

"She's got more tricks," said Anne. "She told me about them."

"What did she tell you," I asked, opening another beer.

Anne looked around, then leaned close to me. I came in closer to her, trying to hear what she said. She put her hand on my shoulder, and I bent down, and suddenly she had my ear between her teeth again.

"Damn it!" I yelled, pushing her off, and she fell on her ass in the grass beside the truck. I jumped on her, and we wrestled until I was able to bury my face in her hair and bite her ear hard. She whimpered, but she did not cry out, and I heard Larry and Ima Jean laughing. Anne and I had wriggled ourselves almost under the truck. When I let go of her ear, she turned her face up, and without thinking much, I kissed her. She lay still and quiet. Her mouth was very soft and open just a little bit. I could taste beer and bubble gum on her breath, and I liked it. When I shifted my weight to get more comfortable, she must have thought I was leaving her, and she held onto me and kissed me harder, opening her mouth and sucking in my breath. God, it was great.

Larry kicked the bottom of my foot. "What's going on down there," he called out. I jerked up, banging my head on the underside of the truck. Anne slithered away from me, and when I crawled out she was already opening a couple of beers. She gave me one as I raked my fingers through the hair on the back of my head, feeling the bump.

Anne said, "I have to pee."

"Use the old double crapper by the barn," I said.

"Where?" she asked. "It's dark." A ribbon of clouds moved across the face of the moon, and the land was no longer bright. "Walk with me," she said.

I hoped Larry and Ima Jean wouldn't follow us, and they stayed by the truck as we hiked along the tree line. There were no lights from the house, and the land was black. We came to the crapper set back in the trees.

Anne said, "Wait for me. Don't leave me alone." The door creaked when she closed it behind her. I could hear her water stream echoing in the hole, and then she was very silent except for some rustling sounds. I remembered sharing the crapper with Ellie when I was only six, her pants way down, how fascinated I had been by her dark place, how I had wanted to explore it. Then, as I listened to the rustling, I forgot about Ima Jean and Larry, because my imagination wandered along Anne's bare hips and thighs, lingering on that dark secret place that had captured my attention as a child.

Anne, dragging me out of my thoughts, cried out, "There's something in here!" I yanked open the door of the crapper. She was almost invisible in the sour blackness. Her hands shot out and clutched me. I said, "What is it? Where?" She turned me around, pressing herself against my back. The door of the crapper swung shut with a bang.

"Where is—"

"No, no. . . . Be quiet! Don't move!"

I froze. Anne did not move, and we were breathing in rhythm. I listened. Her arms held me tightly, and her hands trailed slowly downward. She held my hips.

She moved her fingers like waves.

I inhaled and then held my breath.

I did not move when she opened my jeans.

Her hands were warm.

My legs stiffened, and her hands played with me.

She brought me out and played with me, and I did not dare move.

A feeling like having to pee came over me, but it was different. Urgent. I did not want her to stop, but I was afraid I would lose it. It became stronger and stronger, and it hurt. I was hard, like our stallion. My belly was on fire, and she played with me faster. I could not have told her to stop if I wanted to, because I was frozen still. And then I began to convulse and lose control. I thought how embarrassed I would be if she knew I had lost it on the floor in front of us. My knees were shaking, and she squeezed me hard until it hurt so much, I pushed her back with my arms. I took a deep breath, and all I could taste was the ammonia of the old double crapper. Anne leaned against my back.

"Did you like that?" she whispered.

I opened the door to let in fresh air. I quickly closed up my pants. We stepped outside. I looked at her, and she was fast wiping the palms and backsides of her hands on the thighs of her jeans. She seemed to know something, but she wasn't worried much. I wanted to explain; I wanted to apologize, but she smiled at me and put her arm around my waist, saying, "Let's get another beer." So I didn't say anything. We walked past the house and up the driveway, and we saw Larry and Ima Jean sitting in the weeds. They were kissing hard, and Ima Jean's tee shirt was pulled up. Her breasts were bright in the moonlight. They didn't hear us until we pounded open some beers on the door handle of the truck. Ima Jean quickly covered herself. Larry threw an empty bottle at us, and it soared over the truck and shattered on the road. It broke with a pop, and I thought maybe it would wake up Ellie. No lights came on, and after awhile Anne and I went over to sit under an old sycamore tree so that Larry and Ima Jean could be alone.

I don't know how many beers we drank—we took turns going for new ones. We didn't talk too much either. We smoked cigarettes and kissed a lot. When I looked at the sky the stars were moving around. When I focused on something and then looked away real fast, it seemed to come with me and then stay there when I looked back at it. All objects seemed transparent and weightless. The stars and the moon were spinning in crazy patterns, back and forth, and I found myself alone and out of balance. My stomach caved in, and I rolled on my belly heaving up the beer, hating a universe that tipped over me. The last thing I remember thinking was that I had better go to bed, but I could not remember where it was.

I awakened hot in the sun, sweating and dry mouthed, my whole body aching. I cracked open my eyes, and the daylight was painful. I waited, lying flat on my back. When I was finally able to view the world, the first thing I saw was a black toad sitting on my chest, its yellow eyes half-closed as the sun stroked its wrinkled hide. When I took a deep, agonizing breath, the toad rolled off me into the grass, leaving a cold wet spot on my shirt. I attempted to sit up, but settled for rolling over, trying to push myself onto my hands and knees. My guts were empty, and the earth seemed to push against me. My arms gave out, and I lay in the grass again, trying to think how

Turtle Belly

I had come here. Slowly the night came back to me in vivid fragments—I recalled the incident in the crapper with a groan; I remembered kissing Anne until my tongue was sore. I might have fallen asleep on her mouth or she on mine. Who cared.

Blinking, I began to focus on small things: the static motions of an ant, a scar on my hand pressed near my face, the shredded label of a beer bottle. After awhile, I lifted my heavy head and saw Ellie sitting on the wooden stoop of the old house, watching me. Her face was blank . . . but firm.

She stood up when she saw that I recognized her, and she came over to me. I rolled over on my back. She was as tall as a tree, and she blocked the sun. "It's past seven," she said. "There's work to do."

I crawled up to a tree and slowly hauled myself up on shaky legs. I leaned back and squinted in the sun.

Already the morning heat was strong, and it bent the rays of light above Carver's truck, still parked on the shoulder of the highway. It shimmered like a sacred object in a mirage, a holy vision of a rusting red pickup truck that bore down on me, bringing back memories of the night before. When I looked across the landscape I saw the body of Anne, lying in the grass near the tree line. She was face down with her hair spread like a broad black fan around her shoulders. Ellie came up to her and nudged her hip with her shoe.

"Go home, now," she said.

I stuck my hands deep in my pockets and hung my head down when Ellie came up to Larry and Ima Jean, both sprawled across the driveway. Ellie kicked Larry hard, and he lashed out at the air with swinging fists. "Fuck off!" he said, and he slowly sat up, focusing on Ellie.

Ellie said, "Put on your damn pants."

Larry scuffled in the dirt for his jeans and then stumbled toward the line of trees and bushes past the driveway.

Ellie booted Ima Jean's thigh. "Ima Jean," she said. "Go home, girl."

Ima Jean turned up from the driveway, and her hair was matted flat with dry grass and gravel. She said, with a weak voice and a limp smile, "Hi, Ellie," and then, realizing that she was disarranged, she began to comb out her long hair with her fingers.

Anne, risen and pale like a spirit, came up to me, put her arms around my shoulders, and leaned her forehead into my chest. She hung against me, smelling like stale beer. Slowly, she turned up her face, kissed my neck softly, and said, "I wish I was dead." Then she backed off and walked up the yard to the highway. I watched her until she disappeared beyond the line of trees and the cornfield.

When I shifted and turned around, I saw Tom standing in the doorway of the log house. He said, "Don't look to me."

Ellie helped Ima Jean out to the highway, and she began the long walk home behind Anne. Ima Jean never said good-bye, and she didn't ever look back at Larry. She seemed a shrunken figure as she walked away, and Larry, coming up now with his pants on and his shirt tucked in, sat on the bumper of Carver's truck with his elbows propped on his knees, his gaze locked on the ground.

After Ellie went inside the house and closed the door, I went up to the truck and sat on the bumper with Larry. We were real quiet for a long time, and then Larry glanced over at me. He spoke softly, almost reverently. "What a sweet night."

"I'm dying," I said, poking my shoe at shards of green glass on the road.

Larry ignored me. "I did it," he said. "I actually did it, and it was so sweet. Didn't you hear me howl?"

I looked over at him, and he was bleary eyed and dirty.

"No, I didn't hear you howl," I said. "I was too busy throwing up all night."

"So was I," said Larry. "But in between, I did Ima Jean. She said she loves me."

I hung my head and shook it. "She doesn't love you." I said.

"Then why else would she say it?" asked Larry.

"Because, you dumb jerk, you just happened to be there." I kicked a piece of glass hard. It spun like a top across the highway.

Larry dragged his fingers through his hair and nodded.

"You're not mad, are you?" he asked.

"Why should I be mad?"

"I dunno . . . about Ima Jean, I guess."

"Forget it," I said. "What's done is done."

"No, really, you saw her first. If you wanna fuck her, I don't care," said Larry.

I stood up crazy, fast, struggling to keep my balance, and stared down at Larry. "Suppose she doesn't want to be fucked!" I said loudly.

"Chrissake," he said. "If she'd have me, she'd have you! You may have blue eyes, but I seen you in the locker room. You got a red cock."

And then, without thinking, I swung my fist hard and caught Larry's left eye, knocking him off the bumper. He lay on the gravel, rubbing his face, silent, and I turned my back on my friend and walked away.

Angry
World

Larry didn't come around much after I hit him in the eye. I sort of holed up in my room, painting pictures. Some of them I didn't want to show around. I think they were abstract, at least that's what others would call them. I saw them as perfectly clear. They were *inside me* pictures of stuff that you can't put into words. One of them was really great. It was a white man, naked, using his cock like a chain saw to cut down trees in the forest. He was bigger than the trees, and many Indian people were crying in the forest. Another painting I did showed the back side of Indians, watching a girl with big tits and a big feather headdress dancing on a stage in Las Vegas. The Indians were thinking, like a cartoon caption, "Nice feathers." I saw a show on TV with girls dancing, and I wondered what the old guys would think. So I just made a painting of it. I guess painting tits and feathers was OK.

About two weeks passed, then Larry and I weren't mad. We shook hands, and we both apologized. It was funny. Larry extended his hand up my arm and flopped his wrist and nodded to me to do the same. So we stood there, me puzzled, forearms pressed together flipping our wrists, and Larry said, "Salmon shake, man." He learned it from his older brother, who had just come home from Alaska, where he had been working as a welder on the pipeline. Larry's brother was Russell, and he was like a lot of guys from the rez. He worked a six-month season somewhere far away, and then he came home with a big bundle of money, hung around with his woman and his kids, banged up a car or two, then took off to find a job the following spring. He was a nice guy, and I liked Russell, even though he busted on us. Russell got an old blue pickup truck with a gun rack across the rear window, but he put a pair of lacrosse sticks on the rack instead of a rifle. He'd been a real champion player in high school, and that's why Larry followed in his tracks. Sometimes he'd pitch a few balls around with us guys, but the real reason he carried those netted sticks was to bust up a fight or maybe catch a turtle crossing the road. But one time he got into real trouble with those sticks.

I'd asked Ellie if she'd drive me to the community center, and she surprised me. She was standing at the kitchen table, stirring chopped cabbage and mayonnaise in a bowl with a wooden spoon, and she licked the side of her hand. She turned to the countertop, picked up the keys, and tossed them at me. I jerked and caught them against my chest.

"What's this?" I asked.

"You know how to drive," she said.

I quickly looked over my shoulder through the window at Ellie's old green station wagon, the big eight-cylinder with phony-blond wood panel strips. "No shit?"

"Don't you leave the rez," she said. "I won't bail you out if the cops catch you driving off the rez."

I twirled the keys on my index finger. I'd just turned fifteen, and I was now thinking about all the long straight highways and dirt crossroads, no speed limits, no cops—not white ones anyway—except for a few guys, like cheap security guards, in uniforms with tribal patches.

Ellie said, "And no drinking."

"I promise," I said, my heart drumming over those keys in my hand.

When I turned to rush out the door, Ellie said, "Sam!" and I spun around.

"Keep it in your pants," she said.

I just shook my head and rushed outside, letting the screen door bang shut behind me. Ellie's son, my nine-year-old cousin, Eddie, was skinning out a big snapping turtle, hanging from a tree branch by a metal hook stuck through its lower jaw.

He saw me getting into the driver's side of the old car, and he flipped the butcher knife into the ground and squatted to wipe his bloody hands in the grass.

"What'dya think you're doing?" he asked, coming up to the car as I turned the engine over.

"Cruising, little brother!" I said, putting the car into drive and spinning a circle around him in the dirt yard.

"I'm coming with you!" he yelled. But I left him standing in a cloud of dust as I flew out onto the highway.

It was a cloudless Friday evening, with supper finished, the weekend ahead of me, and just a hint of autumn in the air. The sun was still up, dark harvest orange reflecting through the trees, and I felt like I was flying, unrestrained and light as milk-weed down blowing across the face of the world. I drove faster than Ellie did, making that old car rattle and whine near eighty miles an hour. It scared me to death, driving like that. But I couldn't help going fast, because no one was there to tell me not to. The wind was blowing in the open window and rushing around the car, loud as a freight train. I hit a rabbit and kept on going. I didn't worry about hitting a rabbit—Ellie did it all the time going slowly—but it might have bothered me to hit some-one's dog, knowing how bad I felt when my dog, *Daywahseh*, Number Twenty, got killed on the road. The thought of hitting some kid's dog made me finally slow down, but I still tore up the gravel coming into the parking lot of the community center, barely missing a dog that lurked between an abandoned pickup truck on cinder blocks and a new red Ford Torino.

I drove right up to the side door where a half-dozen girls were swarming in a cluster. I recognized Anne, and Ima Jean, and Carver Hill's little sister, Angie, who was wearing bright red lipstick in public now that she had entered the high school. It looked like big wax lips on her, too big for her face, and she always had it on her teeth. Most of the older girls had grown out of that stage, but I liked the taste of lipstick, as long as it wasn't red. I thought there was nothing worse than having your face covered with sticky lip prints, like you were wounded.

I got out of the car, twirling the keys proudly on my finger, and sauntered towards the girls, calling out, "Has Larry showed up yet?"

They turned to me, and Ima Jean broke stride from them, came right up, and caught me unexpectedly with a hard, stinging smack across my cheek that came out of nowhere, blinding me for a second.

"You son of a bitch!" she said, gritting her teeth.

I got so mad then, I wanted to left-hook her right onto the parking lot, and I would have too, but her friends had come between us. I think mostly they were trying to keep her off of me, because her arms were flailing and she was spitting at me. But my fists were tightly clenched in case we got close enough. I was ready to break her neck if she thought she'd clip me again.

She was screaming at me, "It's all your goddamned fault. If it wasn't for you none of this would have happened, you lousy son of a bitch!"

Then she just started crying and folded up, like a dying flower, in the arms of her friends. Anne pushed me back a few yards and put her arms around my neck. "It's OK," she said. "It's really not your fault."

"Why'd she hit me?" I asked. "I didn't do anything to her."

"That night we came to your house and got drunk in the yard," she started—

But I spoke out. "That was almost two months ago. So what?"

"So what?" she said. "She's pregnant. That's so what!"

"I didn't do it!" I said. "It was Larry. You know that. I was with you all night." And then I paused, fully understanding what Anne had said. "Pregnant? No shit?"

"No shit," said Anne.

"Larry, for sure?" I asked.

"There's been no one else," Anne said. "I'm her friend, and I know it's true."

My face was burning. "So why the hell did she hit me?"

"Because you were there that night."

"You were there, too. Did she hit you?"

"I'm not a guy," she answered, her eyes dark and narrow with sympathy for Ima Jean. But then she put her arms over my shoulders, and she came in close to me. "I know it's not your fault."

I leaned my forehead against hers, and then I put my arms around her for the first time since the night in my yard. We'd seen each other since then. We'd chatted. We were in the same math class at the high school, but we had kept a distance up till now. It wasn't that we disliked each other, at least I didn't think so. Because I liked Anne, and I knew she liked me because she smiled from time to time in my direction. I think we were distant from each other because it was too embarrassing to be together or intimate after that sick, drunken night. But this changed everything, and it felt good to put my arms around Anne, just to hold onto some person. Because I needed it and so did she, and I hoped to close up that awful, embarrassing blackness between us.

I whispered, "Larry's going to meet me here. I just talked to him, and he didn't tell me."

Anne said, "He doesn't know. He came flying by with his brother, Russell and said he'd try to swing by later. We were supposed to tell you. Ima Jean was pretty fucked-up after he left. She went kind of crazy on you, I guess."

"Where'd he go?"

"Caledonia. To play some pool."

I gave Anne a quick squeeze hug and left her to talk with Ima Jean. It was crazy how life skinned you and turned you inside out in the blink of an eye. Just a moment before, Ima Jean was that long-haired girl who wiggled around in her blue jeans, all antsy and hot to trot it out. She was like the temptation to let a mosquito bore into you and watch it grow fat and red with your blood, enjoying the itch. But now she was a red-eyed, angry young woman who just hated everything, but who let me come up to her, let me put my arms around her, and cried with shaking gasps that made me fix my balance and lean into her.

She sobbed, "You're his best friend. You have to help me tell him."

I rocked her and said, "I'll help you." And that was the first time Ima Jean ever kissed me, softly on my shoulder. I felt her breath through my shirt, but it was hopeless to hope for her. She no longer was the Ima Jean of my fantasy, dancing like a wide-hipped mare. She was the Ima Jean of my reality, who suddenly made it seem like there was no hope—that we all just sat around sharpening the very knives that would skin us inside out. Her pain did that to me. It made me feel small. It made me feel that there were forces in the world that just rolled over us and kept on rolling. I said to her, "Let's go find Larry. We'll tell him."

Then Anne pulled us away from the others, and the three of us sat in the front seat of the big old car. Anne leaned against me while Ima Jean cried out the window as we drove down the highway. I didn't feel so free, and I didn't drive so fast. We were leaving the rez, going to Caledonia, a bit of nowhere—me without a license and in Ellie's car—to find the father of Ima Jean's baby. There was no other choice, and when we crossed over the surveyed line into white-mans' land, I sat taller in the seat, looking out for police. But most of all, I was looking at the deepening twilight and seeing the world not as a passenger, but as a driver. I could steer to the left or the right, entirely stop, or go backward, watching the world retreat. And that's mostly what I wanted the world to do—to retreat in a backward spin and make Ima Jean unpregnant and happy, to give the car keys back to Ellie, to just sleep away the future and never have to face it, rushing at me like a car with its high beams blinding me.

Anne shrieked, "Look out!" and I swerved away from the oncoming car, then back onto the highway. "The sonuvabitch almost hit us!" she said, looking back over the seat.

Ima Jean said, "It would serve me right to die on the road like a dog!" Then she pushed open the car door, battling back the high wind, and Anne struggled with her as I tried to slow the car. My heart was drumming, and now I just knew that nothing good could come of this. My hands were all greasy on the steering wheel, and my mouth was dry.

"Don't ever do that!" I yelled at Ima Jean. "Kill yourself if you want, but don't kill us, too!"

Anne struggled to reach past Ima Jean while the car fishtailed onto the gravel and came to a stop—the dust rising up in the headlights like gray highway ghosts come to accept us. But we were not ready to greet them. And when Anne finally closed the door, she shoved Ima Jean over to the middle, sandwiching her between us. And I gunned the car through those ghosts until we were again flying down the dark road.

As we neared Caledonia, we passed a roadhouse tavern with a big parking lot on the right, and I saw Russell Killdeer's blue pickup truck parked in the lot. I quick-braked and wrenched the steering wheel over, bumping across potholes until we slid beside the truck.

I looked over at Ima Jean and Anne and said, "I'll go see if Larry's inside." I got out of the car, then turned back. "Anne, you make sure she stays with you." When Anne nodded, I stuck my hands in my pockets and walked toward the front door of the tavern. The door stuck out from the corner of the building and over it on the roof was a cockeyed neon sign, in red and blue lights twisted like a peppermint stick, that read *The 8 Ball*. I tried to stand taller when I opened the door, but I still felt fifteen years old, and I had never been in a bar.

Larry was big for his age, and Russell had been bringing him along since he got back in August. I guess Larry just fit in, because no one ever questioned how old he was. But when I came into the smoky big room the door slapped shut with a loud bang, and people looked up at me and kept staring as I tried to spot Larry or Russell.

There was a long bar across the back of the room with mirrors and faceted glasses stacked like diamond pyramids, all sparkling and full of hazy reflected faces. There were six pool tables in a row across from the bar, each one illuminated by swinging overhead lights with green metal shades. The smoke from cigarettes hung in the lights, making the green felt tables look like battlefields under siege, with generals in cowboy hats and tee shirts sighting down their cue sticks at the enemy. Beyond the pool tables was a broad, dark open area, flanked by a few tables and chairs and a jukebox. Several couples were slow-dancing in the shadows, playing grab ass to the music.

One of the guys behind the bar saw me and yelled, "Get the hell out of here!" But I ignored him and hurried down the row of pool tables. I could see Larry with his back to me, and

Russell was leaning over the table with one knee up on the corner, trying to make a long shot. I came up fast and grabbed Larry's shoulder, and he spun around, with a cue stick held out in front of him, ready to fight.

"Jeezus Christ!" he said, taking a deep breath. "You coulda' got your fuckin' head knocked off!"

"You gotta come outside," I said. "I got the girls in the car."

Over my shoulder I could see the bartender coming after me.

Larry leaned back, grabbing his beer off the edge of the pool table. "What do you mean *you* got the girls in the car? Who drove you?"

"I drove us. Ellie gave me the car tonight."

Larry shifted the cue stick into the hand with the beer and slapped my palm hard. "Nice going, little Brother."

"Let's get outta here," I said.

"Right now? It's my quarter on the table. I've got the next game."

"We have to talk," I said, then sidestepped as the bartender tried to grab me. "I'm leaving, man. Back off!" I pushed past him and yanked Larry along with me. He yelled back at Russell, "Save my quarter," and Russell nodded.

Outside, the air felt crisp and cool, and I walked Larry fast to the car, where I could see the silhouettes of the two girls, exactly as I had left them, their shoulders pressed together.

Larry leaned into the open driver's window. "Kind of a long way from home, aren't you girls?" They both sat silent and stared straight ahead.

Larry glanced up at me. "Does someone have a problem?"

"Big-time problem," I said. "You and Ima Jean."

He rolled over and rested his elbows on the edge of the

open window. "Oh, yah? So what's this big problem everyone but me seems to know about?"

Before I could answer I heard the awful screech of car tires on the highway, and when I looked up I saw a lime-colored Camaro spin into the lot, slamming into park. It was Ima Jean's older brother, Virgil, and two of his friends, some goons who lived at the lower end of the rez. They just came roaring out of the car, leaving the doors open, and they were heading for Larry. I backed away, and Larry stood up, taking a step forward. But they didn't even say a word. They attacked him like wolves, bringing him down on his knees in the parking lot. Ima Jean began to scream, and she leaned out the open window of the car.

"Stop it! Virgil, you'll kill him! Stop it!" she screamed, and she started to pound on the horn of the car. Anne folded her arms across her body and seemed to melt way down in the car seat, and I wasn't going to get in the way. I was afraid they wouldn't get enough of Larry and would come after me.

Curious people came out of the bar after hearing the screams and the car's horn, and I edged closer to them to be invisible. Larry was lying on the ground, and those three guys were really giving it to him. One of them had Larry's arm bent up behind his back, while Virgil punched his face. There was blood all over Larry's face, and I think he was already unconscious. The third guy was kicking Larry, and I felt sick in my stomach to see the blood splashing on the ground with each punch. In the neon light, Larry's blood was like black tar on the gravel.

Larry's brother, Russell, pushed through the people. He walked fast around my car, opened the door of the truck, and came out swinging one of his long-handled hickory lacrosse sticks. He dropped the guy who was kicking his brother with a blow in the small of his back. I heard a loud crack, and I thought he had broken the stick. But he swung it again and clipped the guy holding Larry's arm under the chin, right across his throat and he fell back choking, one hand holding his throat, and trying to crawl like a baby. When Virgil looked up, Russell brought the stick full-hard into his face, and he fell flat on his back. I could see the pattern of the rawhide webbing cut through the skin of his forehead, and I loved it. Russell came in swinging like a warrior against three enemies, and they all fell. It was different from the way they had come and jumped on one guy, kicking him when he was down.

Russell bent down, still holding the stick in his left hand, and rolled the fingers of his free hand around Larry's shirt collar. He rose up and dragged Larry toward the truck, and I rushed forward to help him.

"What started this, Turtle Belly?" he asked under his breath as we hauled Larry into the truck.

"Larry knocked up Ima Jean, and Virgil caught him."

Russell climbed into the truck. "He didn't say nothing to me."

"He didn't know. I brought her here to tell him, and those guys jumped him."

"Was it a set-up?" Russell asked.

"I don't think so. I think it just kind of happened."

Russell started the truck and threw it into gear.

"Let's get the hell home," he said.

I ran around to my car. Ima Jean was out on the ground with her brother. She was crying and holding his head, and there were other people milling over them.

"Ima Jean!" I yelled. "I gotta go!" Then I heard sirens coming from the direction of Caledonia, and I jumped in my car and started it up. Anne looked all around. She was scared, her face all tight and pale. "You can't leave Ima Jean," she said.

"Ima Jean! Please, get in the car!"

She wouldn't listen, and when Russell gassed it hard I followed right behind him, throwing up gravel and speeding out onto the highway. Looking in the rearview mirror, I saw the flashing red lights of two cop cars coming fast, but they both turned into the parking lot.

Russell was doing about ninety, and I tried hard to keep up with him. Then I saw, far behind me, the flashing lights of one of those cop cars. We turned off the big road onto the small highway that led north onto the rez. We were still a couple of miles ahead of the cop when we crossed the line, but I knew he'd keep coming. All they needed was one reason to cross the line, and they'd get you. Suddenly Russell hit the lights on his truck, threw it into low gear, and slowed. I killed the lights on my car and slowed, and it seemed as if the sound of the siren and those flashing lights were on top of me.

Russell turned onto a dirt side road, slowly, so as not to kick up too much dust, and I hugged onto him for about half a mile. He must have felt it was safe to speed up, but we still drove all lightless through the black country. I saw the cop car racing up the main road behind us, and I gave a short honk. We both pulled over, and I got out. Then Russell got out, and we met between the two cars.

"Where are we going?" I asked. "What're we going to do, Russ?"

Russell squatted down. "I'm thinking, Sam. I'm thinking about it all. Give me a minute."

"Jesus, you really took care of those guys," I said.

He looked at the dark sky, all cloudy with no stars or

moon. "They had it coming," he said, gazing across the land for some answer. He stood up, brushing the knees of his worn jeans. "Maybe it would be best if you took that girl home," he said, pointing his chin at my car.

"I want to stay with you," I said.

"Take her home now."

"Where are you going?" I asked.

"I gotta get Larry patched up," he said, turning back to the truck.

I pricked my ears and looked back. "Another cop car going up the highway. I'm going with you."

"You got no stake in this," he said. "Keep your name clean. You get involved now, and every time you turn around some cop'll be cruising behind you. Now, I told you to take that girl home. Go on. . . . Get out of here!"

Russell went fast to his truck and took off, and I got in my car and followed slowly behind him. I wasn't going to turn around and go back to the main road. I figured I'd take the next crossroad north.

Anne asked, "What'd you guys talk about?"

"Russell told me to take you home."

"Is Larry OK?"

"I don't know. I guess he's pretty beat up."

We were still driving without lights, but once, far ahead, I saw the brake lights of Russell's truck when he slowed at a curve.

"You goin' to take me home?" she asked.

"Do you want to go home?"

"I don't know," she said, curled up small on the seat beside me. "I'm cold. Put on the heater."

"The heater's broken," I said, rolling up the window.

I came up to the crossroad, inched out, and looked both

ways. I saw Russell's brake lights flick on to the north of us, and I turned north too.

"Are you following him?" asked Anne.

"Not on purpose. We're both going the same way."

"You know where I live," she said. "South."

"I'm sorry. I'll turn around."

"No, it's OK," she said. "Just drive."

I speeded up a little and saw the truck brake before it turned east at the next dirt crossroad. When I came up the dust had settled, and I followed. We were traveling through a big wood lot, the place where people came in early spring to collect the maple sap. There were old sugarhouses back in the bush, and some old log houses sinking into the earth. I knew just where we were, because I'd ridden Ellie's horse, Star Blanket, the big Appaloosa stallion, across a concession of land and into the sugar bush last spring. I didn't ride much anymore, but when I did it was memorable, not like driving fast and alone in a car. When I rode a horse through the bush I felt every footstep echo in my body, and I saw every bird and chipmunk. Star Blanket and I would come up to an old log house and carefully, watching for rusted wire and well holes, travel around it, studying the notched logs and the wooden roof shakes covered in moss. I guess I knew pretty well how to build one, if I ever wanted to.

After a while it wasn't so bad driving without headlights. We had gone a long way into the bush, and I decided to turn on the lights. The road jumped into view, unnaturally bright at first, and it seemed funny to see the animal eyes bouncing beyond in the darkness.

We came to a fork in the road, and Anne said, "Go left."

"Why?"

"He's going up to Carver Hill's camp."

"What do you know about Carver Hill and a camp?" I asked.

"One time after church, I heard my Aunt Ruth say that Carver Hill was going to hell for running a still up the left fork of the sugar-bush road."

"How does your old aunt know about stills?"

"It isn't a sin to drink it; it's just a sin to make it," she said. "Aunt Ruth believes that sin gets watered down the farther away from the source you get. She gets away with an awful lot of sin that way."

I drove up the left fork of the road, and after a mile or so I could smell woodsmoke in the air. I rolled down the window and looked up at the sky, and the clouds were moving down from the north. I turned north on the first cutoff, and after a couple-hundred yards, I saw Russell's truck parked off in the woods by a path. I killed the car lights and told Anne to stay put.

"I always sit in the car," she said. "But I'm not sitting here alone in the bush at night."

So we got out of the car and walked close together along the path, smelling woodsmoke. It was birch in the stove, sweet and pitchy, that burned slowly but hot, and we followed the scent through the woods.

Suddenly two people carrying shotguns stepped out in front of us, and we stopped short. I didn't recognize them. They were big guys who held the guns low, pointing at us. My breath was short, and I didn't move. Anne was quiet beside me, one arm around my waist and the other hand hanging onto my shoulder.

They didn't say a word. They just kept those guns aimed at us, and after what seemed a long time, Russell came from behind them, and they put the guns off to the side.

"What the fuck is wrong with you?" he said. "Driving up here with your lights on, banging car doors. You're lucky you didn't get shot dead."

"I want to know about Larry."

"He's all busted up, spitting blood. He's got a broke arm."

"He gonna be alright?" I asked.

"We're taking care of it."

I took a step closer to Russell. "Maybe I'll go talk to him."

"Don't want you here," he said. "Nothing against you, but you gotta get out of here, and you gotta take that girl home. Things'll just get worse if you don't listen to me. Now you go home. You don't talk to nobody. You just been driving around since the fight, clearing your head. You got it?"

"Yeah, I got it," I said. "You promise you'll come by and tell me about Larry."

"Promise," he said, coming in close and shaking my hand hard. He pulled me aside. "You talk to that girl. Keep her quiet."

"She's OK," I said. Then Russell and the two guys disappeared up the trail.

When I pulled up to Anne's place, a nice white frame house with a wilted flower garden, she got out of the car fast and ran inside without saying a word of good-bye. She didn't really even talk during the ride back. I guess she was all shook up, having those guns pointed at her.

I drove up the line and got home close to midnight. Inside the house, Ellie was watching TV. Everyone else was asleep, and the house was all dark except for the glowing TV.

Ellie, wrapped up warm in a quilt on the sofa, said, "I talked to the cops tonight. They were looking for you."

"I didn't do anything," I said.

"Then why don't you tell me what you didn't do."

I looked around the room. "Where'd Tom put his smokes?"

Ellie pointed, and I grabbed a cigarette from the pack on the TV and lighted it. I sat on the couch by Ellie's feet and took a deep drag on my smoke.

"I don't like it when the cops come around asking about you," said Ellie.

"I told you, nothing happened."

"The way I heard, there's three guys in the Caledonia hospital. Russell Killdeer was liquored up at The 8 Ball and went after them with a lacrosse stick. You and him took off together and outran the cops."

"It wasn't like that," I said. "You got it all mixed around."

Ellie's face was set, all frozen with no emotion, madder than I ever knew her, and her voice was hard-edged and brittle. "Then you tell me how it was. You tell me how you come to drive my car off the rez to The 8 Ball, when I told you to stay here. You tell me how you outran the cops."

So I told her everything, and I was honest, except for the ride back to the rez. I told her I was running along behind Russell's truck, trying to keep up and worried about Larry. I told her we lost them on the back roads.

"You fooling around with Anne all this time?"

"No," I said. "I didn't even kiss her."

Ellie's eyes got real slim, and they looked right through me.

I put out the smoke in an ashtray on the floor between my feet. The way Ellie was looking at me made me feel like some giant bird was resting on my shoulders, diggin' its talons into me. It could take off, carrying me away, weightless, so that my feet would never touch the ground again.

"They would have killed Larry," I said. "Russell was only looking out for him."

Ellie sighed. "People getting liquored up, messing around with girls. All that bad feeling off the rez, and now it all comes home, fighting among ourselves."

"Wasn't our fault."

"Doesn't matter whose fault it is. Only thing that matters is that it happened," said Ellie. "Come on now. Tell me where Russell took Larry." There was that damned bird of prey again.

I took a deep breath. "They went up the left fork of the sugar-bush road. There's a camp back in there."

"How bad is Larry hurt?"

"I didn't see him, but Russell came out and said that he was spitting blood and his arm was broken."

"I see," said Ellie. "Your best friend, the father of Ima Jean's baby, and you-all leave him like that in some old sugar shack in the woods on a cold night like this."

Ellie got off the sofa and pulled on her cowboy boots.

"Go get in the car," she said, grabbing up a canvas coat.

"What are you doing?" I cried out.

"I'm going to get that boy and take him to his mother and drive them to the hospital! Now go get in the—" She suddenly stopped because headlights were turning into our yard. "The cops said they'd be back."

I looked out the window. "No, not the cops. I think it's Russell's truck." I went to the door, and it was Russell. I waved to him to drive around the back of the house, and he didn't waste any time speeding through the weeds.

Ellie and I rushed back through the house to the kitchen door, and Tom came downstairs, pulling on his jeans. He was barefoot and shirtless, and his hair was all tousled. He asked what was happening.

Ellie said, "Russell Killdeer just drove in."

Tom looked at me with one sleepy eyebrow raised. "Welcome home," he said. "You have a good night?" He rubbed his forehead and palmed back his hair.

"No," I answered.

"Neither did I. Cops coming around. Trying to sleep. I got my Saturday-morning shift tomorrow."

"I'm sorry," I said. But he waved me aside to look out the back door. Russell came up to the door. His face was gray as a clay pot.

"I think Larry's pretty bad off," he said. "I drove by Mother's, but there was a cop car there."

There was a big guy in the back of Russell's truck, and he jumped out, holding a shotgun. He was guarding Larry, who lay in the back.

Ellie came out the door, and Tom and I followed. She went right up to that big guy and grabbed the barrel of his shotgun. She looked him right in the eyes. "I know you," she said. "You're Norman Lake, aren't you? I remember when you used to poop your pants, and now you're standing in my yard with a gun." She yanked the gun from his grip and ejected the shells on the ground, then leaned the gun against the side of the log house. "Don't you even think about that gun while you're standing in my yard."

Tom, still barefoot and shirtless, was shivering. He looked hard at Russell and Norman. "You boys been drinking?"

"Maybe a little," said Russell.

"More'n a little," said Tom, "judging by the smell of it all over you."

Ellie leaned over the back of the truck. "Larry, it's Ellie.

You're gonna be alright," she said. Then she turned back all tight faced. "What's got into you guys, driving him around in the back of an open truck, on a cold night, all busted up? You got no sense at all."

Tom said, "I'm getting cold without a shirt. I'm going inside to get dressed and call an ambulance, and you guys are staying put. You hear me?"

Russell and Norman nodded and hung their heads like two sick dogs. Ellie draped her arm over the back of the truck and held Larry's shoulder. "You call his mother, too," she yelled after Tom.

I never saw two guys so big act so small. Ellie shrunk them right down and held them in her palm. She was a strong woman when she was in the right, and those guys knew it. She was, in the best old-time tradition, the head of the household, and they were powerless standing in her yard. Now they weren't even talking, not even to each other, and they didn't dare look up at Ellie. One more bad look from her, and they would have dried up like dust and blown away. So they just made themselves invisible. I wasn't far behind them, either. When I asked Ellie how Larry was doing, she did something she hadn't done in years, since I was a kid who would not learn or listen. It was the way of our ancestors, who did not believe in hitting or yelling. What she did was look right through me, making me invisible like Russell and Norman, as though I did not exist. There was nothing worse in the world than when someone you loved didn't know you were alive, didn't hear your voice, couldn't see you, talked to people behind you as if you were a vapor or a wisp of smoke. That's how the old-timers taught you a lesson. Sometimes, I was told, it lasted for days, maybe weeks, or even a month, until you were so ashamed of not being a person that you would do anything to be alive again—apologize to your old grandma, do extra chores—anything to raise the veil of silence.

The first car that pulled in was Larry's mother, and she had brought Russell's woman and kids. Larry's mother was a short, round little woman with a smooth polished face and wiry grey hair. She left the others sitting in the car and came up to the truck. She took one look at Russell but didn't say anything to him. She leaned into the truck as Ellie stepped aside, and comforted Larry with her hands and an almost inaudible soothing voice.

A cop car came in and parked behind Russell's mother, and I was relieved to see that it was a tribal patrol car, not a provincial cop from off the rez. The cop got out, put his Smokey hat on, and came up to us slowly, looking around carefully. He saw the shotgun leaning against the side of the house. He saw the bright red shells scattered in front of the back door. He shook his head, took off his hat and scratched his head, then put his hat back on. "Where have you been, Russell?" he said, and he looked at Norman. "As if I had to ask." He came alongside the truck and looked down at Larry. "Got busted up there, Larry?" That's how it was with those guys. They knew everyone, and they knew everything that was goin' on. They were OK about it, though. They just wanted to keep things quiet and try to handle it themselves. It wasn't the Indian way to talk too loud, because you didn't know who else was listening. I knew that, because Tom once told me that if a tribal cop took off his hat and put it back on before talking to you, it meant he was on your side and wanted to "keep things under his hat," all quiet and private until things could be worked out. But if you gave him a hard time, and he had to arrest you, then it just meant he had an itchy head.

Tom came out, dressed and snapping closed a work coat,

and nine-year-old Eddie was standing in the doorway, watching us mingle in the yard in the bright headlights. Our shadows were long and spidery. When I glanced over my shoulder I saw Russell's wife sitting in the car, silhouetted in white radiant light from the patrol car.

The cop, knowing that Russell had been drinking, gave him a lot of space. He said, "You gotta control that temper of yours."

Russell, who wouldn't dare talk up to Ellie, said, "My brother got jumped by three big guys."

The cop said, "You hurt 'em pretty bad."

"Three on one," said Russell. "They hurt Larry pretty bad."

"I'm going to give you two choices," said the cop. "You can come along to tribal lockup or go home to your mother's house and stay there until we know how bad off they are. If one of them dies, I'll come get you and turn you over."

"Maybe I'll run," Russell said.

"You can run like a dog if you want, or be a man about it. If none of those guys dies, I'll back you up. They jumped Larry first, and you protected him." The cop looked back. "Here's the ambulance now. Think it over."

The cop directed the ambulance around the cars, and it backed up to the truck. It was one of those new ambulances, like a van, so people could sit inside the back. Two guys in white uniforms with red cross patches on the sleeves got Larry out of the truck and onto a stretcher-like cart, covered him with blankets, and strapped him down with buckles. His mother got in with him, and before they closed the doors I saw her worried face illuminated by the sterile lights. She seemed older to me. But Larry was her youngest and he was hurting bad, and I guess it just took some of the life out of her.

After the ambulance left, the cop questioned Russell.

"What do you want to do?"

"I guess maybe I'll go home," Russell said.

"And stay there?"

"Where am I gonna go?"

"Well, don't think about it too hard," said the cop. And then, looking over at Russell's truck, he added, "And give me those damned lacrosse sticks."

Russell reached inside and gave him two sticks. One of them was all bloody.

The cop told Norman to go sit in the patrol car. "Russ, have your woman drive your mother's car. You drive behind her in the truck, and I'll follow. When we get there, you're going to give me your keys."

"That won't keep me put if I decide to travel," said Russell.

"You just spend some time with your kids," said the cop. There were three of them in the car—a four-year-old, a toddler, and a baby.

Ellie didn't talk to me for the next couple of days. I didn't do much talking either. When Anne came by and told me that Larry was home from the hospital, I walked four miles to his mother's house to visit him.

His right arm was broken, up by the shoulder, from when they bent it back. His jaw was wired shut. Ima Jean was with him. She said, "He lost a molar. The doctor just pulled it out with his fingers. That's why he was spitting blood."

Larry grinned stiffly. He had a big cast on his arm and shoulder and a brace around his neck. He spoke with a low clenched slur. "I been hurt worse playing lacrosse," he said. Ima Jean sat beside him on the sofa, and she just stared, in love, at him. "You're gonna be a daddy!" Then she held up a cherry Coke with a straw for him to sip.

When I left I was relieved that things had worked out. Larry had agreed not to press charges against Virgil and the two other guys, so they wouldn't press charges against Russell. Everyone might pay his own doctor bill someday. Everyone would heal someday, but for the moment there was a baby coming. It was a mean, twisted-up world. I knew the world wouldn't get any better, but I sure as hell hoped we'd all be around for awhile. Don't ask me why any of us wanted to keep on going in this world of fucking and fighting and drinking and dying. We just did.

Over
A
Hundred
Miles
An
Hour

I never understood why tourists came to the reservation every summer, especially during hot, dry August when the tar roads buckled and shimmered in the heat and the dirt roads churned up dust like tornadoes. It was funny to see them, the tourists, riding around in cars with all the windows rolled up against the dust, sweaty and baked until their faces turned red, kids crying, moms and dads yelling at each other. We didn't care about the dust—it was just part of summer—and we let it blow in the car, and we drove fast so the wind kept us cool.

Beyond that, there was nothing to see or do, just miles and miles of flat land, tree lines, little creeks, squat log houses, a few modern ranch homes with white vinyl siding, and a horse or two nuzzling a fence post by the side of the highway. The real sites, places with real meaning, were lost on the tourists—places like the Sour Springs churchyard, where so many of the old ones were buried, or the wood-frame longhouses where the traditional people gather to pray. The meaning of these places was lost because they did not stand out as anything different from the outside world. If there was not a sign, no one would know they had just come upon Indian land.

Perhaps because it *was* Indian land, the tourists suffered all the summer heat and dust to satisfy their curiosity. I always had the sense, watching them gas up their cars, grumbling and swigging ice-cold soda pops, that they were disappointed. I didn't care, I wondered how they would feel if caravans of rusty trucks and dented Buicks filled with Indians drove around their suburbs—cameras snapping, kids throwing empty potato-chip bags on the emerald lawns, fenders stained with the blood of their pet dogs and cats. It just never occurred to us to pack the family in the car to go in search of white people.

When I wanted to go on holiday I went to the general store and gas pump at the four corners, where a tar and dirt road intersected, smelling like creosote and fresh-turned earth. A breeze always blew up the Grand River, carrying the corn-pollen musk to tickle my nose. Sooner or later someone I knew always came by, and we'd sit together on the high concrete stoop, still outfitted with iron rings from the time when folks tied up their horses and buggies. Sometimes Larry Killdeer and I sat sipping a soda pop or a beer, watching cars and people, smoking butts, maybe giving some guy a hassle if he asked something stupid. One time a guy, sunburned in a purple tank top, asked us where the action was, and Larry said, "In your eyes, faggot." He was a mean enough guy, a few tattoos on his bare red arms, his hair slicked back, but he walked away from us because the odds didn't seem right, with a dozen other guys hanging around the dry, dusty stoop of the faded wooden store.

Sometimes a person might ask a stupid question, but we didn't get mad, because they were just stupid. Like when a really nice lady with two fat kids asked, "I've been driving around all day, and I can't find any tipis." Larry shook his head and answered, "That's 'cause we only put them up at night to sleep in."

The woman said, "I didn't know that."

Larry said, "Now if you go about a thousand miles west of here, to the plains, those people keep their tipis up all day long."

The woman, her face weary and blotchy from the heat, asked if she could take a picture of her kids with us, and then she herded them around us. She began to focus her camera, and then she looked up at me. "Would you mind, please, moving off to the side. I only want real Indians in the picture."

I slipped off the concrete stoop and stood off to the side while she took a picture. What did she know? She saw a guy sitting there with brown hair and blue eyes, and she just figured he didn't belong in the picture. I didn't take it personally, not like she should've known better. That's how it is with stupid people; you just can't blame them. But you still get mad. Not for yourself, but because the world seems all snaked up and twisted and full of meanness and innocence preying on each other. I guess then I just thought that true meanness and true innocence were about the same thing, because they both resulted in someone being hurt.

I was eighteen that summer. In the fall I was going off to a university, and I didn't want to do anything but sit around the four-corners store with my friends and stare at all the tourists. Soon I would be going out into their world, but for now this was my only world, my one life, and I exaggerated it, drinking down beers, spitting tobacco juice towards the Flying-A gas pumps, sneering at the young guys who strutted around the young girls. Sometimes my cousin Ellie, who was almost forty and still acted like my mother, would come by the store and say, "It's hard to believe you're a university man, sitting around with all these bums."

Larry said, "Who you calling a bum?"

Ellie would knock the top of his head with her knuckles and say, "You go home and look after that woman and baby of yours."

Larry would brush her away. "She kicked me out this morning. I'm just giving her time to come around."

Ellie answered, "She kicks you out every morning."

Larry said, "And every night she comes around. True love."

Ellie wouldn't let up on him. "You could be going to the university, too, if you'd been smart enough to keep it in your pants, where it belongs."

"Jeezus, Ellie, what'd I do to you?"

"Nothing," she said. "I got no problems with you, but you make sure you look after that baby and your woman."

Larry twisted his head around. "I hear you," he said. But after Ellie gassed up the car and left, he turned to me. "Can't she do nothing but bring up the past?"

"I thought she was bringing up the future," I said.

Larry began to speak, but past his shoulder I saw a sporty little red car speeding down the road, the gears low, whining as it slowed and pulled up to the pumps. Larry was talking, but I didn't pay attention. I was looking at the woman getting out of the car.

One of the gas pumps blocked the car's door, and the first thing I saw was a white spiky-sandaled foot and a white ankle, calf, knee, and the hem of a yellow silk skirt with black polka dots, then a yellow silk-pleated hip, jutting out as she leaned her way up from the car to stretch in the hot afternoon. The yellow silk dress left her arms bare, and she waved them. Her fingernails were bright red. Her hair was straight, curled under at the shoulder, and black like a wig. When she turned sideways, her mouth was red like her nails, and her skin was pale and flawless with just a slight blush on her cheeks. She yawned and reached her hands high above her, and her armpits were caked with talcum powder. When she walked away from the car, toward us on the stoop of the general store, her eyes seemed glazed from the heat. And when she mounted the concrete steps, her heels tapping, I could smell a perfume, like sweet cut flowers and spice. She was like a pie fresh out of the oven, all warm and ready to sink your teeth into, but forbidden. I thought maybe she was a movie star or a magazine model, and I got up fast when she went into the store.

Larry said, "Aren't you listening?"

I said, "I'm going to get a soda."

Larry complained, "I'm doing the best I can. You know that. Just tell Ellie to lay off for a while."

I said, "Sure. Whatever you want." And I followed the lady in the yellow dress into the store.

The store was dark after the bright sunlight outside, and it took a moment for me to find the lady. She was by the Popsicle freezer, and she had picked out a paper-wrapped Popsicle and was stroking it across her forehead. Then she dragged it slowly across the back of her neck, rotating her head like a happy cat. I watched the way she absorbed herself and seemed to disappear from this world, so caught up and private that nothing else existed except for the coolness on the back of her white neck. After a while, a thin orange stream seeped through the paper wrapper and trickled down between her shoulder blades, and she jerked up. She opened the wrapper, licked the Popsicle, and aimlessly wandered around the store until she found herself in front of a revolving rack of postcards.

I had no idea how old she was—she might have been twenty or forty—because she looked like a woman but acted like a bored child, shifting her weight as she picked out postcards and read the descriptions on the back of them. She suddenly quick-turned and stared at me, and I looked away. When I glanced back after a moment, she was holding the Popsicle between her teeth while she shuffled postcards with both hands.

When she looked back at me, the twin Popsicle sticks aimed like shotgun barrels, I flinched, and she took a couple of steps toward me. "Hold these," she mumbled, handing me the postcards. She took the Popsicle from her mouth.

"It's so hot," she said. "Thanks."

I handed her the postcards, and she spread them like a bird's tail and fanned herself. "Godforsaken hot in this godforsaken land," she said. She held up the orange Popsicle and said, "You know, someone ought to make these things with vodka. You wouldn't care how hot it was, would you?"

"I guess not," I said.

She laughed and leaned in close. "So what gives around here?"

"What do you mean?" I asked.

"I mean it can't be all postcards and Popsicles." She was so close, all perfume and sugar breath, and her eyes were narrowed, quick and full of fun. I breathed her in deeply, her sweaty perfume, and my heart was beating fast.

"There are things going on," I said. "What do you want to do?"

"I think," she said, pausing with a slow breath, "I just want to explode. It's so hot and dusty, I want to turn myself inside out. I can't wait for nighttime, as long as it's cool. I want to have some goddamn laughs."

At that moment, my eyes lowered to her ankles. Gazing up those slim white legs, I just thought about giving her the right answer, about making this time with her last a little longer. I said, "We could go over to my friend Carver's and see what's happening."

"Who's Carver?" she asked.

"He's alright," I said. "He always knows what's going on."

"Let's go," she said. And as we walked out of the store, she tossed the postcards and the melting Popsicle on the counter, reached into a pocket in her yellow silk skirt, and flipped a dollar bill at the dark girl by the cash register.

I knew that girl. She was Fiona, the younger sister of Ima Jean, the woman of my best friend, Larry. Fiona yelled after me as I went out the door, "You tell Larry the door is locked! You hear me? Ima Jean don't wanna talk to him!"

When I came outside the sun was white hot bright, and it seemed to evaporate the landscape, all shimmery and breathless. We walked down the concrete steps, past Larry, who rolled his eyes at me. "Where you going?" he asked.

"Sightseeing," I said, hurrying to keep up with the woman's fast-clicking walk. At the car she said, "You drive. You know the roads better than I do." Then she reached inside the car and flipped the catches that held the black leathery roof in place and folded it back down behind the two little bucket seats. There was a small suitcase strapped to a chrome rack on the back of the car, and she took a minute to fish a pair of red-framed sunglasses out of it. I didn't even open the driver's door, I just stepped over it and slid down into the low seat. I played the clutch and ran the stickshift through the gears, and I fired up the engine as she got in beside me. She turned to me, and I saw my own grinning reflection in those big black sunglasses. "Let's blow this pop stand," she said, and I did, taking off like a rocket with squealing tires. We hit the tar road fast, and when I slammed the stick shift into second I was exhilarated by the wind and the speed. In third we were flying, her black hair blowing around her face, her yellow skirt whipping up her bare legs. She was wearing yellow satin panties with lace. She said, "What are you doing? Driving your granny to church?" And then I really let the car go full out, faster than I had ever gone before. It all seemed too easy.

"How fast are we going?" she asked.

The wind blew tears back from the corners of my eyes, and I squinted at the speedometer. "A hundred and five," I yelled. I couldn't feel the road, and the horizon was like a dancing mirage.

"Take your hands off the wheel!" she said.

"You're crazy!"

"I've done it at a hundred twenty!" she said. "Go on. Do it now!"

Very gingerly I loosened my grip but did not let go. I held the wheel gently, then lifted my hands away about an inch. They were shaking and I quickly grabbed the wheel.

"Are you afraid of dying?" she asked. And when I looked at her briefly I could see my answer, my ashen face, staring back at me from those damned sunglasses. She was smiling, and then she reached into a little leather purse for a lipstick. She puckered her mouth and kissed the bright red lipstick. She held it up like a bullet and aimed it at me. "Bang!"

So then I punched it even harder and watched the needle's slow climb up to a hundred twenty, the last number, and I put my hands on my lap for the count of five before I grabbed the wheel and said, "Yes, I'm afraid of dying." Then I braked and downshifted to about sixty and turned left onto a dirt road, making a turn that was more like a slide into home plate with flying gravel and dust. We were going, so fast I didn't feel the washboards or potholes.

"What'd this car cost you?" I asked.

"Husband number three," she said. "Number one didn't have a pot to piss in. I got a house out of number two. If I keep going, maybe around six or seven I'll get an island in the Caribbean.

"What's your name?" I asked.

"Honey, just call me Honey."

"My name's—"

"I don't want to know," she said. "I'll call you Sugar, because you're so young and sweet." She laughed at me then and got out a little silver flask from her purse. She took a drink and handed it to me, and I tipped it up, drinking fast, the whiskey melting my throat. She said, "Let's go find that damn Indian friend of yours."

It was then I realized that she didn't know I was Indian. I was just along for the ride. "I'm a damn Indian," I said.

She lifted her sunglasses. "Well, you don't look like one."

"What do you want me to do, wear a damned sign around my neck?"

"You're a touchy damn Indian," she said, reaching for the flask. "Give me another drink, Sugar."

"My name's Sam. My grandfather was the grandson of a warrior."

"Sugar, we're all warriors. We just don't all take scalps. Nowadays we just cut out a man's wallet. Same thing in the long run. Brings the enemy to his knees," she said, drinking hard. "Come on, Sugar. We're looking for laughs. Who needs all that other shit. Let's go!"

We flew down the road, passing ragged fences of dried upturned stumps, their roots like shriveled spiders baking in the sun, until I turned in, past a cornfield, to a turquoise blue trailer propped on cinder blocks. Three of Carver's old trucks were sunk in tall grass, and there was a dog dragging his chain back and forth across the bare packed-earth yard. "Stay here," I said, jumping out of the car.

A big pregnant woman stared at me behind the screen door. Then she disappeared, and Carver came up to the door. He had a swollen eye.

"What happened to you, man?"

Carver smiled, "You know the definition of Indian love? A hickey and a black eye." He pulled back his long black hair, and there was a big purple bruise on his neck. "My woman caught me with someone else and popped me in the eye. How's that for love? The more jealous they are, man, the more they love you. She's a good woman."

I tipped my head back, gesturing. "This woman is looking for some laughs. Anything going on?"

"Forget about me. My woman nailed my shoes to the floor and hid the hammer." He smiled back in the darkness of the trailer. "Give me a smoke." I lighted a cigarette and passed it around the screen door. His voice was almost a whisper. "Nice car. Who is she?"

"I just call her Honey."

"Keep it that way," he said. "God, she's sweet."

"I think she's fucking crazy," I said. "She made me drive the car a hundred and twenty with no hands."

"Nobody makes you do nothing, little brother. You only do the stuff that's waiting to come out, deep down inside you." Carver blew smoke through the screen at me, and I waved it away.

"Something's got to be happening?" I asked.

"There's a ham and bean potluck at the community center tonight. There's bingo at the church. What can I say? There's nothing happening."

"Shit!" I jabbed my foot at a spider's web below the trailer. "What am I going to do?"

"Take her to dinner and bingo."

I looked up at Carver. "Give me a bottle, man."

He disappeared for a minute, then came back and passed me a mason jar filled with yellow corn liquor. "What do I owe you?"

"I'll put you down for five."

"Can I catch up with you in a couple of days?"

"Make it six then."

"You got it." Then I turned away and went back to Honey.

I climbed into the car and gave her the booze. She unscrewed the lid and carefully refilled her flask. She took a quick drink from the jar and shuddered. "God, it's like sandpaper," she said, "but *fine* sandpaper."

"It'll cost you ten," I said.

She looked at me. "What's your cut?" Then she shrugged. "Oh, what the hell. Who cares? Come on, let's get out of here."

I turned the car around and drove out onto the dirt road.

"Go on out to the highway," she said. "Find that motel we passed. I need a cool shower."

I didn't drive so fast now. We didn't seem in a hurry to get to where nothing was happening. She sipped from her flask and stared at the dusty landscape from behind those dark glasses. After awhile she said, "Look at all that land with nothing growing," even though there were fields of corn waving from the river breeze. "Everything's dead here."

She gave me the flask, and I sipped Carver's corn liquor.

I pulled into the Chieftain Motel, and she got out of the car with her purse. A little bit later she came out of the office, twirling a key on her finger. "Number nine," she said, walking down the line of rooms, her high heels tippy from booze.

"Bring in my suitcase," she said, gesturing for me to follow. She went up to the door, unlocked it, and went inside as I unbuckled the straps holding the suitcase on the luggage rack. So what, if anyone saw me. This was luck!

When I came inside the room she had pulled all the curtains closed, darkening the room, and she had already taken off her shoes and dress and was slumped in a chair, in just her yellow panties and a yellow bra, still wearing those dark glasses and sipping the flask. I put the suitcase on a metal frame at the foot of the bed, and she said, "Turn on the shower for me. Lukewarm."

I went in the bathroom. It was a dark little room with a double-thick smoked-glass window up near the ceiling, a toilet, half a roll of paper on the lid, a sink with brown rust stains around the drain, and a shower stall with a mermaid-printed plastic curtain. I reached inside and turned on the water, feeling it until it was skin temperature. I came back out.

Honey hauled herself out of the chair and pushed past me into the bathroom. She suddenly fell to her knees, threw up the lid of the toilet, and began to vomit, and I could see her stomach collapsing in and her ribs distended. I came up behind her and held her shoulders. I rubbed the back of her neck as she heaved up the booze. "God, I need a shower," she said, standing up and wiping her mouth on the back of her arm. She held onto the sink for balance with one hand, and with the other she slipped out of her panties and unsnapped her bra, leaving them all twisted up on the floor. Then she entered the shower and stood there wearing those dark glasses, letting the water run down her body. "Bring me my purse," she said. And when I fetched it she grabbed it into the shower and rummaged in it until she found a toothbrush. She tossed the purse on the floor and scrubbed her teeth with soap. She dropped the toothbrush and gargled in the spray of the shower. Then she pushed past me and walked all dripping wet out of the bathroom, and she pulled back the bedcovers and lay down on the cool sheet. "Got a cigarette?" she asked, and I lighted one for her. She took it and inhaled deeply, and then she butted it out on the nightstand, missing the ashtray.

"There's nothing happening anywhere in the world," she said, stretching her wet arms over her head.

I didn't know what to say. She was a beautiful woman, wet and naked, and I tried not to stare at her because I didn't know where her eyes were behind those dark glasses. She slid her legs together like a cricket. She moved on the bed all lazy and cool. She took a deep breath, arching her back, pushing up white breasts with wide dark nipples. I came up to her and drew up the top sheet, covering her.

"Do you want to get some food?" I asked.

She said, "Get my purse."

I brought her purse out of the bathroom, and she fumbled through it, spilling out some money. I scooped it up and said, "There's a place down the line—an old couple who hired a Chinese cook. They've got sweet-and-sour takeout."

"Go for it," she said, her dark glasses peering around the room.

I left quickly, fired up her car, and traveled down the road fast. I couldn't figure anything out. I didn't know who she was or what she wanted, and most of all I was thinking of her all naked and wet and fucked-up and drunk. She was all so white, with wide hips and a narrow waist and a rib cage like a bird. I could see her heart beating in her breasts, and when she stretched her arms, her hands trembled. Of all the times Larry and I had sat on the stoop of the general store, watching women come and go, this was the first time I'd known one. This was the first time I had entered the world of a stranger, and I was lost.

When I came up to the Thunderbird Cafe I jumped out of the car and rushed inside. I almost knocked over an old guy coming out, and I said, "Sorry, Uncle," but he brushed me away with his hand. I looked at the paper menu at the counter and told the woman to pack up some egg rolls and fried rice and pineapple chicken to go. I gave her money, and then I leaned on the counter, waiting, staring at all the empty tables. There was an old woman back in a corner, dipping a piece of dark bread into a cup of tea, and there was a teenaged couple, sharing a coke with one straw and a pile of french fries dripping with ketchup. I smoked two cigarettes, waiting for the food to come, and when it did, the woman spent a lot of time tossing in little plastic packets of soy sauce and hot mustard. "Give me a couple of those fortune cookies," I said. She tossed them in, then stapled closed the top of the bag.

On the way back to the motel I tore open the bag and chewed on an eggroll. The sun was going down. It was below the western trees and the air was night cool, all August and dusk. The wind blew over me, and it smelled like rain coming. I could see the static motion of bats flipping across the twilight. They came out of the eaves of barns and swooped through the early night air, sucking up mosquitoes and fireflies.

I parked the car outside the motel-room door and grabbed up the food. I pushed open the door, and it moved a couple of inches, then was stuck. I leaned my shoulder against it and shoved hard, like pushing a car out of a snowdrift. Still holding the bag of food, I squeezed inside the room. I put the bag of food on the floor and flipped the light switch beside the door.

Honey was lying there, one arm wrapped with a piece of rubber tubing. There was a glass eyedropper syringe on the carpet. I looked around the room. Her purse was dumped out and scattered all over the bed. There was a candle and kitchen spoon on the nightstand. I kneeled down and picked up her hand, and it was chilly and limp. I stood up. "God," I said. "Why'd you have to go and do a thing like that? I just brought back the Goddamned food! Couldn't you wait?"

Then I was embarrassed for her, blue-naked and lying in a puddle of piss, and I grabbed up her yellow silk dress and smoothed it over her.

I squeezed through the door and took a deep breath as the bats flew low over the cornfields across the highway. The fireflies were amazingly bright this time of night, and the night-time songs of the insects were gathering strength, loud and restless. I walked down the row of rooms to the office and went inside to the counter. A guy was sitting there, watching a black-and-white TV. I slapped the bell on the counter, and when he looked up I said, "You got a problem in number nine." We stared coldly at each other on that hot night.

Later, when the parking lot of the motel was full of flashing lights—both cars from the tribal police, an ambulance from the hospital in Brantford, and a provincial cop—I watched them inside the room, picking apart her life.

One of the tribal cops went through her wallet. "Damn," he said, looking at Honey lying on the ambulance stretcher. "She's got an Indian card. Edna Singer. Band number 13489. Mohawk." He paused for a moment. One of the other tribal cops came over and looked at the card. "Singer? I remember a Singer family. The old man married a white girl. They lived back in the bush. When he died the woman moved off, took a girl with her." He studied her. "She don't look bad."

The first cop went over to her and shook her by the shoulders. "Edna? It's gonna be okay." He shrugged, "They go away, and they come back crazy." He wiped the hair away from her face. "Welcome home, Edna."

The second cop looked at me. "Did you fuck her? There are tests to prove it."

"No," I said. "I just went out for food. That's all."

"Where did the dope come from?" he asked.

"I never saw it. We had a few drinks from that silver flask on the bed. That's all we did. She threw up and went to bed, then I got the food."

I didn't like it when they wheeled away the stretcher like a grocery cart, one of the rollers crunching her sunglasses lying on the floor. I didn't like it when the provincial cop untangled her panties and stared at them before stuffing them in a plastic bag. I didn't like it when everything in the room was swept clean as if she had never been there. I didn't like it, because we had driven together at a hundred twenty miles per hour with no hands, afraid of dying. I suddenly fell head over heels in love with Edna Singer. I guess, because she was all alone in the world and had come home a stranger.

The night didn't ever cool off, but I could not shake the chill that was all over me like an animal. I sat on the edge of my bed under the second-floor eaves of the little log house, wrapped up tight in a gray wool blanket, shivering in the darkness. I was trying to sort through everything I felt about Honey—Edna Singer—and things I felt about myself. I knew the world was crazy, and I knew it made good people crazy. But what I didn't know was if it would make me crazy, too.

Then, pulling the wool blanket completely over my head to make the world even darker, I reached inside the folds of my shirt for Honey's silver flask, which I had tucked away for later back at the motel room. I took a hard drink and shivered until my ears were ringing. It wasn't that I really wanted the booze. It was just that I felt bad, and the booze made me feel good. It tasted awful, and it burned a hole in me right down to my socks. But it put my head in the clouds and numbed my skull. After awhile, sitting under that airless blanket, my spirit was laughing. My spirit didn't care about a thing, and I was flying with the birds that come out at night.

I was still flying, soaring over the crazy world, when Tom

pulled the blanket off my head. The empty flask tumbled out of my fingers and settled on the floor between his feet. I narrowed my eyes and gazed up at him. He was standing so tall over me, his face all pale and limp like a turned-out pocket. I tried to focus on his eyes, but they had no centers, all black and watery.

He said, "Ellie was coming home from her horse-club meeting. She was coming right down the line. Carver Hill blew right across without stopping. They say he was doing over seventy, and he hit Ellie broadside. They say she didn't know what hit her. They say she died instantly."

I squeezed my eyes shut so hard I saw orange fireballs.

"What the hell do *they* know," I said. "No one dies instantly. It just kinda creeps out of you. You think the fucking stars just explode across the sky? You think the sun comes on like a goddamned morning light bulb? Nothing happens instantly. Ask Edna."

Tom said, "It's going to be a long night. I'll make a pot of coffee."

I thought it was so damned funny when I said, "You gonna make *instant* coffee, Tom?"

And then Tom, who had never laid a hand on me in all the years he and Ellie had raised me, reached out and picked me off the bed by my shirtfront. He held me up so he could smell my breath, and he said in a low voice that cut through all the booze, "You sober up like a man, or I'll knock you senseless. You hear me? I don't want to hurt you, but I will. I swear it."

I tried to focus on him. "Go ahead. You think I fucking care what you do? It don't mean shit to me!"

Then he put me down and stepped back. "It's a bright clear night," he said, "full of stars."

He turned his back on me and stood there waiting.

I waited too. Somewhere in the darkness of the night I heard a crow suddenly cry out, and I remembered old Jonas once saying that crows were the smartest birds in the world. He said that they watched over the dead. Tom must have remembered the story too, because he started to sob when he heard the night crow voicing its grief. I wasn't ready to feel grief yet. All I felt was anger, and I just exploded all over the room, breaking everything within reach, as Tom stood there with his face buried in his uplifted hands.

Tom and Ellie's boy, Eddie, appeared in my doorway, rubbing his eyes. He stared at the scene with a look of terror on his young face—he was only twelve—and Tom fell to his knees and held onto his only child. I was weaving in place, breathing hard.

"Where's Ma?" asked Eddie.

Tom said, "She's gone."

"What's wrong with Sam?" he asked, pointing at me.

"He's drunk. He's angry."

"What happened to Ma?"

"A car wreck up the line," said Tom, composing himself.

"Oh," said Eddie, turning around and walking out of my room.

"Where you going?" I yelled.

"I don't know!" he yelled.

"Come back here!" I said.

"Fuck you!" said Eddie. I heard him stomping downstairs. Tom said, "Pull yourself together. We gotta look after the boy. Let's get some coffee into you."

Tom took me downstairs. Eddie was sitting on the worn-out sofa. Tom led me past Eddie to the front door. "You gonna be OK?" he asked, opening the door wide. My head was spinning, but I nodded. "Sorry about this," he said, and then he hauled off and punched me hard in the stomach. "Now you're gonna be better," he said, as I doubled over and began to heave all the booze in my guts out the door.

While I hung onto the doorframe, Tom picked up the phone and began waking all the family for miles around. In the distance I could already hear car engines starting, up and down the line.

Talking
with
Father
in
the
Barn

Nothing seemed real when I looked around at the flat land-scape of the reservation—scrubby fields and ragged tree lines, log houses, tar-paper shacks, broken cars. It all seemed artificial, like a spray-painted model of a railroad set with sponge trees and toothpick fences. The Creator of it all could scoop up arrangements in the palm of his hand and lay them down, in pleasing, temporary layouts, the way kids line up green plastic soldiers and sweep them away. The world was that unstable when my mother, or rather, Ellie, died. And I got riotously drunk after the funeral, cruising through the artifical world with a couple of guys 'til almost dawn, when they dropped me off at home, a sagging house of square logs with a tin roof set off from the road among a grove of sycamore trees. The yard was hard-packed earth, hard as our lives, and hope sprung sparingly from that land.

Ellie, the woman we buried in the yard of the Mohawk Chapel, wasn't my real mother. I don't remember much about my real mother. She seemed as ghostly as a dream and faded from memory as I grew older. But Ellie, my mother's cousin, was real during those twelve years, and when I bore the weight of her coffin across the churchyard, feeling the roughness of the earth through my moccasins, I hated the earth for taking Ellie away from me.

She wasn't too old, only forty-four, and I was eighteen and getting ready to leave the rez and go to college with an art scholarship. Ellie had joked about that when I was a kid, lying in the dirt yard, pounding up colored sandstone with a rock to make a water-paste paint. When I got that scholarship, she said, "I hope they got a driveway where you're going, so you can pound up your little paints!" That was Ellie's way. She could make you feel big as a mountain by reminding you that you'd come a long way scrabbling in the dirt. "I never thought

155

I'd see anyone in this family go to college." I didn't either. I wasn't great in high school, but I wasn't that bad. Mostly it was art that kept me going. That and reading. Math and science could go fuck themselves. So when those colleges started sending reps around to the rez, I figured I'd see what they knew. I got to check the little box that said "other" when it came to race. They wanted lots of "others" at their schools to get more money and show how sincere they were. Christ, it made me laugh when they raced after me to sign up. So I did. Because I didn't want to work in the slaughterhouse or the Sheetrock factory for awhile, and I figured four years would be a helluva-long paid vacation.

I remembered how proud she was of me, an artist, when we buried Ellie. And I connected earth and paint and color and death and the shortness of life and her pride in me and my sudden loss in a web of human frailty, because nothing, not even my scholarship, mattered. So, I went drinking with my friends, and I got drunk. And I didn't care if the world stopped dead in its tracks, because someone else would come along and give it another spin. That's what it was about, eh, the time between the spins. And when I got home and the world had stopped spinning, I went out to the barn to feed and water Ellie's horses.

For a while I sat on a bale of hay, listening to the horses snorting in their stalls as the sun came up. The light of the sun slowly seeped an orange tide across the hay-strewn wooden floor, and I sobered up sick, watching mice scuffle underneath the straw. Our old grey cat, who had frozen off his ears so many years ago, listened to the scuffling mice from a dark corner but could no longer see them. I kind of respected that old cat, blind as he was, for catching mice, but I didn't worry if he lived or died. He was just a blind, earless old cat who was too dumb to know how worthless life was. I mean, sometimes I got the feeling, watching people walking around with stupid smiles pasted on their faces, that being happy was for idiots. Well, maybe when they were just little kids who didn't know about dying, it was okay, but that was still no better than a dumb cat. Then, once you did know you were going to die someday, it was just as bad even trying to be happy. What's the sense in that? The old-timers—the real traditional elders—had an answer for everything, and we young ones were supposed to believe all that stuff about the Creator and meeting your relatives when you die and all the spirits in the forest. Sure, one time I had knocked myself unconscious riding a horse and thought I had seen a tiny little man under a fern in the forest, but what the hell good is that? Go on, knock yourself in the head and see God. Knock someone else in the head, and they'll see God too. I ought to start up some crazy church and hand out Louisville Sluggers, so all the Indians can bash their brains out in a squirming frenzy of faith and blood. See your dead relatives and meet the Creator. A case of beer and a quart of bourbon and I came damned close to the Creator, everytime. And I had some strong words for Him. But he didn't answer, not once. Coward. I'll tell you what really happened, especially for all those people who say God is dead or who seek proof of his existence. Put yourself in His place. If you fucked up and created an imperfect world of pain and suffering, would you show your face? Coward. Not one apology. All those other folks are doing plenty of apologizing though: "Sorry your mother died." What the hell are you apologizing for? I want to hear it from the Creator, from the mouth of the horse we been forced to ride since man first dodged lightening bolts on the mountain top.

That's how it was as I scooped oats with a cut-down plastic bleach bottle and dumped them into the feeder of Ellie's favorite horse, the stallion Star Blanket. I must have been arguing with myself pretty loud, because the horse was crunching oats and his eyes were all rolled back, white and fiery, staring hard at me.

"What the hell are you looking at?" I pulled apart a bale of hay and pitched it at the stallion's feet. "Eat your damned fill, you dumb, happy animal, but think about this: Do you know what happens to your kind? You end up on the back of postage stamps, mucilage, glue, in case you didn't know."

Star Blanket rolled his eyes back even more, snorting at me like I was a stranger. I guess he was scared seeing me so angry, especially because Ellie had raised him with her quiet, gentle voice. "Ellie's gone. Things change. I can't do anything about that," I said, quietly. "Now go on and eat." But he snorted hard and tossed up his head.

A shadow passed over us, and I turned around fast.

The morning sun silhouetted the figure of a man standing in the open barn door, his hands in his pockets and his legs braced apart.

"Who the hell are you?" I said.

The man took a step forward. "Heard you yelling all the way out to the road. You in the habit of fighting with horses?"

I eyed the dark figure carefully, trying to make out the details of his hidden face. "You in the habit of busting in uninvited?" I said.

He took another step toward me and turned slightly, and I saw a partial profile that slowly resurrected old memories. "I didn't come here to mix it up with you, son," he said. "I just wanted to see how you was getting along."

In that second, my blood turned into ice water and my heart began to shiver in my chest, and I saw in his profile the long-buried nightmare of my youth—the night twelve years ago when he had found my mother and me. I had no sense of order about that night, but rather a mosaic of vivid stark images like a shattered stained glass window: the broken front door of the log house and the rain pouring in, the glint of a knife stabbing through the air, the darkness all eerie blue from the light of the black-and-white television, a woman's song now ugly shrieking, my mother's silent open mouth as she lay rumpled on the floor, blood black as tar, the deafening roar of Ellie's shotgun, the dogs ripping into the stranger. That was the night my heart first turned to ice, freezing images that would sneak up on me as I slept unsuspecting, always catching me off guard, then vanishing. There was nothing to grab, nothing to hold onto.

Here now was the maker of those night terrors, something to grab and pin down, and I just leaped forward like a cage door had been sprung suddenly open. We collided hard and scuffled across the straw-strewn floor until he lost his balance. He went down with a grunt, like an old man, with me on top, struggling to push his arms apart so I could wrap my fingers around his throat. I buried into him and caught hold of his neck and squeezed my fingers hard, staring down into that faceless nightmare made real. The sun washing across the floor illuminated him, and I saw close-up the jagged scars the dogs had left on him, one ear split in half, his hair peppered gray, his voice silent, and his face chalky white, then blue as I choked the life out of him. I also now saw in the face-to-face struggle what his dark silhouette had concealed—his coat was black, his collar was a white band around his throat, and a crucifix on a twisted cord nuzzled my hands. A small Bible lay in the straw near his shoulder.

I flinched. I don't know why exactly, but I let go of him like he was something filthy. Maybe I should have strangled him to death.

159

He rolled out from under me and lay gasping in the straw. I leaned back against a stall, my arms wrapped around my knees as I watched him slowly regain his breath and his color. He spotted his Bible, clutched it up with his left hand, and turned a pious face toward heaven, closing his eyes as if in meditation. There was straw on his profile.

"You some sort of preacher?" I said.

He looked towards me across one shoulder. "Son," he said, "I am the walking word of God."

He pushed up his sleeves and thrust out his arms. One was holding the Bible, but the other, which I hadn't noticed before, had a cap on the wrist from where the hand had been amputated after Ellie's shotgun blast. Mounted on the cap was a silver-and-ivory Crucifix. That fragmentary image came back stronger, and I saw him falling out the front door as his fingers were blown off, into the rainy night where the dogs descended on him.

On the other hand were the scars of those dog bites, and he held them up and tipped his head off to one side.

"Those are dog bites," I said.

"The serpent's tooth that spiked our Saviour to the cross," he said, "comes in many forms."

"You killed my mother. Ellie shot you, and the dogs ripped you up."

"All these years," he said, "and that's all you've come to know? Well, that's not surprising. I used to be just like you until the word came to me. Sitting in prison all those days and weeks and months, staring at the holes in my hand, I was reborn. The second I realized that it wasn't me who killed your mother, but the Satan *in* me, I was purged and the spirit of the Lord came into me and told me to go out among the people and speak the gospel. Just as Christ was made to suffer, I too was spiked with the serpent's tooth and was reborn into the kingdom of God."

"You're crazy," I said, squeezing my knees even harder.

"And you ain't, you and your people, stuck on bears and birds? There ain't no truth in a feather, a claw, or a pipe bowl of burning weeds." He firmly shook the Bible. "This is truth. This is the truth that freed me. The parole board seen that I was reborn, no longer the man I used to be, and I was freed to spread the word."

I pointed at his Bible and then drew back my hand.

"That book," I said, "never helped anyone around here. No more than the bears and the birds, probably less."

"It ain't the here and now you ought to be concerned with. It's the blessed Hereafter and how to get there. If only I'd known it sooner, your poor mother wouldn't be suffering in hell right now. Maybe if you pray with me, we can ease her torment."

"There's no such place as hell, and even if there was, I know my mother isn't there."

"You're not listening to me, son. She didn't die with the grace of the Lord. She died because Satan wanted her and made me his instrument. Sshh, quiet. Listen now! Can't you hear, very softly, your mother crying for your prayers?"

"The only thing I hear is you blowing hot air."

"You're my son. And just as I once had Satan in me, surely he is in you now, making you fight me and despise me, because I have walked all this way to bring you the word."

I stood up fast and kicked a pile of straw and horseshit at him. "Son of a bitch! You come here and expect to be forgiven because you wave a Bible and wear your collar backwards?"

"Only the Lord can forgive me," he said, lowering his hands to brush the dirty straw off his lap. "You have a duty to accept that."

Turtle Belly

"But you can judge me?"

"Until you are reborn, I have no other choice." He stood up, facing me squarely.

"I'll take the damned bears and birds," I said.

"And be damned for it," he added. He reached into his pants pocket and brought out a forged-iron spike. "Take this and hold it," he said, forcing it at me.

I pushed the nail away, and he held it up. He leaned back against an upright post. Tacked to the post above his head, instead of a sign reading INRI, was a thermometer in a tin cutout of a Coca-Cola bottle. It was seventy-three degrees. He looked like an idiot, spread out as if he would fly right up to God, covered in straw and horseshit with a Bible tucked in the waistband of his pants, gazing up past the image of a bottle of soda pop.

"What are you doing?" I asked.

He squeezed his eyes shut, pinching his face. He was pressing the point of the nail against his left palm. "Suffering for you," he said. "My God, the burning nail!"

"Go right ahead," I said, stepping back near the stallion, who was stamping his foot in the stall. Next door to the stallion, in an adjoining stall, was a delicate Appaloosa mare, who hung her head all sleepy with this talk of God. I looked over then at the stranger who was my father, and I saw him in such contrast to the natural, relaxed way of the world, his face all wrung up like a washrag, forcing God into his soul. I knew right then that he didn't know anything. That his faith was contained only within the pages of a lifeless book and not from seeing the real work of God and the arbitrary winds that swept across the world. His God was different from mine, His God was the god of his own angry soul. To believe in his God was to believe in him, and nothing less would make him happy.

Leaning my arm over the stall gate and stroking the muz-

162

zle of Ellie's stallion, I smiled broadly at my father's self-torment.

"When you're done suffering for me," I said, "you can get the hell out of here."

He relaxed the muscles in his face and opened his eyes.

"I figured you all wrong. I figured growing up here all these years you'd be ignorant-like. Figured you'd be just another corn-eater like your mother—goddamn that woman could eat corn. But you got something on the ball. Ain't you the smart one? You're no kid. Nosiree. You're a man with a head on his shoulders."

I wasn't smiling anymore, and I could feel my jaws, so tight my molars ached.

He continued: "You're not so dark, either, not like your mother's side. You leave this place and you wouldn't even look like an Indian. You ever been anywhere *but* this place? Well, I been places—Chicago, New York, Toronto—I seen it all. You don't know what the world has waiting for you!" His voice rose in pitch like a radio preacher. "There's a whole world out there, and you're passing it all up. Now you just stop and think a minute. Think about your old man here, coming to this place on a rainy night to get his little boy back, this Godless place of voodoo spirits, and Satan comes into me and makes me kill like a crazy man—'cause I didn't know right from wrong without Jesus—but then I found the Lord and paid my debt and came back again—RESISTANT! Came back to save my boy all grown into a man! But a man with the ways of a godless corn-eater, a man afraid of the real world without the Lord to guide him! You and me could be a team. I am the living testament, and you are my son. Just as the Lord of Hosts sent his only begotten Son to suffer on earth, so have you suffered only to be risen. You *are* the son of God!"

I nodded my head and smiled through clenched teeth. "So you want me to go with you and preach?"

"Oh, it don't seem like much right now, I grant it, just me and you, but think about it down the line. You see we starts up small, like the shepherd with a small flock. But it grows, you see—a truck to start, and a tent to hold meetings in, and I even thought maybe a lion in a cage, a tame one of course, like Daniel lay down with, to show the beast that dwells in each of us. It could grow bigger and bigger—Brother Billy's Circus of God! A three-ring circus like the Holy Trinity—Father, Son— that's you—and Holy Ghost. I even been thinking of an act— imagine a high wire with silver angels going back and forth on bicycles and the ceiling of the big top painted with golden rays to catch the spotlights shining up. Then suddenly down below comes a bunch of Indian savages all painted and hooping and hollering, and out of the middle of them comes you in dia- mond robes on a rig, see, that pulls you up to heaven! When you get way up in the air, you open a bag of silver dollars and throw them out for all the kids, sort of like the riches of heaven, only they won't be real 'cause it would cost too much, you know. Oh, I got lots more—Adam and Eve juggling apples on a trapeze—listen to the crowd gasp when they fall from grace—only they land in a net, the net of the Fisherman. Gets you down deep, don't you think?"

I nodded again, "Yeah, it gets me."

"You could make a life for yourself. A *good* life, if you know what I mean."

I rubbed my chin like I was thinking about his offer.

"Let me get this straight," I said, walking up to him and standing by his side. "You're telling me there's money to be made in this preacher business?"

"Son, you ain't heard the half of it," he said. Then lowering his voice, he put his arm around my shoulder and turned me to look out the wide barn door. "There's a whole world of lost people out there, who are willing to pay the cab fare home. The meter is running, boy. The meter is running."

His arm felt like a snake draped on my back, and I slid away from him. I turned and looked in his ugly face. I wasn't sick or hung over anymore, and I remembered how I felt about the world when I first came in the barn alone at dawn. I guess in this instant I sort of changed my mind about a lot of things.

"Look out there," I said. "There's more world in a square acre than you'll ever know. The problem with you people who get down on your knees is you look at the sky instead of the earth." I backed away then, because I was sick of him.

"Don't damn yourself!"

"I think you better be going now."

"I walked all this way to save you!"

"I want you to go."

"You'll regret it. One day you'll need me."

"Get out of here."

"You're turning away a hungry prophet! The least you could do is offer me a meal. I haven't eaten since yesterday, and I'm tired. Maybe you could run down to the house and rustle me up some breakfast before I leave. Then I'll go."

"Can't do that. My dad—I mean my cousin Tom—might wake up."

"You're half Indian. You could sneak inside, grab some bread and jam, maybe a bottle of milk."

"No. Tom's whole Indian. He'd catch me, then he'd kill you." I was afraid I'd start laughing, and I bit down on the inside of my cheek. "No, there's no food, except maybe the—no, I couldn't do that."

"Do what?" he asked. He really did look hungry.

"The sacred corn," I said. "It's stored out here in the barn, but it's sacred."

What's so sacred about it?"

"We use it to feed the medicine man when he comes to the house."

"Who the hell is the medicine man?"

"Sort of a preacher."

"A preacher? Well, who the hell do you think I am? Same difference, don't you think?"

"I don't know," I said. "Maybe you're right." I paused. "I'm not sure I should. There isn't much, and it's awful sacred."

"I'm awful hungry," he said, "and it's all I'll ask. I promise I'll leave after I eat."

"Promise?"

"On my Bible."

"You wait here." I slipped around the corner into a small grain room and scooped up a coffee-can full of dry cracked corn that we fed to the chickens. I brought it out to him.

He took the can and dipped his fingers into it. "Not much to it, is there?"

"I shouldn't have given you that much," I said. Then I reached out and covered the top of the can. "I don't know if this is right," I said. "The old-timers believe that anyone with a dishonest heart who eats sacred corn will get sick."

"You think I'm dishonest?"

"That's up to you. I ain't telling you not to eat it."

Then he really dug into the dry cracked corn, and the dust from it made his lips yellow. "Not much taste to it," he said. "Not like the cooked corn your mother gave me."

"It'll fill you up and keep you strong all day," I said.

"Don't see what's so goddamned sacred about it," he muttered, but he kept shoveling it in his mouth.

After a while he tipped up the can and crunched up the last of the corn. "Dry as a mummy's bones," he said. "Got anything to drink?"

I took the can and filled it with water from a spigot near the horses' stalls.

"One thing up here," he said. "the water tastes clean."

He drank down the whole can.

"Got a cigarette?" he asked.

I gave him a smoke from my shirt pocket and told him to keep the matches.

"I guess you better go," I said.

"Not so fast. I got expenses. It ain't easy walking around, spreading the word. You got any money?"

I pulled my wallet out of my jeans and opened it. I gave him a five and three singles and showed him the empty slot. "Get on now, before I call out for Tom."

He stood in the door of the barn and smoked his cigarette. "Look at that sun," he said. "Every morning it rises on a world of opportunity. Like the Bible says, 'Seek and ye shall find.' You don't know what you're missing, kid."

"The sun's coming up fast. You better go before Tom comes out."

"Can you spare a few more cigarettes?"

I gave him the pack. He flicked the burning butt into the weeds and stepped outside the barn.

"I been waiting a long time to save you," he said, "but you got too much of your mother in you. You got them blue eyes, though. Maybe there's hope yet."

I don't know what exactly came over me, standing blue eyes to blue eyes, but I suddenly caught him under the chin with an uppercut that spilled him backwards, knocking the cracked corn out of his teeth.

He got up and brushed himself off. "Born in hell," he said. Then he turned and walked away, and I felt angry at myself for hitting him.

He walked boldly along the line of trees past the log house, then turned onto the highway and quickened his stride until he was far down the road. I watched him go, wondering if I might still catch up with him and kill him and bury him in the woods. That's how much I hated him. But I really knew that enough was enough. I just sat down in the door of the barn and crossed my legs and felt the sun's healing warmth all over me, my head tossed back.

I was startled to hear the back door of the barn slide open on rusty runners, and I turned around fast. Tom came inside the barn and he came right over to me and sat down.

"A whole can of corn?" he asked.

"A whole can."

"A whole can of water?"

"A whole can."

"I once saw a sheep burst from that combination, after the dry corn swelled up," he said.

"I think I was with you. I was about twelve."

"Of course a man is bigger than a sheep," he said, "so I don't think he'd explode. He might just crawl along the road for a day or so." Tom grinned wide. "I never heard it called 'sacred corn' before. Those lucky chickens."

I reached over to Tom's shirt pocket and dug out his pack of smokes. "Give me a match." I lighted my smoke. "When the hell did you come out?"

"Awhile ago. Heard you talking about the serpent's tooth."

Tom listened to Ellie's horse, Star Blanket, snorting back in the barn. "I got up this morning thinking that maybe we ought to keep the stallion. Ellie loved that horse."

"I don't mind feeding him," I said. "He doesn't like me the way he liked Ellie, but we get along."

Tom grew sort of silent for a moment. Then he laughed and put a warm, comforting arm around my shoulders.

"Never asked nothing of you," he said. "Never figured I had a right to. Figured your life was pretty much your own."

"I guess I always acted that way," I said.

"Things sure happen fast," he said. "In a moment Ellie's gone. Now you're leaving, might not come back. A person sure does take on a lot of the things around him. Even a horse. Take Star Blanket. I never saw a stallion like him. Ellie bottle-fed him from a foal. Quietest, gentlest stallion I ever knew. I guess that horse has more of Ellie in him than any living creature. More like Ellie than horse. I guess what I'm really saying is, I hope you don't forget us when you go away."

Then Tom got up, real slow and tired, and I listened as he went back to Star Blanket's stall. How could I forget my cousin Tom. I looked back saying, "I won't forget." But Tom was in the stall with his arms wrapped around the thick neck of the stallion, and he was holding on as if his life depended on it.

I got up real quietly and went to the house to begin packing.

Around dusk my friend Larry came around to say bye. We were sitting in the last low sunlight of the stoop, drinking beer. Tom was leaning against the tailgate of his truck. Eddie was scaling a pile of rock bass he caught in the creek.

Larry thought I was crazy to leave. "You gonna learn so much out there," he said, "won't nothing ever be enough to make you happy. You're gonna have a big head, so big you won't be able to hold it up."

Then he sort of snapped alert. "I almost forgot. Tribal cops found some white man crawling along the road two lines over."

I glanced over at Tom, who just kept quiet.

"So?" I said to Larry.

"Dumb sonovabitch got into some dry corn. His guts all swollen up. Took him to the hospital in Brantford."

Tom perked up his ears but stayed quiet. I caught him glance at me with a half smile.

"Dumb sonuvabitch," I said.

"He could have exploded!" said Larry. "They said his belly was hard as a rock, big as a basketball. A real fucked-up white guy with a cross for a hand and a black suit of preacher's clothes."

After Larry left, Tom said, "Don't it mean anything to you?"

"Don't mean nothing," I said. "A person ought to know what he's filling himself with. Nope, don't mean a goddamned thing to me."

Tom said, "You're leaving tomorrow. You want me to find out what happened to him? Write you a letter maybe?

I said, "You gonna write me a letter about every stranger who passes through?"

"Guess not."

Then I lowered my voice so Eddie wouldn't hear. "He got what was coming to him. I don't feel a thing for him. He didn't belong to me, and I didn't belong to him. I'm glad it's over."

Tom said, "You better take the truck. Go say your good-byes to the family before it gets late." He tossed me the keys and went inside the log house.

Eddie, whose face and hands were covered with shiny

scales, whistled low. "Can you imagine that, swelled up with corn till your guts almost bust? What a dumb sonuvabitch!"

"I can't imagine nothing worse," I said, climbing into the truck. As I drove towards old Aunt Molly's, I tried to feel bad for the guy, I really did, but I just couldn't work up any feelings for him. I realized then that I didn't even hate him. A stranger would have evoked more sympathy in me than my natural father did, and I felt as if a terrible burden had suddenly evaporated. I got to thinking about our stories—we tell a lot of them—and about some old French missionaries. I still remember their names, Brebeuf and Lalemont. Those guys were dumb, Catholic dumb. Around 1640 they got it worse than corn. Necklaces of red-hot tomahawk heads, on chains put around their necks. We told them, "You should be grateful to us, little brothers, for letting us allow you to test your faith. Thank us now for letting you meet your Jesus. See if Jesus recognizes you without your hair, eyes, or tongues. Scream your hallelujahs loud so your God welcomes you!" I don't remember which one it was who died right away on the first day under the knife and fire, but the other priest lasted a long time, a couple of days in the coals, so I suppose he got a better seat in heaven. No, I didn't feel bad about my father—he wasn't tested at all.

A
Long
Bus
Ride
Across
Mother
Earth

I didn't just say goodbye to the living but to the dead as well. I drove out to the Mohawk Chapel to spend some time with my thoughts about leaving home. It ain't a bad idea to talk to dead people once in a while. First off, you can say whatever you want and they never argue back. Second, they never try to borrow money or take your last beer or smoke. Dead people have manners, unless they haunt you in dreams. But usually they only do that when you're about to die yourself and they're making sure you know it.

When I got out to the chapel there were a few white tourists wandering around, like always, but one family caught my attention. They were having a goddamned picnic, with a blanket spread out among the tombstones. Damn, they sure fit the bill. Dad was pasty white, like flour, in shorts and a stretched out tee shirt, stuffing his mouth with chicken. An older kid about fourteen was dressed up like G.I. Joe in some damned army outfit. Mom was a skinny little redhead with tugboat-sized shoes, who kept swatting at gnats on her bare scabby knees. A couple of little ones ran around, climbing on the gravestones. I didn't like seeing that, but I didn't own the dead and I kept quiet, watching their dachshund sniff the earth.

My thoughts turned to the old army duffel bag in the truck. We didn't have a lot, but Tom had shared what we did have to help me pack the bag. He was quiet as we packed. The college said that each room had a bed, a desk, a chair, and a dresser. So we packed a set of sheets and a pillow, two towels, and a washcloth. We wrapped the towels around a small lamp without a bulb. "Go buy a bulb when you get there," said Tom. I thought it was stupid, but Tom gave me a necktie. The rest of the bag was filled with a couple of shirts and some jeans, socks, underwear, and a canvas coat. It was just about everything I really owned. I had two hundred dollars, rolled up in a pair of socks, plus forty bucks in my wallet to buy food and smokes during the bus ride. We also packed a couple of photographs. One was really nice. It showed me standing with Tom and Ellie just before Ellie died. Ellie's Appaloosa stallion, Star Blanket, had picked up her long black hair in his muzzle, and Ellie was laughing in that picture. Not very far away from where I now sat was a stone marker for Ellie.

I was distracted by a low beeping noise. I looked around but I couldn't tell where it came from. I began to count out my family, staggered among the stones—Ellie, Uncle Lewis, my grandparents, my great-grandfather, and all the ones who traveled back to the old days. The oldest one was the warrior Thayendanegea, Joseph Brant he was called, entombed in a stone crypt protected by a spiked iron fence right beside the chapel. I heard the beeper noise, and when I looked around I saw the older kid from the picnic family coming out of the bushes on the embankment. He was carrying a metal detector and a little green army entrenching tool.

He said, "Dad, check it out! It's an old axe and a leg bone!"

I narrowed my eyes and followed the boy as he came up to the picnic blanket. He waved the bone in his mother's face, who pulled back saying, "Throw that dirty thing away."

The father took the old iron tool and scrutinized it with a little magnifying glass from his pocket. "Mid-eighteenth-century trade axe, Hudson's Bay touchmarks. Nice find." He smiled at his son, who was, I guessed, about fourteen years old. The boy clicked his tongue at the dog and threw the bone in a high arch toward an open field. The dog caught it and ran in fast circles, flipping the leg bone up and down.

I didn't say anything as I got up and walked past the family to where the dog lay in the sun, gnawing the bone. The dog looked up at me with dark possessive eyes and growled as he tightened his jaws on the bone. I didn't even have to think about it. I kicked the dog under the chin so hard he flipped over backwards and lay squirming and howling. I reached down and picked up the bone as the father charged over bellowing, "What the hell do you think you're doing!"

I pushed past him, but he grabbed the back of my shirt and sucker-punched me in the eye when I turned around. I just stood my ground, though it blurred my vision for a few seconds.

"Are you fucking crazy?" he said, his fists tight.

I stuck the leg bone in the pocket of my jeans and then, quick, reached out and grabbed his shirt collar with both hands, squeezing tight so he couldn't breath. He was bigger than me but mostly fat, and I dragged him breathless while his family circled us until we stood in front of a gravestone.

I pulled his face close to mine.

I spoke low under my breath, so he would listen carefully. "There lies my mother."

I let go with one hand and pulled up the leg bone from my pocket. "This is my grandfather." I pushed him away, and he fell on the ground gasping.

"You don't look like any fucking Indian I ever saw," he said, wheezing. His wife stooped to help him up.

I walked over to the picnic blanket and went crazy. I kicked their potato salad to kingdom come. I threw the chicken at a tree. I picked up the metal detector and whirled it against a gravestone. I went into the brush and covered over the leg bone and the axe where they wouldn't find them, and when I came out he was holding up the little shovel like a weapon. I walked past him and got in the truck and started it up. He followed me.

"I've got your fucking license plate!" he yelled.

175

I drove away slowly.

"I'm calling the cops!" he bellowed.

I stopped the truck and leaned my head forward for a second, thinking about really having it out with this guy, a real shit-kicking fight, and then I drove away. I had a bus to catch.

Tom drove me down the line to the gas station on Highway 6 where the bus rolled by. He looked at the side of my face, all swollen and dark. "You gotta control your temper."

"I did."

"Don't look like it. Now you gotta ride six hundred miles with a busted face."

"I'm fine," I said.

"Get yourself a cold can of pop and hold it against your cheek. You shouldn't show up at Dartmouth looking like a prize-fighter who lost. You gotta be a winner," he said.

When we got to the gas station, I got out of the truck and grabbed up my duffel bag. Tom said, "You take care of yourself down there. Send me a phone number. I'm not much for writing letters."

"You better get off to work," I said.

Tom looked at his watch. "Shift don't start till three. Still got an hour."

"Then you better go and feed Ellie's horse. I think I forgot to feed him this morning, with all the packing."

"I remember you going out to the barn," Tom said.

"You sure?" I said. "Maybe you'd better check."

"I'll check." Then Tom shook my hand. "You'll do okay out there. Don't you forget us up here."

I thought for a moment, and then I told Tom, "Thanks for taking care of me all those years."

Tom said, "You're family. Where else were you gonna go?"

I said, "You better check on the horse."

Then Tom climbed back in his truck, started it up, and said, "Onen'kewahi." I go now.

I watched him drive up the line. Then I bought a cold can of soda from a machine. The two-o'clock bus rumbled off the highway, and I climbed on. I sat way in back and held the can of pop against my face as I watched the road whiz by me. I transferred to another bus in Niagara Falls and crossed over the Rainbow Bridge into the States. A customs agent talked to each of us, and when he came to me I showed him my papers, and he nodded me past.

About six o'clock that night we pulled into a rest stop on the New York State Thruway. I was glad to stretch my legs and walk around the parking lot. All sorts of people were hustling inside, holding in their piss. In the back of the parking lot I saw a guy in a black leather jacket pissing by the trunk of a beat-up brown sedan. All the doors were open, and there was a girl, wearing a tiger-skin leotard, hanging her bare feet on the pavement. She was drinking a beer, and I came up to the guy just as he rolled his hips while zipping his jeans. When he turned around I said, "Got an extra beer?"

He glanced at me. "Fuck off." Then he climbed into the car and rocketed out of the parking lot while his woman slammed the doors.

I bought a couple of burgers and brought them on the bus. I ate them slowly as we traveled east, the sun behind me. The land was flat out here but not as beautiful as home. I'd never been too far from home—Brantford, Hamilton, and once to see a Maple Leaf hockey game in Toronto—and this land was raked over, weak and haggard like an old woman who wanted only to die and be reborn young and fresh. I noticed that was what the white man did to the earth. They used it all up and never gave it a chance to breathe. That's why all the land looked so tired. It made me tired, too, watching it all pass by, greying factories and billboards, glass and steel corporations with names like DATEX and MICRON. Sometimes I saw an old deserted place, a metal warehouse or rubber tires piled up big as black mountains. It didn't bother me that they were used up, abandoned—nothing should last forever except the stones. What bothered me was that all this had come from the earth and had been changed so that it could never go back. So it just lay on the earth in great lasting piles of death.

At the bus terminal in Rochester a few people got off and a few people got on, and I didn't really pay much attention until the last person boarded. It was a young woman with long stringy blond hair. She was wearing a tie-dyed tee shirt, a paisley-print cotton skirt, strings of beads, and a backpack. She was barefooted and her legs were unshaven, and she moved down the aisle of the bus, offering a daisy from a limp bunch to each passenger, saying simply, "Peace," with a frozen smile. When she came to me, the last person on the bus, I took the flower and watched her settle into the window seat across the aisle. She hummed a repetitive chant to herself, while rocking and smiling and staring out the window, as the bus pulled away. I thought she was maybe drunk, or else kind of simple in the head.

It was dusk by then, the inside of the bus cast in milky shadow, and a few overhead reading lights came on along the aisle. During daylight it was not as noticeable, but as darkness crept in and the windows became grey mirrors, the strong odor of the bus hung in the air, a sweet, oily city smell mixed with cigarettes and sweat. To really see outside the bus, I had to cup my hands around my eyes, peering through my own reflection in the dirty glass. It didn't matter. The lights and the darkness rushed by so fast. It was like spinning on your back while watching the stars. I just leaned my head back and waited. I was all tight inside, the way I'd feel when I dreamed I was falling, not knowing if I'd land in one piece. Sometimes I got that way when I was away from home too long, feeling that there was nothing to hold onto. I wasn't tired, but I think I must have fallen asleep, because I dreamed, or else it was a vision, that the old ones were singing a "One-of-Us" song. There was a big piece of red cloth, and everyone was cutting it up to make shirts for themselves. When they finally got around to me there was only a small square of cloth left over, and an Old One said, "If you can make yourself a shirt, you will belong." Somehow I made a shirt, but it was too small. I was still fighting to get into the shirt when my dream ended.

I looked around fast to clear my head, and everything was quiet on the bus. The girl across from me was prying apart an orange with her thumbnail. She saw me staring at her and held out an orange section. It smelled bittersweet and fresh, and I reached across the aisle and took it, saying, without thinking, "Nia:wen." Thanks.

She nodded but asked, "Is that, like, Chinese or something?"

"Mohawk," I said.

"Oh wow, that's, like, Indian. Do you speak Indian?"

"A little," I said.

"Far out!" she said. "How would you say *celestial sunflower* in Indian?"

"In Mohawk?"

"Yeah, whatever."

"I don't know what you mean."

"That's my name. Well, like, my real name is Celeste Downey, but Downey is Gaelic or something—O'Dunnagaigh—which means, 'brown-haired warrior,' and since I don't

have brown hair and war is, like, wrong, I changed it to Sunflower, because the sun makes all the flowers grow. See? And
Celeste sounds like *celestial*, which only makes sense, because
we all share the same universe, ya' know. How would you say
that, like, in Indian?"

I was sort of looking down at the floor between my feet as
she was talking, and I answered her with a word that reminded
me of my Aunt Mary's kitchen: *"Ienhk:skarah'kwa."* Linoleum.

"What's that?" she asked, digging out a pencil nub and an
old envelope from her backpack.

I sounded out the word, and she scribbled the sounds on
the paper, repeating them to herself. "Far out! From now on I'll
call myself 'Yankee-scare-a-squaw.'"

"That's not quite right," I said.

"But it's close, isn't it?"

"Close enough."

"How do you know all this?" she asked. "Did you live
with, like, Indians? I never actually knew anyone who lived
with Indians."

"My mother was Mohawk. I was raised on the reserve."

She dragged her backpack across the aisle and sat beside
me. "You're an Indian? You don't look like an Indian. I always
wanted to meet an Indian, and now that I have I didn't even
know it. I mean, like, I do now, but it's so exciting because you
people really know about things."

"What things?" I asked.

"You know, things like animal spirits, making it rain,
Mother Earth. I read once that Indians say you should never
judge a person until you've walked a mile in his moccasins.
That's so beautiful! Do you know who said that?"

"No, not really."

"It doesn't matter," she said, reaching into her backpack. "The only thing that matters is that we all share."

Her backpack was stuffed with oranges and carrots, and she gave me a carrot. In the dim glow of the reading light I saw that her hands were tinted an ugly pumpkin color. We ate some carrots.

"Where are you going?" she asked.

"New Hampshire," I said.

"I'm going to Woodstock. Were you at the concert last year?" I shook my head no.

"It was incredible! I mean you could feel the love in the air. Everybody was in love. Everybody shared. Anyway, I met some really groovy people, and they started a commune in the hills, and that's where I'm going. It's going to be really cool. We're growing all our food and all our own pot, and it's on, like, private land, so no one can tell us what to do. We're going to have babies and raise a new generation out on the land. Doesn't it sound beautiful?"

"I hope you do well," I said.

She fell kind of quiet for a while, and then she leaned close to me. "Maybe you could come with me."

"Why?" I asked.

She reached for my hand and squeezed it. "You could be our Earth Father. You could bring rain."

"I don't really do that," I said.

"I understand," she said, tightening her fingers on my hand. She paused and leaned a little closer. "Do you think it's wrong to love people?" she whispered.

"No," I said.

She tipped her cheek against my cheek and waited a moment.

181

Her mouth was next to mine. "It's beautiful to share," she said, her breath sweet as a carrot.

"Yes," I said. Her cool face was against my swollen cheek, and it felt good.

She slowly rolled into me and kissed me, and we hung onto it for a long breathless minute.

She pulled away and looked down the dark aisle of the bus. She whispered, "Let's go back."

I slipped out of my seat to the bench seat across the rear of the bus. She pushed me down and unzipped my pants. It was an old bus without a toilet closet, but it was late enough and dark enough that no one saw us. She just hiked up her skirt— she had no panties—and spread her legs across my thighs, sitting right down on my cock. She made a little high-pitched squeak with each bounce, and the vibrations of the bus rolled through us like waves. Even though we were pretty quiet and it was so dark, I worried that people might smell us—we were pretty rank with sweat from being on the bus all day, and we were steaming it up even more. At least I could smell her, a tangy pissy odor that excited me—I'd never journeyed this far before—and Linoleum and I really had fun. I didn't get any sleep.

She sat beside me as we came into Albany.

"I really wish you would come with me," she said.

"You'll do alright."

"Do you know what I hope? I hope I have a baby. An Indian baby from you. Wouldn't that be incredible? It would have a big family at the commune, and it would be sort of like a symbol of the land. Oh, I hope I have your baby. I'm really fertile, you know, because the moon is in my favor."

I didn't speak. The bus was coming into Albany, and people were waking up.

"I guess we have to change buses now. Are you sure you won't come with me?"

I opened a cellophane package of beef jerky and offered her a bite.

She looked at it. "Is that meat? Sorry. No way."

"It's pretty good," I said.

"I'm into life, not death," she said, shouldering her backpack full of carrots. She grabbed up her wilted bunch of daisies from the opposite seat. "Sooner or later there will be no one left to eat," she said. "Grow it; don't kill it."

When the bus was empty I got off and dragged my duffel bag inside the terminal. I drank a cardboard cup of coffee from a machine and found my way to another bus. It was almost empty when it groaned out of the terminal. This time I sat in the middle, so that anyone who came on would go past me. No one else came on. The bus came into Vermont and stopped at Bennington, and then it rocked and weaved across mountains until we stopped in Brattleboro. After that I dozed as the bus headed north—even half-awake I sensed my direction—and finally we came to a motel stop in White River Junction.

It was a truck-stop diner with an orange roof, gas pumps for big trucks, and a sleepy guy at a ticket window, and I asked him about getting to Dartmouth.

"You should've stayed on the damned bus," he said. "It goes right up to the inn."

"How do I get there now?"

"Call a cab."

"Maybe I could walk?"

"Sure—cross the river and five miles north." He turned away and muttered. "Ivy League idiots."

I backed away, hoisting my duffel bag on my shoulder. It was four-thirty in the morning, I still hadn't slept, and the sight of the polished Formica counters made me hungry. I was so tired all I wanted was food. There was a waitress visible in the coffee shop through a plate-glass window in the waiting room. She was leaning on the counter with one elbow, holding a glass pot of coffee off to the side while she smiled into the face of a man bent over his plate. She tossed back her head and laughed. She leaned over him again, and her breasts were inches from his face.

I carried my bag into the coffee shop, straddled a stool at the counter, and lighted a smoke. The waitress came over after a minute, carrying the coffee pot from habit. She gave me a mug and filled it. "What else?" she asked, tipping her chin at a menu stuck in a little metal holder beside the napkin dispenser.

"Got any corn?"

"What?" she asked, leaning back and tucking her chin down.

"Corn. Plain-old yellow corn?"

"Yeah, we got corn. Comes as a side dish on hot roast beef."

"I'll have a bowl of corn. A big bowl, please."

"Now you say please. Someone teach you some manners from the look of that black eye?"

"I'm just tired and hungry, and if you got corn I'll have a big bowl, please. And keep the coffee coming."

She refilled my mug. "You been on the bus long?"

"All night," I said, drinking the coffee slowly.

"Where you going?"

"Dartmouth College."

"Why the hell didn't you stay on the bus?" she asked.

"Because nobody told me to, that's why."

She leaned over the counter at me, one hand on her hip,

the coffee pot held back and to the other side. "You always do what people tell you?"

"Hardly never." She was wearing a pink uniform with a white collar and apron. The top was unbuttoned like a shirt, and I was staring between her breasts.

"Don't see too many of you rich Dartmouth boys coming in by bus. Mostly your rich mommies and daddies drive you up from the Hamptons. You run away from home to college?"

"Ain't running from nothing," I said. "And I ain't no rich boy."

"You sure you're at the right place?" she asked.

"I don't know," I said. "Now can I have that corn?"

She stood back and adjusted her uniform. "You can have anything you want."

She brought me back a little bowl, hardly bigger than an ashtray.

"What's this?"

"A bowl of corn, like you wanted."

"That wouldn't even feed a little person in the forest, let alone someone my size." I looked behind her. "You see those big oval plates there? You start filling one with corn, and you think it can't hold no more, put on two more scoops. That'll be about right. And bring me a stack of dark bread."

"Whole wheat?"

"Whatever."

I really dug into that food. It wasn't the same as home though. The corn tasted like tin, and the bread didn't have any body to it. But it filled me up, and she only charged me two bucks. She really kept that coffee coming. I liked her. As I filled up I felt better, and she came and leaned over the counter again. I was seeing more clearly with food in my belly, and she had a great young smile set in a lined and tired face. I guess she was about thirty-five, with hair the color of a grouse pulled up under a net. She had bright red nails and lipstick. She didn't look too bad.

"Where you from?" she asked.

"Six Nations. Grand River country."

"That don't tell me nothing."

"Canada. West of Toronto. Where you from?"

"Here. I'm from right here."

"You like it here?"

"It's as good as any place, I suppose."

"You got that all wrong," I said. "You're supposed to love the place you come from." I held out my hands. "See that dirt under my nails? My mother is buried in that dirt. See, you're only thinking of this place here and now because of the people walking on it. You gotta think of all the people who came before, who made this place what it is now."

"What are you, some kind of poet?"

"Just thinking about the land."

"Well, I'll tell ya', honey, I got too much shit to worry about besides the land, unless that includes rent, which is too goddamned high since all you rich guys started renting apartments around the college. Sorry, forgot you're not a rich kid." She filled my cup.

"You got family?" I asked.

"Was married for a while. French guy from up-north Vermont. He split. Took the kids to his mother. I see 'em once in a while."

"I always thought kids should stay with their mother," I said.

"What could I do? He was the only guy who ever gave me roses. He was a real shit, but I couldn't say no to him. I even got a tattoo on my ass—a heart with a dagger through it. It says 'edualC' on the blade. That's 'cause I can only see it in a mirror. It really says 'Claude'. Claude liked tattoos. Oh, fuck him. What the hell."

She looked through the big window at the clock in the bus waiting room. "I get off at six. You want a ride?"

"Sure," I said.

"You should've stayed on the bus," she said. "Better yet, you should've stayed on it till it went back. See what you done? Got me talking about Claude."

"Then don't talk about him."

"I'll make you a deal," she said. "I won't talk about Claude if you don't talk all poetic about death and stuff."

At six another waitress came on, and we left.

She drove an old grey Volkswagen. It was like riding in a noisy turtle through the dawn. There were a lot of mountains and pines, and I liked the feeling I got from the land. I had a sense that this was a very old place—not the buildings or the roads—but a place where many, many people had come and gone over thousands of years. I thought maybe the mountains were sleeping giants covered over with moss and trees. This was a very old place, but it was all wrapped up in the present.

I don't know how many coffees I had, but I was all lit up inside. Then I asked, "What's your name?"

She said Judy.

"Well, Judy, where the hell can we buy some beer?"

"You want beer at six in the morning?"

"I gotta cut through all this coffee."

"How old are you?" she asked.

"I fucked up," I said. "Let me start over. Where the hell can we buy some roses?"

"Roses?"

"If I give you roses, you won't be able to say no to buying the beer."

"Goddamit!" she said. "I'll buy the beer, but I draw the line at any more tattoos."

By ten o'clock that morning we were getting kind of loud, parked down a lane near the Hanover Country Club. We were having a great time with a case of beer, watching people out on the golf course. I fished out an envelope and read the letter. "I'm supposed to be at McNutt. What's a McNutt?" I asked Judy.

"It's a building, I think." She lobbed an empty beer can into the back seat.

"Let's go find it."

We drove that old turtle all around the Dartmouth campus. It was a beautiful place, with a huge green field surrounded by brick and stone buildings. One of them had a tall tower with a clock. We drove around reading the names of the buildings. "McNutt!" I said. "Park here!"

"I can't park here."

We drove around looking for a place to park. We went behind the building, down narrow lanes. "There's a space!" I said.

"The sign says 'reserved for president.'"

"You mean Nixon has his own parking space at Dartmouth? What a world."

"No, you jerk, the president of the college."

"Well, he must have taken the day off. Park there."

"Why don't I drop you off."

"No, come on in. Just park the fucking car and come in with me."

"I don't belong in a place like this."

"Neither do I. Who gives a shit? You're my guest. I invited you."

And so I arrived at Dartmouth College—late for registration, drunk with a black eye, towing along a waitress named Judy in an unbuttoned pink uniform and a hair net. I told the admissions officer handing out packets with room keys that Judy was my sister. I don't think he believed me.

I didn't give a shit.

Judy and I tried to act pretty cool, but she kept laughing and ducking her face into my shoulder. That guy—he was buttoned right up under his chin—wasn't having any fun at all. I was having a great time, because Judy was giggling so much. I told the guy she couldn't help it. "My sister has a condition."

Judy doubled over laughing.

"See?"

The guy gave me the packet and my room key after checking all my papers. He said, "You better straighten up your act."

I looked at him. "Tell me one thing—if I buy you roses will you get a tattoo like this one?" I pulled at Judy's skirt hem, and she leaned into me, laughing so hard tears rolled down her face.

We later found our way to Chase Dorm, a big old brick building with narrow corridors, and got into my room on the third floor. It was a small white room with a blue-striped mattress on a single bed, a desk and chair, and a chest of drawers. I carried up the duffel bag, and Judy brought the few remaining beers.

We sat on the bed and leaned back against the wall, our legs splayed out towards the desk. "You as tired as I am?" I asked.

"How tired are you?" she asked.

"I'm so tired I don't even want to see your tattoo."

"I'm so tired I don't even want to show it to you."

"Some other time?" I closed my eyes.

"No way," she said.

"Are your eyes closed, too?"

"You couldn't open them with dynamite."

Then we fell asleep. Together.

Judy was gone when I woke up. She left a note with a telephone number on the back of a restaurant check.

I wasn't doing too good. The dean of freshmen called me to his office, and it was the same buttoned-up guy from registration. He put me on probation for the entire term.

A few days later, I doubled over in the crapper taking a piss. The pain went right up into my belly. Then came the yellow pus and the fever. I spent a couple of days at "Dick's house," the infirmary, and got some shots in my ass. I didn't want to talk about it to anybody. Getting the clap from Linoleum on the bus wasn't something I wanted to talk about.

I didn't call Judy. The phone was in the hall beside the bathroom, and someone was always on it or hanging around listening. I couldn't think of anything I wanted to tell her and I figured I'd just get myself into more trouble. Already word, had gotten out about all my troubles. When I came out of my room, guys in the hall would clap their hands once to let everyone know I was coming. I got the feeling that everyone was watching me, so I didn't use the phone and I just stayed in my room. After a couple of days I wasn't even hungry. I mostly slept, and when I was awake I thought about my dreams. They were always about home. I thought about what all the people were doing at that moment. I could see my old aunts frying corn bread and beans in butter. I could see Star Blanket stomping his foot in his stall. Now that Ellie was dead and I was gone, he was a tired and sad horse. I could see my little cousin Eddie, now twelve, running in a pack with all the little brothers of my friends. I could see the young women, tossing their dark hair around their shoulders, taunting us. Sometimes, lying facedown on my bed, I couldn't tell if I was thinking or dreaming. It was powerful enough to lift me off the bed and take me all the way home.

One night someone knocked very lightly on my door. I ignored whoever it was, only they knocked harder.

I was dream-thinking again and yelled out in Mohawk, "*Sakwatee!*" Go away!

A voice said, "Don't be like that little brother. Let me in so we can talk." He had an accent that sounded like home to me, and I rolled off the bed and unlocked the door. Then I lay down again.

A few moments later I heard the door open slowly. The light from the hall was white and harsh. "Close the door," I said.

He closed the door and came into the dark room. He found the chair at the desk and turned it around to face me when he sat down. His silhouette loomed big in the dark. He waited for a moment then he said, "How's it goin'?"

When I didn't answer, he dragged the empty metal trash can by my desk between his legs and lighted a smoke. In the light of the match, I could see that he was an Indian guy.

"Did you come from home to get me?" I asked.

"No."

"Where did you come from?" I asked.

"Arizona. My name's Vincent Begaye, Navajo. Just heard you were having a rough start."

"I think everybody's talking about me." I said.

"The dean of freshmen told me you haven't gone to any classes. He said no one has seen you at meals."

"It's a prison here," I said.

Vincent nodded like he understood.

"It's a little different. You can leave if you want. You want to leave and go home?"

"Yes."

"I don't blame you, little brother. That's how I felt when I first came to this place. This is my third year here. It seems like it at first, but it's not really a prison."

I leaned up on the bed and spoke right out at him. "I got put on probation the first day! Just like a criminal. As soon as I walk out of this room, I'll do the wrong thing and go home in shame. I'd just as soon go home proud on my own."

"Maybe we can talk to the dean about it, make things right. Sort of explain how it is where you come from? Where was that again?"

"Six Nations. Grand River country. I'm Mohawk. Wolf clan."

"I don't know how things are where you come from, but I know when I came to this place it wasn't like home. I remember my old grandma crying on the front porch and squeezing her hands together over me. She was afraid I'd drown in the ocean. She don't speak no English, see, but she said I'd sink in the big blue-eyed water. I cried on the bus, that's how sad I was to leave my old granny. When I got here, alls I could think about was old granny spinning wool, my brothers looking after the sheep on their ponies—"

"You got horses? We got a real good horse, a stallion named Star Blanket. He was Ellie's horse—she raised me until she was killed this summer in a car wreck."

Vincent shook his head in the dark. "I know how it is, little brother. My dad, he got drunk and drove off the road two summers ago. I guess when it's your time to go, you have to live with it."

"Ellie wasn't drinking. It was some other guy. He walked away, a little busted up."

"What about your mother and your old man?"

"My old man killed her when I was six. I saw it. A knife right through her heart."

"Sorry to hear it."

"He got out of jail and came sneaking around, acting like a preacher. I sent him away. He didn't belong."

"You do what you have to do," Vincent said. "Just like now. You're gonna have to decide what's right for you. Nobody but you can decide that." He got up from his chair. "You mind if I pull open the shade?"

I shrugged, and he opened the shade on the window between us.

"You look out that window there at the Baker Library. Millions of books in there. All that knowledge. You think our people needed all them books to get along? My old granny didn't need those books to be happy. She knows about her world, and everyone respects her. She's an elder who knows things. But these white men don't learn anything at home. The only way for them to get respect is to buy their knowledge at these here colleges. Sometimes they pile up degrees to get even more respect, because, like money, they can't get enough and they want to be big shots. That would be okay if we could put up a fence and live our own ways, but we can't do that. We gotta walk shoulder to shoulder across this earth, so we buy white man's knowledge. You just gotta figure out how much cost you can afford. Sometimes the cost of leaving home is too much. Nothing wrong with setting your own price, little brother."

"I can't think about anything but home," I said. "I never had this much trouble at home."

"There's more of it, too. Think of it like going away to war. If this place kills you, your people will sing your name. My older brother Benny got killed in Viet Nam last year, and my younger brother is there right now."

"I have two cousins over there, too," I said, "and a good friend."

"I guess it's harder on them than on us," said Vincent.

"I guess so. Much harder."

"So some of us go in the army, some of us go to college, some of us stay home and work the sheep and the corn. It's all hard. No easy choices. Not like the old days when you knew your station in life."

"Too many choices," I said.

Vincent lighted a couple of smokes and handed me one. "Listen," he said, "I was sort of thinking maybe you'd like some fresh air. Maybe we could scare up a few beers. I see that you don't have a pillow or sheets. Maybe we could pimp some from one of the frats."

"I got a pillow and sheets in my bag."

"Maybe after we get some air and some beers we could sort of unpack them and get you more comfortable, just for tonight, until you decide what you want to do."

"We could do that," I said.

"Well then, let's go. Let's get this show on the road."

As we came outside the dorm into the cool, dark night, Vincent said, "I heard your sister was an old waitress."

I laughed a little, "That wasn't my sister."

Vincent said, "I didn't believe it. How was she?"

"Nothing happened," I said, walking fast to keep up.

"How'd you get the clap them?"

"That was on the bus ride. A hippie. I gave her an Indian name and she gave me the clap."

"What'd you call her?"

"*Linoleum*. She don't know it though."

Vincent laughed. "I once gave a guy a name that meant *bloated testicle*. He was fat and full of himself. The same day I fell off my horse and broke my arm. I guess you gotta watch what you say."

"I guess so."

"Especially here, if you know what I mean," said Vincent. "Find other ways to channel it out of you. What sport are you going out for?"

"I don't know. We play a lot of lacrosse and hockey back home."

"Those are good. You get to carry a big stick. Game's so fast, you get out a lot in a short time. Good luck."

We came to a big house, all lighted up, on a street lined with similar houses. People were hanging around everywhere. "What is this place?"

"Phi Delt, little brother. The home of the never-ending keg of beer. The basement battlefield. The place veterans always talk about. In a word, paradise for people like you and me." He slapped my back hard. "There are no rules, and you're on your own."

We passed through many people in the entryway, and we turned sideways to squeeze downstairs to the basement, rubbing past people on the narrow wood-paneled staircase. The odor rose up to us, hot and moist like a hog barn. It was so sour. And when we finally got downstairs to the concrete basement floor, I knew why. The floor was an inch deep in foamy liquid. We sloshed across the floor to a long room with a bar crowded with people. It was all smoky and dim. A blond guy in wire-rimmed eyeglasses and a blue button-down shirt was filling plastic cups with beer from a tap and lining the counter. Vincent grabbed a couple of beers and gave me one. The music was so loud, he yelled at me: "Just help yourself!"

"How much do I owe?" I yelled.

"Nothing! They don't charge for beer!"

"Where did all the girls come from?"

"WHAT?"

"I SAID WHERE DID ALL THE GIRLS COME FROM?"

He leaned close to my ear. "I don't know! Smith College, Brown, Bennington. Who cares?" He pointed down the bar. "Check it out!"

There was a red-haired guy leaning over the bar with both hands clutching the rail, and people had given him some room. His shoulders were rolling back and forth, and his face was limp. Suddenly his mouth opened and he vomited across the bar. Some girls on the other side screamed and slid away, and everyone was laughing. People began to chant, "PHI DELT! PHI DELT! PHI DELT!" The red-haired guy wiped his mouth on his shirt sleeve, and someone handed him another cup of beer. I watched him tip it up and drink it in one gulp.

"I bet that guy is worth a million bucks!" yelled Vincent. "He'll go on to business school and own half of Connecticut by the time he's thirty!" He pointed at another guy wearing a green-and-white striped shirt. He was weaving in place with his dick sticking out, pissing against the bar, surrounded by women. "I know that guy! His father *owns* the Bank of Boston!"

"I never saw anything like this!"

"You thought *you* had it hard! Think of those poor rich sons of bitches!" he yelled. "There's more ritual in the white man's world than in all the Indian nations combined: which fucking fork to use at your meal, what kind of tie to wear, who sits next to who at your fancy dinner! All that money pressure! The basement of an Ivy League fraternity is the white man's descent to heaven, 'cause for them it's hell up on earth! They can't wait to throw away the lessons their mommies and daddies taught them! They've been brought up with so many rules, and they *know* they're going to spend their whole lives with rules. This is their one and only chance to piss on walls, and they are going to do it, little brother! No matter who is in the way! So don't you be afraid of them, because now you know they're just animals underneath. And animals give themselves to you to be eaten if your heart is strong! A good hunter, with a clear mind and a strong heart, will never go hungry! Do you want another beer?"

I nodded, and we sloshed over to the tap and grabbed some more beers. Vincent gulped down a beer and looked at me. "Drop it!"

I let my beer fall on the floor.

"No, drop a beer!" He grabbed another one and tipped it up in one gulp. "Don't worry, little brother I'll look out for you!"

I took a beer and tipped it up and swallowed so fast it burned.

"If you gotta piss, you piss! If you gotta boot it up, you boot it up good and loud, over the bar and everyone standing in the way! Upstairs, in the daylight, put your fucking napkin on your lap, hold open doors, get out of the way of fast-moving objects! Be a smart and hungry hunter!"

The
Pink
Waitress

Turtle Belly

It wasn't that I was ashamed of Judy, the pink waitress I had met at the bus terminal in White River Junction, it was that I was ashamed *for* her—I was eighteen and a freshman at Dartmouth, and she was thirty two, divorced, loud, too colorful to be hanging around with a guy at an Ivy-League school. She wore too much makeup, and her hair smelled like french-fry grease from the coffee shop. But I liked her. And I knew she was uncomfortable coming to the school to see me, especially after she'd given me a lift and we'd gotten drunk and created a scene at registration.

She was surprised when I finally called her. It was about a month later, after the clap was gone. I went to a pay phone in the library, so the guys in my dorm wouldn't eavesdrop.

It was night, the first week in October, and I was shaking all over. I said, "Judy, it's me, Sam."

There was a long pause, and I explained, "I'm the guy you brought up to Dart—"

"I *know* who you are," she interrupted. "I just about forgot about you. It's been a long time."

"You know how things go," I said.

"No, I don't," she said. "You gettin' along with all those rich kids? You got one of them blue blazers with the gold patch on the pocket?"

On the phone her voice was soft, singsongy. It was relaxing, and I needed it. I could hear her breathe when she spoke, as if she were standing by my shoulder, whispering in my ear.

I said, "I don't know about this place. I'm just trying to stick it out till Christmas."

"I wouldn't know," she said. "It might as well be the moon, for all I care."

I waited a moment.

"You still there?" she asked.

"Yeah. . . . Listen, what are you doing?"

"Right now? I'm waxing my legs."

"What?"

"Never mind."

"Maybe we could do something?"

"What'd you have in mind?"

"I don't know. I just need a break."

"After this long, you need a break and call me in the middle of waxing my legs? I'm watching an old movie."

Her voice was slushy.

"I'm sorry," I said. "I'd better go—"

She laughed loudly, "Where are you?"

"In the library."

"You go stand out in front of that big tower, then. And you better be there, 'cause I'm not getting out of the car to go looking for you."

"You're gonna get me?"

"Ten minutes," she said. "Bye-bye." Then she hung up.

It only took me a minute to get from the phone to the walk. I hung back in the shadows of some tall trees, watching the night movement on campus, people walking across the green. I was startled when a hand slapped my shoulder, and I wheeled around.

"How you doing, little brother?"

It was Vincent Begaye, the Navajo guy who took me to the fraternity house one night.

"Got a smoke?" he asked. I gave him one and lighted it for him. "Got any bucks?" he asked. "I'm kinda low. I'll pay you back sometime."

"No, I don't have any money. I gotta be going," I said, and turned to walk away.

"Where you going?" he asked.

"Study," I said.

"Fuck it. Let's go to Phi Delt."

"No, I'm behind," I said, turning in the opposite direction from fraternity row.

"Later," he said, going off alone.

I walked some distance, and then, when I was sure he was gone, I turned around and hurried back to wait. I didn't want Vincent around when Judy came. I didn't want him to know or to be talking about it. I knew those guys would give me a hard time and make fun of her. They were that way, rough on people they didn't know. Ugly mean. I just didn't want to hear it. They'd say I couldn't do no better than an old waitress. Maybe I didn't want to do no better than an old waitress. It was my business, I guess, and maybe she couldn't do no better than me. That was her business.

I heard the Volkswagen before I saw it, rumbling into the square. It sputtered around the green like a German army helmet. Only since the last time I saw it, she had pasted big yellow-and-orange flower decals all over it. She rolled around up to the library, and I came quickly out of the shadows and yanked open the door, jumping in. In the brief light I could see she was wearing a pink bathrobe, faded blue jeans, and big, pink fuzzy slippers. She wasn't wearing a hairnet, but her hair was sort of loosely pinned up and hanging in strings at the nape of her neck.

"Hi!" she said, smiling wide at me, her mouth a big pink crescent of lipstick. She did a double take in the mirror and rubbed a smudge of lipstick off her front tooth.

She looked at me. "You look a hundred years old."

"You look like a big piece of bubble gum," I said.

"You gonna try to blow me up?" she said. Then she laughed and threw the car into gear, and we jerked away from the curb.

We didn't go too far, across the Ledyard Bridge into Vermont, down a winding road, only a few miles. She turned into a big farmhouse with barns out back.

"This your place?" I asked.

"I wish," she said. "No, I got a little apartment out back."

She parked behind the barn, and we got out by a wing addition. "It ain't much," she said, "and the rent's too high, but it's private and I got a garden."

We entered through a small wooden door. "Goddamn it! I left the stove on!" The place was all smoky. There was a pan of wax on the stove. She left the door open and fanned smoke outside with a kitchen towel.

I liked it a lot inside. It was the closest thing to home I'd seen since coming to this place. We were in a kitchen that was the short end of an L-shaped room. The rest of the L was the living room. There was a small woodstove in the corner. Between the L was a bedroom and a bathroom. The furniture wasn't much, just like home, only it was fixed up with India-cotton throws on the sofa and strings of wooden beads hanging in the bedroom doorway. She had a Formica table and some books on a shelf beside the TV set. There was a record player and a lot of albums.

When most of the smoke was gone, she closed the door and pointed at the fridge. "Help yourself," she said.

It was full of beer and some wine. She had a lot of vegetables, too. I grabbed two beers and tossed one to her.

"I'm sorry," I said, when she came back and opened it

with a metal key hung on a white string from the door handle on the fridge.

She kicked off her pink slippers, and they landed in a dark corner. Then she peeled off her blue jeans and wrapped up tighter in the bathrobe. She carried the pan of hot wax to the coffee table in front of the sofa and put it down on a pile of magazines. Then she turned on the TV set, and we settled back on the sofa.

"It's not really cold enough," I said, though the night was chilly, "but I sure miss a woodstove."

"You want a fire, light a fire. I don't care." Then she began cutting strips of muslin cloth with a pair of scissors on the table. The TV blared. It was the only light except for a glaring bulb shining from the kitchen ceiling. I went over to the wood-stove. All the fixings were there—newspaper, kindling, chunks of dry wood. I opened the damper. In a little while I smelled the smoky sweetness of a fire, and even though it didn't put out much heat yet, the chattering sound of the burning wood made me feel warm.

I came back to the sofa, and Judy had poised one leg on the table and was smoothing hot wax on her leg with a wooden spoon.

"What are you doing?" I asked.

"I told you, waxing my legs."

Then she laid a strip of cloth on the wax and pressed it down. She waited a second, took a deep breath, and suddenly ripped the cloth up with a little gasp. There in the wax were dozens of fine hairs, and her shin was pink and shiny. She blinked a tear out of the corner of her eye. She let out her breath in a long sigh. "That was a good one!"

"My mother—well, the woman who raised me—didn't have hair on her legs. None of the girls I know are hairy. Why do you do that?"

Her bathrobe was open below the waist, and her right leg was trembling. "I only have to do it every couple months. It keeps my legs smooth."

"It looks like it hurts."

"It's not exactly pain. Sometimes it hurts if I'm not in the right mood. Sometimes I like it."

She prepared another patch, along the outside of her calf. I could see her other leg, too, and it was like polished white marble. She bit her lower lip and tore up the hair. She tossed the cloth onto a pile on the table.

She drank some beer.

Behind us in the corner, the stove was really hissing.

On the TV set, Jimmy Stewart was running down a snowy street yelling, "Merry Christmas, you ol' building and loan!"

Judy's hair had fallen apart and was tangled around her shoulders.

The air was electric all around me.

Judy kept on waxing her legs. I got another beer.

After awhile she said, "I never did this with anyone. But this is the hard part, and I always botch it up. I can't reach." Her knee was pulled up to her chin. "Help me out. Pull this off the back of my leg. Just hold it firm, and then pull it away fast.

I put my beer down, and she pulled her skin tight with both hands. I slowly reached for the back of her thigh and held the strip of cloth. "You sure?" I asked.

"Do it," she said.

Then I ripped the cloth away from her skin, and she jerked forward. She relaxed back, and her chest rose and fell.

"You okay?"

She wiped away a tear. "I'm fine," she said. "Help me with another one."

She parted her legs and her bathrobe and spread some

wax on her inner thigh. Her voice was quiet. "I'm real sensitive here. Do it fast."

I reached around, but she said, "No, come in."

I slipped past her naked foot and crouched between her legs.

My heart was beating fast. "Let me light a smoke," I said. I got out a butt and flicked a match. "Want a drag?"

She reached over to a bowl on the end of the couch and got a thin, twisted cigarette. "Smoke this," she said. We smoked it, and it was bitter and dizzy.

"Do it." she said.

I gripped the strip of cloth and pulled it, and she cried out, pressing both her legs against me. She laughed and shook for a few seconds. She reached past me for the pot of wax. "No! Don't look!" she said. Close your eyes!" She relaxed her grip, and when I started to move back she closed her legs again. I didn't move when she opened her legs, and I kept my eyes closed.

She said, after a few moments, "Open your eyes."

I looked at her. Her bathrobe was open. Her breasts glistened. They were long and streaked with white lines, hanging to either side of her chest. I looked down at her panties, bright orange-and-lime psychedelic paisley. On either side of them was a waxed strip of cloth.

"Will you do it?" she asked.

"Yes," I said.

She put her hands around my neck and pulled me down. We kissed for a long time. She pushed my hands down until we found the cloth. "Wait!" she said. "Not until I say!"

Then she unzipped my jeans, and my cock was standing out like crazy. I held onto the cloth strips, as she pulled aside her panties and pressed up around me, then I dug deep into her. She rocked back and forth, and I did too, my eyes squeezed shut, my fists curled into her groin as I held the cloth. She began to shudder. "Pull them now!" she grunted. And I ripped them up, and she screamed out, "Yes!"

I felt like I was flying, waving those strips of cloth in the air until I was airborne, and then I crashed into her, breathing hard. The woodstove was popping, and on the TV some kid said, "Every time you hear a bell, an angel gets his wings!"

I guess then some fucking angels were flying high, because my ears were ringing.

Judy reached over with one hand, while the other arm held me tight against her, and she grabbed a phone off the table. She knocked the receiver off the hook and fumbled to dial a number. She picked up the receiver. "This is Judy. I won't be in tonight. Yeah, I hurt my leg." Then she put down the phone. "Your timing was great."

I was still trying to get my breath back. It hadn't been too long, but I'd put all my energy into it. She brought her leg right up over my head and then lifted herself off the sofa to take off her panties. She wiped herself with them, tossed them aside, then sat up. I put my arm around her, and she leaned into me.

"You wanna stay?" she said.

"Yes," I said. "You mind if I keep the woodstove going tonight?"

"It smells nice," she said. Then she stretched out her smooth shiny legs. "I wanna take a shower."

She turned off all the lights and lit a candle.

We went through her bedroom and into the bathroom, and we got into a real hot shower. I never washed a woman. I got to touch every part of her body, *every* part, and it was slick

207

and steamy skin. Some parts of her were firm, other parts were soft and jiggly. I played with the jiggly parts, squeezing them, letting her ass and breasts slip around under my soapy hands. She pushed me down until I was on my knees, and she put one leg over my shoulder. She hooked her calf around the back of my neck and pulled my face right up into her. I never did that before either, but I liked it. It was kind of hard, though. The water was running so fast and hitting me in the face, and I was trying to breathe, but she was wriggling and moaning. I just took deep breaths and held them, so I wouldn't drown. Then she lost her balance and wiped out, landing with a wet fleshy slap on the drain. Her eyes were big as saucers, and her knees were quivering.

"Are you alright?" I asked, wiping water away from my eyes.

"God, what a come!" she said, leaning her head back in the corner of the dark stall. The water was beginning to run cold, and it raised goosebumps on her arms and breasts.

When we came out to the dark bedroom, all wet and carrying towels, I snapped on the light by the bed. "Where'd I leave my cigarettes?"

When I looked over, she was in the corner, trying to cover herself with the towel.

"What's wrong?" I asked.

"Turn off the light!"

"Why?"

"Because I look like a skeleton with droopy tits and stretch marks!"

I quickly turned off the light and we stood for a moment kind of quiet. I went in the bathroom and brought out the flickering candle. I put it on the chest of drawers.

I came up to her and took her towel away. We were standing only inches apart. "I guess you look alright," I said. In the dim yellow light she did look alright. Her breasts hung down with pointed nipples, and her ribs stood out. Her belly was kind of rounded between the hips. Her collarbones jutted out a bit. "You just look like a naked woman," I said.

"You don't think I look too old?"

Her hair was still wet, and it was down now, long, light brown and wavy. She had a sweet, upturned mouth and wide eyes that sparkled in the candlelight.

"I think you look like you. I like you."

"Oh, I look like a drowned rat!" she said.

"I never saw a drowned rat. I'm no judge."

And that was the truth. Until then, until that shower, I'd never seen a real-life full-naked woman. The first time I ever screwed was on the bus to Dartmouth. When I looked at Judy I just saw a bunch of parts. I liked Judy, so I liked her parts, too. I said, "You look OK to me."

She let the towel fall away. "You're sweet," she said. Then she walked over to my clothes and found my smokes. I saw the tattoo on her ass: *Claude*.

"You really do have a tattoo!"

"You think I was lying?" she said, lighting some smokes.

Then we got into the bed. It was a wide brass bed with soft flannel sheets and a heavy wool blanket. We lay there for a while, with our arms outside the covers, smoking, and we could hear the fire popping in the woodstove.

After we put out our smokes she said, "I'm all topsy-turvy. I should be working right now. I'm not used to being in bed now." She turned to me and draped her leg over my hip. She pulled me close. "Do you wanna fuck again?"

"Yes."

I wasn't sure what time it was when I woke up. I first thought maybe I was late for class. Then I thought that it was Friday, and I didn't have a morning class. No, it was Thursday, and I did have a morning class. Judy was draped over me, but when I turned she was propped up on one elbow and was looking at me.

"What time is it?"

"About ten," she said.

"It's Thursday, right?"

She nodded. Her hair was dry, long and fluffy and curled around her face. Her eyes were green and sleepy.

Our faces were only inches apart. "Thursday. Ten o'clock. I have a class."

"I'll drive you," she said.

"I don't want to go. I'd be late anyway. I hate being late. Everybody stares at you."

She smiled. Her lips were naturally pink. I kissed her.

She said, "I went out early. I bought some corn. Then I came back to bed."

I blinked and looked around. "You've been up?"

"I kept the woodstove going."

I could hear the woodstove hissing in the next room.

"Get up, and I'll make you some corn and coffee. You want toast with that?"

"Sure. Got some jam?"

"Don't press your luck."

She rolled out of the bed. She was naked and tattooed, and she padded around to my side and lighted a cigarette and gave it to me. I sat up and swung my legs over and kept my groin covered. She left the bedroom and went around the corner, and I found my pants. I followed her, and she was opening a can of yellow corn at the stove.

She didn't look at me at first. "You were so tired. I mean, you didn't even budge, so I loaded up the stove and drove out for the corn, 'cause you really seemed to like—"

She looked at me wearing jeans.

She grabbed a kitchen towel and covered herself.

"Oh, God," she said. "I'm really sorry."

She tried to push past me, but I blocked the way.

"You lied to me!" she said. "You said I looked OK, but now you got dressed first! I mean isn't that what it's all supposed to be about? Being honest? I mean, I don't know too much, but I know what I read. I thought I was supposed to take off my clothes."

I held onto her hard.

"I don't know what you been reading, Judy, 'cause I probably didn't read it. All I know is I didn't lie to you, and I just got up and put on my pants. You want me to take 'em off, I will. You wanna get dressed, go ahead. I don't care. I never before sat around buck-naked eating corn, but if you want me to I will. I guess it just seems that there's all kinds of rules. Maybe you and I ought to forget the outside ones and make up our own."

She sort of relaxed. "You didn't lie to me? I'm not old and ugly?"

"I guess not," I said.

"I never walked around without my clothes on, not even when I was married," she said. "I read it. That's what you people do."

"I never did," I said. "But I guess it's alright."

She slipped by me into the bedroom, and she put on her

big pink bathrobe. "It was kind of fun, at first, but I didn't really like you staring at me. It's OK at night, but not in the morning."

"I wasn't staring at you."

"I felt like you were staring at me."

"Maybe I was, but it wasn't in a bad way."

"It was still staring," she said, clutching her robe tight at the neck with one hand as she poured the cups of coffee. "Staring is staring and staring is rude."

I took a cup of coffee and sat at the table near the woodstove. The coffee really opened my eyes. It was hot and black, just like at home. I told Judy, "I never saw a woman's tits until I saw my mother—I mean Ellie—feed my little cousin Eddie. I didn't know where life came from till then. That's why I was staring at your tits—'cause I could see that they been used. That's all. You're the one who got all jumpy about whether they were good tits. Tits is just like corn 'cause both is the source of life."

"You saying there's no difference between my tits and a plate of corn?"

"I never turned down a plate of corn."

"So you're saying you'll take any tits that come long? Is that what you're saying? My tits is just like any old meal for you?"

I drank my coffee hard. "You sure are fired up about tits and corn," I said.

"If you could have a choice, right now, what would it be—tits or corn?"

I jumped right up and pulled off my jeans. I grabbed her big pink bathrobe and pulled it open, staring at her long breasts. I looked her right in the eyes. "Both," I said, reaching for the pot on the stove and pulling her to the bedroom.

She shrieked and pushed at me, but it wasn't very loud. Then she was laughing and lying back on the bed.

"Go on. Make a bowl," I said.

"You're crazy," she said, cupping her breasts and pushing them together to form a hollow on her chest.

I tested the corn with my finger, and it wasn't too hot.

"NO!" she cried out when I tipped the pan over her, the buttery water trickling between her breasts and down her sides. "You're a PIG!" She was laughing so hard then, as I sat very politely eating the corn with the spoon from the pan, which I had tossed on the floor.

"You've made a mess of everything!" she said.

"Hold still," I said. "You're the one making the mess."

She was shaking all over, trying to hold in her laughter. "I can't help it," she gasped.

Then I dropped the spoon and rolled over on top of her.

She wrapped her arms and legs around me, and we really went at it, no holding back, the corn flying, saying all kinds of things like, "Don't ever stop," and "I'm dying."

I never thought people could be so crazy, like there were animals lurking inside us. I guess it wasn't that way with all people. I guess you both had to have the same animal in you, and you knew it when you got close enough. Then it really wasn't like you were howling and biting and sweating—it was the animal.

When we were both exhausted, the bed all ripped apart, Judy said, while trying to catch her breath, "We need another shower." She pushed herself up with both arms and hung there a moment. Then she looked back at me and smiled. I never saw a more peaceful beautiful face. She was glowing and blushed, her lips translucent pink. Her thin ribs reminded me of a birdcage. Her breasts were swollen, her hips were wide, and her legs long and tapered. I didn't want to ever leave.

Maybe she had the same animal in her. She said, "Will you stay with me today?"

"I'll stay as long as you want," I said.

We lay on the couch all afternoon. We didn't get dressed, and we couldn't stop touching each other. We wanted to do more, but we were both so sore we acted like old people, getting up slowly and taking small steps to get another cup of tea or change the albums on the record player. We listened to James Taylor and Joni Mitchell. We smoked some grass.

She asked me what classes I was missing, and I had to think about it.

"Cultural anthropology, classical mythology, chemistry," I said.

"You understand all that shit?"

"Not much. Maybe I'll do alright."

"I hope you do great," she said, rolling into me. She was warm and smooth, and I closed my eyes, feeling a million miles from college. After a long silence, Judy whispered, "I think I'm in love with you."

I started to say something. I was going to ask her why, but she softly pressed her fingers against my lips and said, "Please don't say anything. It's OK if you don't love me—I just don't want to hear you say it."

I kissed her fingers, and I didn't say a word. I think at that instant it would have been easy to say I loved her, but I wondered if it was just the lurking animal.

The sun was going down behind the mountains, and the place was cast in shadows. "I really should go to work tonight," she said.

"I really should do some studying."

"You can study here anytime you want," she said. "I won't bother you."

Then she got up and stretched in the shadows. She went into the dark bedroom and began to dress. She leaned over, nesting her breasts inside a bra. She pulled on a pair of purple-and-orange polka-dot panties. Slowly she was transforming herself into the bus-stop waitress, and I got up and went to her and held her from behind. She paused and leaned her head back into my shoulder. She was silent.

I kissed her ear.

"I think we went too far," she whispered. "I think *I* went too far."

I kept holding her tightly. She wrestled around to face me, and she buried her face into my neck. "You'll go back and tell all those rich boys about me. You'll go to parties with all those young girls from fancy schools." She clicked her tongue. "I always end up doing this to myself."

I let her go, and she continued to dress herself in the bathroom while I found my own clothes.

I waited for her in the living room.

When she came out she was the same person I had met, what now seemed so long ago, and she seemed unrecognizable as the person I had spent the past twenty-four hours with. She was in her pink uniform and hairnet, white-heeled sandals with painted toenails, peach lipstick, and purple eye shadow. She seemed shy now. "How do I look?"

"I like it," I said. "Nobody but me will know what you really look like, how beautiful you really are."

"Do you mean that?"

"I wouldn't lie to you."

But in a sense I really was lying. We had a story back home about how the twin boys, the left-handed one and the right-handed one, formed the world. They molded human beings out of clay and baked them. Indians were baked just right, black people were baked too much, and white people weren't baked enough. I didn't think Judy was baked enough. Her skin was so pale and milky, almost fragile, like she might fall apart. I thought she *was* beautiful, in her own way, but not a Mohawk girl. She had that mouse-colored opening between her legs and that light hair, sort of vulnerable. I guess I did lie, because I liked Indian girls more. But I liked Judy a lot, because she didn't act like those Dartmouth people. Even the secretaries at Dartmouth acted like they were queens, real snobs. Some of them even thought I was some kid coming in to fix something, just 'cause I didn't talk all the *fah-fah-fah-la-la* stuff and stick pennies in my shoes and wear expensive aftershave.

Then she grabbed her purse and we left, driving the few miles to campus, where she dropped me off. She leaned way over and called through the passenger window, "You sure you don't want a key to my place?"

"I'll give you a call," I said.

"Last time it took nearly two months."

"I promise. I'll call."

Then she drove off fast, screeching around the corner in her decorated Volkswagen. The pink waitress, late for work.

The
Lecture

It was the anthropology course that really got on my tits—Judy said that a lot, and I sort of picked it up, like, "Get off my tits, Asshole," when some guy was bugging me to get off the pay phone. The professor in the anthro course didn't know what he was talking about. He was a smart guy, too smart. You could see all that learning bubbling out of his head, but he was still as dumb as a chicken pecking at its own reflection in a pool of water. That guy in anthro saw only his own autograph stamped on all the students.

He was talking about some stuff that didn't interest me much, Neolithic man and hunter/gatherer culture, and I was staring around at the room. It was pretty shabby for a big-shot college like Dartmouth. We were in half-circle rows like bleachers that overlooked the lecture podium, and the walls were streaked with water stains that seeped from the ceiling like spilled coffee on white paper. There was a big wind outside, and every once in a while curled brown-and-yellow leaves blew around in little whirlwind patterns. It was the same wind that blew at home, and I remembered watching the leaves whip around outside the elementary school. I guess I just didn't like listening much.

But then I sort of perked up when the professor started talking about tobacco. He was explaining about Iroquois tobacco, which I knew a lot about. He said how we smoked clay pipes to send prayers up to the Great Spirit. I must have clucked my tongue a little too loud, 'cause he heard me and looked at the seating chart. For such a smart guy he still couldn't remember who I was or how to pronounce my name, so he pointed at me way in the back.

"You there," he said. "Do you have something to say?"

I shrugged and got kind of small. Everyone turned around and looked at me.

"Come on, out with it," he said.

"Only that Iroquois people don't smoke pipes like you say. We burn it on a stove or a rock to pray and give it as offerings, but it's not like you say."

He pulled off his reading glasses and squinted at me.

"You are an authority on this subject?" he asked.

"I sort of grew up with it," I answered.

"I would suggest that you are the victim of a cultural demise. You do not even know your own history," he said. Then he went on to explain how these theories were formulated by leading scholars—anthropologists, archaeologists, historians—who not only uncovered the past but were doing Indian people a service by reintroducing their culture to them.

"You're wrong, sir," I said, feeling my heart tremble.

He stood there with his mouth agape.

"We don't need you to teach us our culture. We need you to stay out of it," I said. I just didn't give a shit. I knew he was already pissed off, so I said what I had to say. You'd have thought I called his mother a whore. I guess those old grey professors were like that about their work, big babies.

The classroom was like a still photograph. I didn't even see a blink or hear a breath. The prof slowly put his specs on and slid back to his notes. He ignored me and continued with his lecture.

Afterwards, while I was walking alone across the green, a guy from class passed me, saying, "You're fucked now. Ol' Widwicke won't forget you."

I guess it wasn't enough that we learned what they lectured, we all had to believe it. Some of these guys were trying to teach me that two and two made five, but I knew better. Where I came from, it made four.

Snow Night

I tried to study, first at the library until it closed at midnight and then in my room. It was Saturday, and I wanted to be alone, away from all the people. It was Halloween. There was a party going on in the dorm. Music was blasting down the halls, and there were weird people everywhere, in ugly masks and wigs, crashing against my door, hanging out in the halls with beer or bottles of hard liquor. I could hear the voices and the laughter of young women.

When I came out of my room about two in the morning, the hall was crowded and smoky, and I had to squeeze by people to get to the bathroom. The bathroom had four stalls and a row of sinks beneath a long mirror. The mirror made the room seem twice as big and twice as crowded. People were sitting in the sinks, and there was a swarm of young women milling around an aluminum keg of beer floating in the icy water in a big garbage can. Most everybody was drunk and talking too loud. I recognized a guy, coming toward me, who lived in a room down the hall. His name was Robert Dudley Sturtevant the Third, and he was an upperclassman with a red convertible. His friends called him BoDudley. He was a big brash guy with a yellow square-topped brush cut. He yelled at me, "Hey, Chief! Where have you been keeping yourself." He came right up and looked down at me. He was the biggest guy I ever saw.

"I've been studying," I said.

"Knock off the books!" he said. "Join the team!"

"What team?" I asked.

"This team! Look around. See all the women? We need teamwork. If one of us scores, it's a goddamned moral victory for all of us."

"I don't understand."

"Let me explain, Chief. We got to work as a team to keep

the pressure on them, otherwise they figure they're just in it for the free booze and dancing. What's in it for us? Dartmouth men are warriors! *Wah-hoo-wah!*"

BoDudley was about as drunk as a standing man could be.

"You got that, Chief? No free lunch at Dartmouth!"

"No free lunch," I mimicked. He wasn't listening.

"Let me give you some advice. First thing you do is find out what school they're from. Smith girls are the hardest to conquer; Bennington girls are the easiest. In between you've got Vassar, Holyoke, Manhattanville, forget them. Bryn Mawr, Colby-Sawyer, they're not bad, but you have to establish their credentials right up front."

"Why?"

"Remember: Smith to wed; Bennington to bed. Sometimes it's a matter of averages, but mostly it boils down to religion and economics. The worst are Catholic girls; the best are Jewish girls; because they don't have all that guilt about sin and hell hanging over their heads. You also won't get a dose of the clap from a Jewish girl, at least *I've* never heard of it. Smith is very Catholic; Bennington is very Jewish. However, if a Catholic girl from Smith is on financial aid, she might just put out. It's an economic thing, gaining acceptance among her peers by snagging a rich guy. Conversely, if you can weed out a Baptist girl, it's almost a sure thing. When they leave home, they go nuts for sex! It's unbelievable. Overall though, the best sex is outside your religion and economic level."

"It all sounds very complicated."

"Not at all. It's based on human nature. Trust me, Chief."

"Teamwork," I said.

"Don't be a fucking fairy. Chase Dorm is counting on you."

"Alright, Robert."

"BoDudley," he said, punching my shoulder hard. "Now, I just happen to know that girl over there," he said, pointing across the bathroom. She was short and chubby, with long, curly dark hair hanging almost to her waist. She was leaning back against a stall with her blue-jeaned hips tossed out.

"Bennington. She's a dancer. Her name's Becky."

Then he started waving at her, and when she saw him he motioned for her to come over.

She was rocking her hips to the loud music and drinking a beer as she squeezed over to us.

She looked up at me. "Hi."

I nodded at her.

"Isn't this great?" she said. "I'm having the greatest time!" She had big brown eyes and oversized front teeth. She looked like a thumb-sucker. "I'm Becky, from Bennington. Where are you from?"

"Just down the hall."

BoDudley walked past me, whispering, "Teamwork," as he melted into the party.

"You're Dartmouth? You don't look Dartmouth. Are you on an exchange program?" asked Becky.

"I'm from Canada."

"That explains it," she said. "Do you like it, here in America?"

"Not really."

"I don't blame you. Did we ever have a war with you?"

"Not directly," I said. "We might have shared a war or two."

"I'm a dancer." she said. "What are you?"

"I haven't figured that out. I'm just going along."

"I danced at the summer festival in Central Park last summer. I was really good. They want me back next summer. I might be an assistant choreographer. Or maybe I'll have the lead. I haven't decided yet."

I didn't know very much about dancing, but she looked too short and fat to be a dancer. I said, "Good luck."

"There's no room to dance here," she said. "If we go to your room, I'll show you how I dance."

I led the way down the hall.

When we got inside my room she closed the door. "It's really bare in here. You ought to fix it up." She cocked her head, listening to the music echoing down the hall. "Anyway, this is how I hear it. One-two-three-four, snap, left five-six-seven-eight, snap, right two-three-four." She stepped, with a spin, back and forth several times, rolled her shoulders and threw her head back, then forward, so her hair cascaded across her face. She pulled her hair away with both hands and waved her arms in the air. She breathed kind of fast and hard, spun around, and collapsed on my bed.

She pushed herself up. "What do you think? It's called *interpretive*. Sort of a modern updating of Isadora Duncan. Do you know she strangled on her own scarf? At least I think she did. Anyway, dance is only the physical release of expression in response to music, so who's to say what's right or wrong? Don't you think so?"

I said, "I never met anyone like you before."

She smiled and her teeth stuck out at me. "Really?"

"Honestly," I said. "In all my life I never met anyone who talked so much bullshit."

Her smile evaporated, and her eyes narrowed. "You wouldn't know art if it poked your eye out!"

"I suppose then I'd just smell it," I said. I didn't care. When you've got someone whirling around in your room like some crazy moth, you just don't know what to do.

"You son of a bitch!" she said, jumping up from the bed and flinging open my door. "All you care about is . . . is . . . SPORTS!" Then she ran out of my room and slammed the door.

I might have felt a little bit bad about hurting her feelings, but it was her own fault. Back home you could bust on someone and they'd bust you right back. Becky was a lightweight. I hadn't been here very long, and my studies weren't going great, but I had learned how to take it. I figured if Becky had any spirit she'd come back fighting.

That's why I liked Judy, my pink waitress. She could dish it out.

I wanted to see her again, and I decided to go and get a cup of coffee at the bus terminal in White River Junction.

I didn't mind running. I liked to run, and it was a clear, crisp quiet night. I covered five miles in less than an hour, and I paused to breathe outside the bus terminal. I came through the waiting room, and the big clock showed four A.M.

I saw Judy through the big window. I stopped and watched, because the top of her uniform was open and she was leaning over the counter in front of two truckers, laughing so her breasts would jiggle in their faces. She was holding a coffeepot on her hip. I backed up and leaned against the door. I watched her turn and whisper into another waitress's ear. She put the coffeepot down behind the counter. One of the truckers got up from his stool and came out of the restaurant. He walked past me, and I leaned forward, lighting a smoke. He went outside and climbed into the cab of an idling semi truck. I saw Judy come from out back, and she climbed up inside the cab. They were hidden in the shadow of the big truck, and I waited. About five minutes later, the passenger door of the truck opened and Judy climbed out. She walked quickly around the back of the restaurant, and when I looked through the big window I saw her come out of the kitchen and pick up her coffeepot. She went along the line of stools, pouring coffee. She was smiling and chatting with people. She looked around laughing. She looked out the big window at the clock on the wall. Her eyes passed over it. Then her eyes passed over me and stopped. She stopped smiling. She stared at me as if she saw a ghost. All the color in her face drained away, and that is how I knew everything wasn't right.

A kind of energy ran down my spine, and it came straight through me and knotted up my stomach. I felt sick inside. I thought maybe I had the clap again. I turned and pushed out the door to breathe fresh air, but outside it was thick with oil and gasoline hanging in the darkness. There was no fresh air anywhere. I started to run. I spun my arms in circles, like the crazy Bennington dancer, and shook my head to clear away the dizziness. I heard Judy calling out in the night sky. She said, "I want to talk to you! Please let me talk to you!"

I just kept running through the darkness until it was all quiet, until the only thing in my head was the sound of my blood pounding. I don't know how long I ran. I just kept up a steady pace, breathing in and out, like a rhythmical anger, until I was caught up in the headlights of a puttering car.

"Please! Get in!"

I just kept running.

"I'm going to lose my job! Please, get in and talk to me!"

The car nudged me off the road, and I stopped and leaned forward, holding my knees and breathing hard.

Judy got out and came up behind me. She tried to hold me, but I pushed her away and walked in a tight circle, staring down at the gravel on the side of the road.

"Please, come back! Don't run along the road like this! You drive, then go to my place. I'll get a ride after my shift. We can talk."

"Talk about what?" I turned and faced her, all unbuttoned in the harsh headlights of the car. "Talk about you whoring in a truck?"

"You were spying on me!"

"I came to see you and get a fucking cup of coffee!"

"Please take me back before I lose my job. I won't leave you out here."

We got in the car, and she spun it around and raced back down the road. She pulled into the truck stop and got out. "Just take the car home and wait for me. I'll get a ride. I'm going to lose my job. Please, listen to me. You don't understand!"

She ran back inside the restaurant, leaving the driver's door open. I sat for a while, and then I climbed over the stick shift and sat in her seat. I closed the door and released the brake.

About six thirty she came home, just as the sun was coming up. The land was all shadows and grey when I heard a car door slam. I still hadn't turned on any lights, and I waited on the sofa. She came quietly, carefully, through the kitchen door. She walked into the living room and stopped, letting her purse just fall on the floor. She slipped out of her shoes and leaned back against the bedroom doorframe with her arms folded in front of her.

"You saw it all, didn't you," she said in a hushed voice.

"I couldn't help see it all."

After a long silence she tried to talk, but her voice crackled. She wiped her nose on the back of her hand and then brushed at her eyes. "Why'd you have to come and see that?" she said. "It's nobody's business but mine."

She rolled around the corner into the bedroom. I heard the water running in the bathroom, and then the toilet flushed. She came back out wearing her big pink robe. The sun was glinting through the windows now, and she went around the room, pulling all the shades and curtains. "Don't stare at me!" she said.

"I wasn't staring," I said.

"Yes, you were." She retreated to the darkest corner, just inside the bedroom door, and looked out at me. "You're spying on me right now. You're looking right inside me!"

"No, I'm not," I said. "I'm just trying to understand things."

"You don't understand anything!" she lashed out. "The most money I can make in tips is seventy-five, maybe a hundred bucks a week, tops! I never fuck anyone! Not once in six years did I ever drop my panties. All I do is blow 'em or rub my tits on 'em, and I always spit it out! I get two ten-minute breaks a shift, and even then I work—Twenty bucks for a blow job, and the night manager gets his cut. You almost ruined everything."

I was thinking about the party in my dorm and what Bo-Dudley said. "What's your religion?"

She was shaking in the doorway. "I'm Catholic."

"Don't you worry about going to hell?"

She stiffened. "I'm already there," she said. "Nothing I can do will pull me back."

"Why do you do it?" I asked.

She slipped back in the bedroom, then reappeared waving a tattered envelope. "I got nearly two thousand dollars in here, tax-free! Every year I got this much money by Christmas. My kids, they don't know where it comes from. They don't care. Somebody's got to give them presents. Sure won't be their old man. Imagine that: Santa Claus giving blow jobs in a fucking truck stop."

"You shouldn't do that," I said. "You're spending yourself all up."

"I think about it all the time. I want to know, if you commit a sin to help others is it really committing a sin? I think a priest would damn me if I asked, so I just do it and figure there's enough time later to work it all out."

I took a deep breath. "You said you loved me."

Her eyes were narrow and burning, and they picked up the light from the crack in the shade behind the sofa as she stared at me. "That was before you spied on me! That was before you knew what I was doing! It's all off! Now you think I'm a whore, don't you? And that's no kind of love. If you could have loved me at home, if you didn't know what I did on my ten-minute breaks, maybe we could have gone on. I'm really sorry. I just didn't want you to know. Every time I lie, I blow it."

"Were you lying when you said you loved me?"

"No."

"Why'd you yell at me for staring at your tits?"

"Because I didn't want to be a whore. I shake my tits and make ten bucks on my break. I wanted you to like me. I was scared I was bringing the whore home."

"Will you stop what you're doing?"

229

"Are you asking me to?"

"I don't know what I'm asking. I don't know what I'm thinking."

She came out of the shadows really fast and knelt on the floor beside me. She put her hands on my knees. "I don't know either! I swear I never fucked anyone for money! All I ever did was blow them, and it was only a job. Most of the time I didn't even try to talk. I was thinking about making more money. I don't even know their names. Just their faces, and even then they all seemed just a bunch of lonely old truck drivers. Can't you understand? Afterwards they went away, and I came home. I didn't love any of them!"

She seemed to melt against me, all limp and dead, and she began to cry. "Don't hate me," she said. "I never tried to hurt you."

It would have been easy to just push her away and leave for good. But I was thinking back, trying to remember some story old Jonas or someone else might have told me that would help me work this out. I never had a problem like this. And I was thinking how my spirits weren't prejudiced, so why should I be? Maybe I didn't like knowing what Judy did, but she didn't try to hide nothing. I knew girls back home who fucked and lied like bandits. Some of them didn't even know who the daddies of their babies were. No one judged them. That's just how it was.

I leaned over Judy, pressing my cheek against the back of her neck. "Sshh, don't cry," I whispered. "It doesn't matter."

She turned her face up and held onto me hard. She said, "I'm so tired."

I got up with her, and we went in the bedroom. We stood on opposite sides of the bed. I got undressed and slipped under the covers, and she curled beside me. Her hair smelled like potato oil, and her breath was all toothpastey. The blankets were over our heads, and everything was black. In that blackness she said, "I'm no good at life. I just know I'm going to screw this up. I always do."

I said, "You need to sleep."

Then we fell silent, and I began to sleep. In my head I saw whirling stars, dark roads, ancient relatives, and distant friends, and they were all singing my name, *Turtle Belly*.

Autumn had been full and glorious after the wounding of the Great Bear—Onkwali Kowah. That was one of the stories—how the Big Dipper was a great bear pursued across the heavens by hunters, how their arrows made all the blood and grease fall out of the sky bear to color the leaves red and yellow, and how the bear hibernated and healed throughout winter to be reborn high in the sky in the greening of spring—that I told Judy. She thought it made perfect sense. We were raking leaves when I told that story. It was November, and the bare branches of the trees rattled when the wind came up.

Sometimes I lied to her. Sometimes, when we walked in the heavy woods behind her little garden patch beside the barn apartment, I made up stories. I told her that wild mushrooms represented the penises of fallen warriors, and that the spirits of the warriors would come after her if she picked those mushrooms. I told her that I knew of a woman who ignored the warnings and got no rest at night as long as she lived. Later, I told her I had made it up, but after that she never knew if I was lying. I figured I'd keep her guessing about me.

When she wasn't working at the truck stop, she was a

different person. Most of the time she wore faded jeans, a blue work shirt, and old hiking boots. She let her hair hang down. And sometimes, working outside in a brown canvas coat with a corduroy collar, her hair got all tangled, and I'd help her brush it out before she got ready for work.

It was always quiet just before she went to work. We didn't talk about work at the truck stop. She arranged a new schedule, working from four in the afternoon until midnight. Every night when she got home she put all her tip money in a red coffee can on top of the fridge, then she went in the bedroom and dug out the tattered envelope from her panty drawer. Next she went in the bathroom and scrubbed her face and let down her hair, and she came out wearing an old flannel shirt, just that and nothing else. Then we went to bed and made love. Every night we let the animals go free, and every morning we locked them up again. Somehow we both knew that was how it had to be. I think it was the same animal in her that came out when she was working and when she was with me. The only difference, and it was what I came to accept, was that she was the pink waitress at work, like she was wearing a mask, a disguise, but she was her own self when she was with me. That's the only way both of us could live with it. Sometimes we made love with such violence it scared me. It was as though we were fighting when we made love, a grunting tug-of-war. We worked out our anger and our passions. One time she broke blood vessels in her forehead—that's how hard she was bearing down—and they looked like little red spiders on her face the next morning. Aside from fucking, we never raised our voices at one another.

She had to work on Thanksgiving Day. I could have stayed at the college and eaten my fill at Thayer Hall, the big dining room on campus, but instead I came to Judy's. I studied for a while, then drank some beer and watched TV. Judy came home a little after midnight. She brought me a big plate of turkey roll, stuffing, and gravy, covered in tinfoil. I didn't even let her re-heat it in the oven. I ate it cold and soggy, but it tasted great. She did a lot of things like that for me—bringing home food, buy-ing beer and smokes—I didn't mind. She said it made her feel good.

Snow came the first week of December, on a Sunday night that Judy wasn't working. I was studying for finals at the kitchen table, and she was sitting on the sofa, wrapping Christ-mas presents for her kids. She'd spent all her free time during the past week shopping, and she showed me all the clothes and toys. I told her I never had that much as a kid, and that she shouldn't do it either. I said, "You might not always be around. You shouldn't get those kids used to having so much. Just when you think you're riding easy, you get a flat tire."

"It's my money," she said. "And if I want to spend it on my kids, I will." Then she looked outside. "Oh, *look*, it's snowing!" Sometimes, when the topic of money or work turned up, she changed the subject with a syrupy, high tone, as though noth-ing in the world was wrong or could go wrong.

"Let's go out in the snow. It's so fresh and clean!"

"I have too much work to do. My exam starts at eight in the morning."

"Well, I'm goin' out!" She bounced off the sofa and pulled on her hiking boots. She grabbed some brown-paper bags from under the kitchen sink and some other things—I didn't pay much attention. I looked up when she opened the door.

All she had on was the flannel shirt and boots. "At least put on a coat and some pants. You'll freeze your white ass off."

"Who cares," she said wistfully. "It's so pure and beauti-ful." Then she turned out the door and was gone.

After a while, when she didn't come back, I got up and called out the door, but she didn't answer. I stepped outside. Her tracks led around the side of the barn toward the garden and the woods, and I quickly followed them. The snow was coming down in slow thick flakes. Everything was white and the air smelled icy, but it wasn't very cold. Off in the distance I could see a strange amber glow, and as I drew nearer it split apart into four orange balls of light shining through the whiteness. I found Judy lying spread out in the garden with four candles lighted inside paper bags arranged in a big square around her. She was unbuttoned and naked, letting the fat snowflakes land on her skin and melt, trickling down. Steam was rising from her. I stepped into the square of candlelight and reached down for her hand. "Are you crazy?"

"No, it's alright. I saw it once in *National Geographic* magazine. People in Switzerland, or maybe it's Sweden, roll around in the snow to stay healthy. It's good for you!" The snow was landing on her closed eyelids, her nose and lips. She opened her mouth, curling out her tongue. The she closed her mouth and pursed her lips in a kiss, waiting for the snowflakes to trickle down her chin. She said, "I invented my own way of doing it. I do it once a year on the first night snowfall, because it has to be dark. Every snowflake that touches you is like a little shock, and after awhile you don't know if you're freezing or burning. You keep your eyes closed, and you can't even feel the ground—it's like you're on fire in space—your body doesn't even belong to you anymore. Then, when I think I can't possibly stand it for another second—not even a fraction of a second—I touch myself, and it feels like my arms and legs explode off my body, and I just hold it there, my fingers getting warm again between my legs. That's when I crash back to earth, when my fingers thaw. Then I run inside to a hot, hot shower. I call it Snow Night, and not another living soul knows about it."

I knelt down close to her. I could see her eyeballs flickering back and forth under the pink frozen lids. "Why don't you come inside."

"No, you go inside. This is between me and the snow. I'm not hurting anyone. You don't have to watch if you don't want to. I'll be in later."

I moved off a few yards and waited, but she didn't get up. She began to shiver. Her jaw muscles tightened, and her legs twitched. She breathed faster and faster, and a low moan rose out of her like it was rising out of the earth. Suddenly she clasped both hands between her legs, curled up in a ball, and rolled over on her side in the snow, panting great gusts of steam.

I quickly turned and went back to the house, and sat at the table over my books. In a minute she came inside, smelling of the singularly peculiar acid odor of frosty sweat. She was ragged and limp, her hair matted.

She said, with a low raspy voice, "I'm going to take a shower."

Later, when we went to bed, I rolled against her and moved my hand over her skin. She pushed it away and barked, "Don't touch me! I can't take anymore!"

Snow Night was the first and only time she said no to my touch.

Christmas
1970

The dormitories closed during the middle of December for Christmas break, and I used Judy's car to bring my duffel bag to her house.

During the entire time I had been away at college, I had not received a letter from home. My cousin Tom was not much of a writer. I didn't write any letters either. I guess I just knew they were thinking of me, and they knew I was thinking of them, so it didn't make sense wasting time gushing out all your feelings on paper. It seemed an awful waste cutting down trees just to tell people what they already knew.

So, I was surprised when I checked my mailbox to find a package from home. There was a letter from Tom inside.

Dear Sam,

I don't know if you're coming home for Christmas. I sent you this stuff. Aunt Bess died last month. She was 94. Star Blanket is OK, too. Jimmy Sky's house burned down. Merry Christmas.
Your Cousin
Tom

Inside the package was a bag of Indian tobacco, a pair of socks (Aunt Molly knitted them), and a twenty-dollar bill. It seemed like big trouble for Tom to go through, but I knew he was thinking of me. I didn't have enough money to go home, so it was good to hear from Tom.

When I got back to Judy's house there was a strange car parked right up by her door. I got out of the car and walked slowly up to the house, and Judy came lumbering out with her arms full of Christmas presents for her kids. An elderly woman followed her, and she was carrying a load of packages. Judy saw me and said real loud, "Oh, good! You got the car fixed! If you wait a second, I'll be right with you!" Then she and the woman went inside for another load, and I went back and waited by her car. After the woman's car was packed with presents, the woman got inside and started it and Judy said goodbye. The woman stared at me as she drove away.

Judy said, "That was Claude's mother. They have the kids, but my life is my own business! I hope you don't mind?"

"I don't care," I said. And I didn't. That pinch-faced old woman didn't mean anything to me.

I brought my bags inside and loaded the woodstove.

Judy looked at my package. "What's that?"

"A package from my father."

"I thought your father was gone."

"My cousin Tom."

"Oh, yeah, I forgot." She looked at the clock. "I gotta get ready for work."

When she was halfway out the door in her disguise-that's how she seemed to me now whenever I saw her as the pink waitress—I said, "I'm gonna use your telephone, if it's alright. I want to call home."

"Sure, go ahead." Then she left.

It was quiet after she left. The winter sun had slipped below the mountains, casting the valley and the house in yellow shadows. I'd spent a lot of time in the house alone, but it seemed different now that my dorm was closed up until after the New Year, when the next term started. I grabbed a beer out of the fridge and took down the red coffee can. I counted Judy's tips. There was fifty-three dollars—two tens, a five, and singles—after three days of work. A little more than two bucks an hour. I never looked at her money before, and I don't know why I did then. It just occurred to me to see how she was doing. A little bit later, I got off the sofa and went in the bedroom. I opened her panty drawer and found the tattered envelope. There was one ten-dollar bill in it. I put it back and got another beer.

I sat on the sofa and lighted a smoke as I dialed the phone. Tom's number rang and rang and rang. When I hung up I figured that maybe he was at Aunt Molly's, because it was Friday. I dialed Aunt Molly's number, and after four rings she picked up the phone.

"*She:kon! Skenago!* Hello! How're you doing! It's me, Sam. I miss you!"

"Sam!"

"Yes!"

"How can that be? You died a lot of years ago."

"No, Aunt Molly, not your brother. I'm Tom and Ellie's boy. Sam!"

"Where are you?"

"I'm at Dartmouth."

"Are you comin' for dinner? I made a ham."

"No, Aunt Molly, I'm a long way from home. I just called to say Merry Christmas."

"Merry Christmas to you, too. Who is this?"

"Your nephew Sam!"

"What do you want?"

"I'm real sorry to hear that Aunt Bess, your sister, died. I loved her a lot."

"Bess died in her sleep. She was ninety-four. I'm ninety-seven."

"I know, Aunt Molly, and I hope you're alright."

"I chopped my own wood today. Are you coming for dinner? I made a ham."

"Yes, I'll come for dinner, Aunt Molly."

"Who is this?"

Then I heard Aunt Molly say, "I don't know who it is, but they're coming for dinner."

Someone else got on the phone. I recognized the voice as my cousin Rita, Aunt Molly's daughter. "Who is this?"

"It's me, Sam."

"Sagolee! Greetings! I thought you dropped off the rim of the world."

"I just called to wish everyone Merry Christmas."

"You doing OK out there among all those *Oserunih*—Englishmen?"

"I guess I'm doing alright. Aunt Molly sounds kind of different."

"Mother had a stroke last month. She doesn't remember a lot, but she's strong."

"I sure was sorry to hear about Aunt Bess."

"Gee, it was a nice funeral. Some Longhouse people came down and burned tobacco, then we gave away all her belongings. Tom saved a quilt for you."

"Listen, is Tom there now?"

"Tom took Eddie to hockey practice. I guess they're coming over for dinner later."

"Tell Tom I called, OK?"

"I sure will. Where are you?"

"I'm at Dartmouth College."

"Where's that?"

"A long way, in New Hampshire."

"Well, I guess so. Good-bye, now."

"Onen:kewahi."

I hung up the phone and lay back on the sofa. It was really dark outside. I reached over and turned on the lamp and lighted another smoke. Maybe later I'd call back and talk with Tom and thank him for the gifts.

I stood in front of the little black woodstove and opened the bag of Indian tobacco. I took out a pinch and placed it on top of the hot stove in the center of a round burner plate. I waited and watched as it slowly darkened, began to glow orange, and give off the smoke. The smoke rose up past me, and I could smell it, sweet and pleasant, and I said one of the prayers I knew in Mohawk for Aunt Bess.

I thank him and heaven,
for he lives,
the Creator.

Then I repeated it for Ellie, and for my mother, and for all the people who were gone or having hard times. I prayed over and over again, and I kept burning tobacco so the Creator would hear me. I had never done that before, prayed with tobacco like the old-timers did. But I needed to do it, because I was so far from home, and I now realized that some of the people wouldn't be there when I returned. I knew that Time didn't care if I was gone. Time was selfish and, like all the others, it was waiting for me, too. That's why I prayed in the old way, to keep Time and the Creator happy.

"She:kon! Tom! It's me. How are you? Did I wake you up?"

"No, I was just goin' to bed. You doing OK?"

"They closed up the dorms for Christmas. I'm living with an old woman. She's thirty-two."

"Are you gonna stay with her?"

"I don't know yet."

"Let's see. When you're eighty-six, she'll be a hundred. Are you sure you wanna live with a hundred-year-old woman?" He laughed real hard.

"Thanks a lot for your package. I burned tobacco on a stove for Aunt Bess and Ellie."

"They got stoves down there?"

"This woman does."

"Well, that's what tobacco's for. That's why the Creator gave it to us."

"I talked to Aunt Molly."

"Yeah, I heard."

"She doesn't sound too good."

"No, she's alright. She just doesn't remember anything. She's like a little kid, eh. You were that way. Life comes full circle, they say, if you live long enough. But she's real strong, and she cooks for everybody," Tom said.

"I sure miss everyone," I said. "I wish I could come home but I can't afford it right now."

"We got your room just the same. Didn't touch a thing. Hey listen, Ima Jean had another baby just last week."

"I didn't know she was pregnant. I just thought she was getting fat."

"She didn't tell anyone until she had to. She and Larry busted up 'cause it wasn't his."

"I don't think Larry looked after her very well."

"I think he tried. He's still pretty wild. He wrecked his car."

"The red one?"

"No, he traded that for a blue LTD. He went right through

the windshield over on the third line. If he wasn't drunk he would have died, that's how limp he was."

"Tell him I said to stop fucking around and get a job."

"I'm not a miracle maker. Listen, I'm working early shift tomorrow, so I'm going to bed."

"Merry Christmas, Tom, and same to Eddie."

"Merry Christmas, Sam. Don't let that old woman wear you out."

"I won't. Oh, wait, I passed all my exams. My Anthro prof gave me a D, though, so I'm on probation again."

"What's meant to be is meant to be. Bye."

"Onen:kewahi."

I hung up the phone. It was getting late, and Judy would be home a little after midnight. I turned on the TV and watched an old movie. I drank a beer. After a while I closed my eyes and dozed.

I snapped up when Judy pushed open the snowy door. "I'm sorry for being so late," she said, shaking off her coat and kicking her shoes into a corner. "One of the waitresses was late, and I covered her shift. I probably should have called you. You don't mind." She put her tip money in the coffee can on the fridge then went into the bedroom. I looked at the clock and it was almost two A.M. I heard her rustle in the panty drawer then go in the bathroom. Five minutes later she came out herself, wearing the old flannel shirt, and she collapsed on the sofa beside me.

She leaned into me and sighed. "I'm so tired. Want to go to bed?"

"It's two in the morning," I said.

"I told you, I covered for another girl. If it happens again, I'll call. Don't be this way. Come on. Let's go to bed."

When we went to bed, I hardly had a moment to breathe. She shimmied down under the covers and wrapped herself on top of me with a fierceness that left me paralyzed. I could not move. She held me down and moved like a roller coaster.

She was so exhausted afterwards, she wouldn't respond when I tried to push her off me. So I squeezed out from under her and went into the bathroom and pissed a long, hard painful stream of dark urine. Sometimes she had a way of fucking me so long everything shut down.

I came out of the bathroom and stared at her. She was face up on my pillow, her mouth open, the air catching in the back of her throat with a dry, painful-sounding rasp. I went over and opened her panty drawer, and in the tattered envelope was a ten-dollar-bill and two fifty-dollar bills.

I went out to the kitchen and counted the money in the coffee can. There were twenty-one more dollars. I went back to bed and shoved her over. Then I lay there, wondering about her money. I didn't sleep very well. Bad dreams.

In the morning she was so happy. She said, "I have two days off, and I haven't felt so excited about Christmas in years!" She was all bundled up in her robe and wool socks, sipping a hot cup of tea in a rocking chair by the woodstove as the sun poured in the window. "It's been so long since I put up a Christmas tree. Let's cut a Christmas tree and put it up! We can hike out back and cut one, and I have a box of stuff in the barn—did you put up Christmas trees?"

"Yeah, Ellie used to. I don't know if Tom will now."

"Well, we will, and we can take a picture for you to send home. When I was a kid we always had a big tree. My dad had to have the biggest tree, and we worked really hard to make it the best tree. It always was. With a white Virgin Mary on top. Dad always waited until the tree was done, and then he put the

Virgin on top. I remember one year he stuck her on the tree, jammed her right on top, and he looked at me, laughing, and said, 'I hope she's still a virgin!' With that spiky top under her white robe. Mother just thought he was being rude, but I understood."

"If you want a tree, I'll cut you one."

"I really want a tree. I want to have the best Christmas!"

After lunch we hiked up behind the barn, and I cut down a small white pine with a rusty bow saw I found in a shed. I dragged it back through the snow, and we set it up on a base nailed of short boards. Judy made me turn it around and around to find the right side, then she stretched a wire to the wall so it wouldn't fall over into the room. There wasn't much in the box of decorations—a string of old lights that didn't work, some broken glass balls, a few painted wooden soldiers on strings.

"This will never do," she said. "I'll go shopping. I'll make it the best tree!"

Then she rushed out, and I waited all afternoon. When she came back at dinnertime I helped her carry in all the bags. She didn't even want to eat. She worked all evening on the tree, and I did what she told me to, hanging balls and stringing lights. I never knew so much junk could be hung on a skinny pine tree. When it was done it looked like a ride at an amusement park. She said, "Isn't it wonderful!" Then she opened up a package. "It's a Virgin, just like we used to have. You do it. You put it on top!"

I stood on a chair and put the Virgin doll on the top of the tree, and Judy hugged me when I stepped down. "That's perfect!" she said. She kissed me really hard, and she was shaking. She stood back and looked at the tree. "It's a better tree than we had—better than Father's!"

As Christmas approached, Judy could not have been more happy. Every morning she turned on the lights on the Christmas tree before she even made coffee, and when she drank her coffee, she stood in front of the tree, cupping the coffee with both hands, admiring the lights and tinsel and spinning golden balls.

I counted the money in the tattered envelope every day when she came home from work and was in the bathroom. It got up to four hundred dollars. Two days before Christmas, the envelope was empty. I didn't ask what she did with the money, and I didn't want to know how she got it.

On Christmas Eve she disappeared into the bedroom just before she left for work. She emerged with a bag. "Go on, open it."

I was sitting on the sofa, and I opened the narrow bag. It was a record album of Christmas songs.

Her face was glowing. "I want you to have Christmas music tonight, and when I come home, we'll listen to it and have hot brandy. I bought a bottle." She adjusted the collar on her pink uniform. She took a deep breath. "Someone's gotta work on Christmas Eve—and those truckers and people on buses. Maybe I can get off early if it's not busy."

But she didn't get off early. She didn't come home until 1:30.

She came in the door, her face beaming, and she squeezed me so hard I lost my breath. "It's officially Christmas! I love you so much!"

She disappeared into the bedroom and came out in the flannel shirt. "Brandy time!" She heated a pan of brandy and added slivers of butter and a sprinkle of nutmeg. We drank it from wine glasses while we sat on the sofa listening to the Christmas record. The TV was on, with no sound, and we watched an old black-and-white Scrooge movie. The tree glistened like a Cadillac. Judy said, "Will you wax my legs?"

I got up from the sofa, going into the bedroom, and reached underneath my side of the bed. I came back out with a dozen red roses. "My cousin Tom sent me twenty dollars. I walked into town and bought you these."

"You didn't!" she said. She narrowed her eyes. "You have to wait till morning. Santa doesn't come till good boys are asleep." She got up and took each rose and placed them all over the Christmas tree. "A Christmas tree with roses! I never saw nothing so beautiful. I love you so much!" She hugged me again, and I had to squirm away.

"Wax my legs!"

Then I waxed her legs, and we fucked while Burl Ives sang "Have a Holly Jolly Christmas".

She must have gotten up during the night, because when I awoke there were gifts under the tree and one of her wool socks was hanging by the woodstove.

She was waiting there on the sofa. "Open your presents! Stocking first!"

There was a Christmas card in the stocking, and a key was taped to it. "What's this?" I asked.

"You'll see," she said.

There were some chocolates and a tangerine in the toe of the sock.

"Open your presents."

I sat on the sofa, and she handed them to me one at a time, her eyes bright. I got a red wool pullover sweater, a pen-and-pencil set in gold, a pewter beer mug, a silk tie. There were more socks, two blue-button down shirts, and a pair of beige chinos.

She hovered at my side as I opened each present.

"I can't wait any longer!" she said. "Get the key and come with me. We're going outside."

I followed her. She was all wrapped up in her pink robe and scuffling through the snow in her boots.

Down the lane past the farmhouse, parked on the side of the road, was a brown-and-tan 1963 Rambler sedan.

"I know it's seven years old," she said, "but there isn't a spot of rust on it, and I had it worked on from top to bottom. It's like new! Go on, get in!"

I got in the driver's seat, and she came around and sat beside me.

"Open the glove box."

I reached inside and pulled out some papers.

"The title's in your name! Free and clear. And there's fifty bucks gas money! I love you. Merry Christmas, Sam."

She leaned over and hugged me. "Maybe some night we can go parking? Maybe a drive-in movie?"

I couldn't find my voice.

"Go on," she said. "Start her up."

I put the key in the ignition, and the car rolled right over, smooth and clean. I listened to the engine for a minute, then I shut the car down.

I put my hands in my lap. "I been counting your money," I said. "You've been coming home late with a lot of money. I never asked you about it. I don't want this car. I don't want none of those presents. You can't afford it."

"Who gave you the right to count *my* money!"

"You were coming home late. You put twenty in the pot and a hundred in the drawer. I don't want to be a part of that."

"What difference does it make? I fucked a few guys—I did it for you, so I could make this the best Christmas."

"If you did it for me, it makes me a pimp."

"No . . . no . . . no! You're not a pimp, 'cause you never asked me for a cent. I did it 'cause I wanted to!"

"Why would you want to do that for me? Can you answer that? Tell me, because I don't understand."

She started to cry, and she leaned over the dashboard.

"Stop crying! Tell me!"

"Because you're the only man," she said, looking up, "who didn't tell me what to do!"

I looked at the papers. Free and clear. It was all there— title and registration, insurance card—all paid in full, all in my name.

"It ain't my way."

"I promise, honey, never again!" she said, throwing her arms around my neck. "I just wanted this to be the best Christmas ever! It was, wasn't it? Nobody ever gave you a car, did they?"

"You gotta slow down," I said.

"I swear, after Christmas I'll be home on time every night. No more fucking around. . . . Only blow jobs!"

I was thinking about the rez. Thinking about that car gassed up in the snow outside.

So after she left for work that afternoon, I loaded all my stuff in the car and set out for home. I left her a note that read:

Thanks for everything. I decided to go home. I'm not sure I even like college. Take care of yourself. Love, Sam.

I left it in the bathroom, stuck in a crack in the mirror.

Flying Away

It was different driving than taking a bus. I flew across the land, and I drove all night. Like before, the distance between the rez and Dartmouth was a great black gulf of automobile headlamps, highway lights, and tollbooths, like intergalactic space stations floating in an endless universe. At rest stops I did not feel like my feet were on solid ground, because those places seemed not real, temporary, with a transient spirit. The people passing through them had no expressions on their faces. They were ghosts who did not know where they belonged. I wondered how many of those people really had homes—not just a house, but a sacred place that conjured the past and filled them up inside. They seemed empty, like peanut shells.

After four months away I was returning to my home, and the closer I got to it the more the emptiness inside me filled with hope. I don't think any of us on the rez really knew *what* we were hoping for, but it was enough to live on. Just being on our own land was enough to live on, even if some of us were starving. I figured I'd rather starve the Indian way with no food than the white man way with no spirit. Maybe someday my spirit would be strong enough so I could go back to places like Dartmouth. Maybe not. It wasn't important enough to worry about. I just didn't want to end up like that Navajo guy, Vincent Begaye. Although he was always bumming money and smokes, I knew he was pretty rich—private school in Santa Fe, new clothes. He didn't talk much like an Indian, either; he sounded more like a politician. I had a feeling he'd make a million bucks and have an office in Washington, be a professional Indian, and get busted by the tribe for skimming federal money in sheep futures. Don't get me wrong, we had our share of the Vincent Begaye guys, too—all tribes do—but I didn't wanna be one of them. We all knew about that stuff, whether it was Canada or the States: Give enough government money to divide up the factions on the rez; then buy the land out from under them. I just wanted to go home. Home. I didn't want all that political or scholarly stuff. I just wanted to know that the tombstones were still standing up with all the names intact.

It only took me twelve hours to reach the outskirts of the rez. I arrived at five in the morning, before dawn, the day after Christmas. It had begun to rain, and a warm breeze was coming off Lake Erie to the south. It should have been snow, but for some reason it was raining. The log house was all dark when I rolled in beside Tom's truck. I got out and tried the door, and it was locked. "Goddamn it!" I pounded on the door. "Let me in! Open the fucking door!"

The rain came down really hard.

I moved to the side of the door and dug my fingers under the window. It creaked and slid up, and I jammed it hard. I leaned over the window and started to climb in. A dog growled. I didn't know Tom had another dog. I began to whisper to it in Mohawk, the way I knew Tom would teach it to understand. Then I saw a shadow-figure move in the kitchen. Before I could say a word, I saw the hot-white blinding flash of a shotgun, like a star exploding in my face with a deafening roar. It caught my left shoulder, and I was blown out the window to lie on my back in the rain. The dog came after me through the window and tore into me. His jaws locked on my neck, ripping at me with shakes of his head. I looked up to see Tom aiming the gun out the window.

"Don't kill me, Tom!" I screamed.

When the shotgun blasted again, the dog was blown apart, and my head fell back on the icy ground. I was weightless and spinning, numb all over and shaking, and the world closed in on me, all blackness with no stars. Then there was nothing.

When consciousness seeped into me, it came with the

sound of laughing voices and the sharp odor of alcohol. Then all was silent again. There was a bright light burning through my eyelids and a pain that gripped my whole body, throbbing downward from my shoulders. My head was heavy and seemed detached from my body. I slowly opened my eyes and tried to swallow, but my throat wouldn't work. It was all closed up. I saw the bright overhead lights and the white ceiling. Then some faces slid in over me, dark faces I could not focus on.

A voice said, "You're gonna be alright, brother. You got busted big time!"

A woman spoke next. "Don't try to move, Sam."

Another woman said, "I'll stay with you, Sam."

A guy's voice said, "Where'd you get the car? It's, like, cherry new!"

"Oh, shut up about the car," said a woman.

"You shut up."

"You can't tell me what to do anymore!"

"Sam, can you hear me? I got your car up to seventy in ten seconds! Too bad it has to be a Rambler. But it runs so sweet!"

Then I drifted away, and the voices became a drone that put me to sleep.

When I really did wake up, I saw Tom sitting on a chair in the corner of the hospital room. He was staring at a TV mounted on the wall near the ceiling. I said, "Tom, I never saw you look so bad." He was pretty worn out, dark circles under his eyes.

He turned and looked at me. "You don't look so good yourself. I didn't know it was you. No one up to any good ever

climbed in my window at five in the morning. You was supposed to be at that college."

"I wish I knew you had a dog."

"Not anymore. I blew his heart out."

"I wish you hadn't done that."

"He had you by the throat. Wasn't time to think about
something like that."

Tom got up and moved his chair right up beside my bed.
He shook my hand.

"I sure am glad to see you," I said.

"Welcome home. Your room's still the same."

I tried to move and winced, shut my eyes, and breathed
deeply while the pain subsided.

"You shouldn't move too much," he said.

"How long have I been here?" I asked, opening my eyes.

"Two days. I got you good," he said.

"What'd they do to me?"

"They put a stainless steel ball in your shoulder—a whole
new joint—stitched up your neck, a few other things."

There was a cast on my body that wrapped around my
chest and shoulders and went down my left arm, where it was
connected to my body with a metal rod. My right arm was
free, but I didn't move it. I just lay there, trying to feel and
sense the different parts of my body. I said, feeling something
strange, "I think they did something to my dick."

"It's a *cathedral*, or something, so you don't have to get up
and piss. It's a tube that goes to a bag hanging on the side of the
bed."

"I don't think I like that much. Who did it to me, a man or
a woman?"

"I don't know."

"How long I gotta stay in here? I sure wanna go home."

"I guess you're gonna be here a long time. They got a special program to help you use your arm again."

I was thinking about a lot of things. "How much trouble you in, Tom?"

"I guess I got some," he said. "It all depends on what you say to the cops. There's a rumor going around that you went away mad and I shot you when you came back. The cops wanna know."

"It was just an honest accident. You aren't mad about anything, are you?"

"When have I ever been mad at you?"

"We better explain it," I said. "Listen, I remember hearing someone say they were driving my car. Was it Larry?"

"I let him use it to bring up Ima Jean, Anne, and a few others yesterday."

"You get the keys back?"

"Not yet. He's still got your car."

"You go tonight and get them keys back. That car means a lot to me. That woman I told you about gave it to me. You don't let no one drive it. Promise?"

"I'll take care of it."

I was beginning to feel tired, and I closed my eyes.

Tom said, "I'll let you get some rest," and I nodded. When he was gone, and I was lying there, opening my eyes every few minutes to look at the TV, I suddenly heard water trickling. After thinking about it, I realized the bag on the side of the bed was filling up. I didn't feel like I was pissing. I felt like a brain inside a numb shell.

Around midnight a pasty-white nurse, with a moon face and red hair tucked under a starched cap, came in with a needle and stuck me in the hip. It hurt like hell, but everything else was hurting like hell, and I stared at the ceiling. After she left I began to fly off the bed into a spinning room. I never landed before I fell asleep.

A few days later I was going nuts to get out of bed. It was worse than a goddamned prison. Larry was visiting me.

"Pull the fucking tube out," I said.

"I don't know how to do it," he said.

"You reach under the sheet and pull the damn thing."

"What if I pull your dick off? Maybe it's connected."

"You can keep it," I said. "I just gotta get out of this fucking bed."

"No, man, I don't want to be responsible."

Larry sneaked a glance over his shoulder at the door.

"Just grab the cathedral and pull it out. I can take it," I said.

"Alright, here goes."

I expected Larry to slide it out slowly. I didn't expect him to act like he was trying to land a fucking catfish. I came right out of that bed and landed on my feet.

"Jesus!" I moaned, doubled over in my plaster suit of armor. "What the hell's wrong with you?"

"You *told* me to pull."

"It's not a goddamned come-along hitch!"

"Stop bitchin'. You're up aren't you?"

He had a point. I moved around the room with my arm frozen—out in the cast. "I think I'm gonna piss right here on the floor," I said, but I didn't. It was just the pain high up inside, and I stood my ground and waited for the pain to pass away.

"Maybe I should call the nurse. It was, like, an accident and you just rolled out of bed, pulled the tube right out!"

"Just shut up," I said, standing a little straighter.

"You okay now?"

"Doing better, " I said. Now that I was hovering in one

spot, I wasn't sure what to do with myself. I'd never been in a hospital before. "What's there to do around here? You been coming and going."

"Nothing. Just lie around and be sick, I guess."

I took small steps toward the door, opened it a crack, and peeked out into the hall. It was a long corridor with doors, metal carts, and a few people with blank faces walking around in bathrobes. "God, they all look like they're dying. I gotta get out of this place."

I turned around and very carefully sat back on the bed.

"You tell Tom I gotta come home."

"What if he won't listen?"

"Then you take me home."

"Can I have your car keys back?"

"They're in the drawer. Take 'em."

Larry got the keys and slipped the ring over his finger.

I looked at him. "I heard you busted up with Ima Jean. You ought to be looking after her and the kids," I said.

"She was fuckin' around."

"The gal who gave me that car was fuckin' around. She always came home. I guess she was alright."

"Was she Indian?"

"No, she wasn't Skin, just a white gal."

"Well, that's different. It wasn't like you was gonna live your whole life with her," said Larry. "Not like me and Ima Jean."

"No," I said, thinking about Judy. "It sure wasn't like you and Ima Jean. My gal loved me."

"No, don't get me wrong. Ima Jean loves me. Remember, I'm the one who left."

"Oh yeah, I forgot. You're the one who left, and she's sittin' at home."

"She's a fucking whore."

"It don't matter what she done, she still loves you. I guess you two got along pretty well. If it's over, it's over."

"What are you, some damned expert?"

"I just been thinking. It just seems like when people love you, they're gonna fuck up."

"You got that right."

I tried to relax and get comfortable. "You go and tell Tom I gotta come home."

Larry spun the key ring. "See you later."

Tom wouldn't help me get out of the hospital. He said I needed to rest. I think he was feeling guilty, seeing me all shot up and in a cast. I didn't blame him.

Larry and Anne got me out. I got dressed as best I could and put a big coat on my good arm and draped the other sleeve of the coat around Anne's shoulder to hide my plaster arm sticking out. We looked like lovebirds, and we just breezed out of the hospital. I sat all stretched out in the backseat of my car while Larry drove with Anne beside him. We roared out of Brantford, and I said to Larry as we drove through the darkness, "I still got some gas money left. Let's go get some booze from Carver."

Larry said, "He doesn't do that no more. Not since he killed Ellie."

"Someone must have a drink around here."

Larry reached over to my glove box. "I do." He opened the box and brought out a bottle. He handed it to Anne, and she tipped it up, then handed it back to me. It was good whiskey, and it sure as hell burned. "Larry, light me a smoke."

Then we cruised around for a while.

Anne said, "Some woman bought you this car?"

"No strings attached," I said.

"You didn't have to do anything?"

"Hey!" I said. "I didn't ask for it. She loves me."

"I don't know why anyone would love you," she said.

"Like people are buying you cars everyday?" I asked.

"Guys do plenty for me. I just don't sell out to the first one who comes along with an old car."

I drank some more whiskey, and it really went to my head—maybe it was all the shots they'd been giving me in the hospital. "I didn't sell out for a car."

Anne glared at me with black eyes. "Somewhere along the line you sold out! Leaving all your friends and family, taking up with some white woman who gives you a car!"

She grabbed the bottle out of my hand and drank hard.

"You're just jealous," I said. "You've got weak pussy hair."

She reach over and started slapping at me. "What do you mean by that!"

I pushed her back over the seat. "I heard a guy once say a pussy hair can drag a battleship across sand. You never been able to keep a guy, and you know it. You can't even give it away."

"I give it away plenty—I mean if I felt like it I would." Her eyes were really flashing. She was breathing hard through her teeth.

"Trouble is you never feel like it, so I hear."

"You ain't heard nothing! Bastard!"

Larry, sitting quietly all this time and bouncing the car around the dark back roads on the rez, turned around and looked at me, his face glowing green from the dashboard.

"She loves you, eh!" He flipped his palm over the seat, and I slapped it with my good hand.

"I do not! I hate him!"

Larry winked about six times. "So how come when he went away you cried, 'I never got to say good-bye,' and then you moped around for a month like a starving dog. Then when he got back you were crying, 'Oh, if he dies, I'll die too.' It sounds more like love than hate to me."

Anne turned around in the seat and scrunched down low, folding her arms tight across herself. She stared straight ahead. "I hate him."

I said, "Why Anne, I didn't know you cared so much," nudging Larry's shoulder. He was grinning from ear to ear.

Anne looked sideways at Larry. "You shouldn't say things I said! That's private!" She looked out the side window, embarrassed. "Take me home right now!"

Larry turned the car around, and we drove over to the third line. Anne got out of the car and slammed the door, and we drove off. Larry said, "Did I set you up or what!"

"Did she really say all that?"

"Word for word," he said.

After a while we cruised home, and Larry helped me get out of the car. He guided me into the house, and I leaned back stiffly into the couch. "I wonder where Tom and Eddie are?" I said, because the house was quiet and empty. "Give me another smoke."

We watched some TV, drank a little whiskey, smoked.

About a half-hour later Tom and Eddie drove in. Tom stood in the doorway with Eddie beside him. He said, "Where the hell you been? I was worried."

"I had to get out of that place, Tom. It was driving me crazy."

"Come on, we're going back right now."

"No way, Tom. I'm fine. I swear. I don't need to go back."

Tom looked at Larry. "Take a hike."

Larry got up from the couch. "See you later, man."

He ducked past Tom and Eddie and drove away in my car.

Eddie flopped down on the couch. I guess he was about to turn thirteen. "Man, it was like you broke out of prison. Everyone was going nuts looking for you."

Tom picked up the phone in the kitchen. I heard him say, "Yeah, he's home. He's alright. He went joyriding with Larry."

Eddie said, "I made junior lacrosse this year. I broke my wrist in October."

"Not bad," I said. "You get the other guy?"

"Naw, I'm waiting for the right time. Maybe I'll kneecap him or something."

"Just make it look like a foul," I said.

Tom got off the phone. "You shouldn't have been drinking with all that medicine."

"Stop worrying about me."

"That college called on the phone, and I told them what happened. I guess you won't be going back for this term, have to go back in the fall."

"Don't bother me none," I said. "I need a break."

Tom said, "I guess I'm to blame. If it wasn't for me you'd be going back to school."

"Forget it," I said.

Tom looked at me, rigid in the plaster cast. "You won't be able to get up the stairs."

"I'll watch some TV, sleep on the couch."

When Tom went to bed Eddie got out his lacrosse stick and showed me some moves. He really juggled that ball, and he was fast. "I practice about two hours a day. There ain't a ball I can't catch," he said.

"You're a real warrior," I said.

Eddie sat on the couch. "You really think so?"

"You bet," I said. "You're the fastest with a ball I ever saw."

"There are guys who are faster," he said.

"Just 'cause they're faster don't make 'em better. You got what it takes. Better than me, anyway."

"You were a great lacrosse player!"

"No, I wasn't, and I'll tell you why. I was always afraid of what was behind me. It's such a fast game. I was always checking out my backfield. I always got hurt from the front, and I never learned. I quit playing when I was fourteen. You don't remember."

"I remember, and you were a good player."

"But I wasn't a great player. *You'll* be a great player someday."

Eddie reached over for one of my smokes, and I swiped his hand away. "What do you think you're doing?"

"I smoke all the time, and besides, Dad's in bed."

"Eat some bubble gum," I said.

"Come on, give me a smoke."

"Alright," I said, and I even lighted it for him. When he was puffing away I said, "Now give me your lacrosse stick."

"What for?"

"You owe me now. That's how it is. That's how it was with me, and that's how it'll be with you. Give me the stick now."

Eddied handed the stick over to me and sighed. He knew what it meant. "Will you give it back?"

"I now own this stick," I said. "It's mine."

"It took a lot of work getting the rawhide pocket all broken in."

"I appreciate your work," I said. "Maybe I'll let you borrow my stick sometime."

He leaned back on the couch beside me, smoking. "How'd you get a woman to give you a car?"

"Now you want a car?"

"No, I was just wondering."

"Don't wonder about that stuff. It'll make you crazy."

"You didn't go crazy. Someday I'll find a woman who'll give me a car, too. If you can do it, so can I."

"Worry about filling your jockstrap first."

"I'm not some little kid."

"You're only thirteen. Sure you are. Nothing wrong with that. Lean over, give me a hug."

"You asked for something! Give me back my stick!"

"Take it," I said. "Now give me that hug, you little shit, and go to bed."

Eddie leaned next to me fast, then grabbed his stick and started to climb the steep ladder-like stairs. He paused and looked at me.

"We never talked much before. I was kind of wondering, did you miss your mother when she died?"

"I was pretty little. I don't remember much. I guess I did," I said.

Eddie said, "I sure miss my mother. I was thinking that when you're born your mother is there, like, to take care of you. Then I got to thinking that she ought to be there to take care of you when you die, too. So you don't always have to feel alone."

"That's how it already is," I said. "Your real mother is the earth. You're not alone." I looked at Eddie poised on the stairs with his lacrosse stick.

"I sure missed you, too, Sam," he said.

"When I get better we'll pitch some balls."

"I'm real glad you came home."

Then he went upstairs, and I got comfortable on the couch, taking a deep breath before I slept.

I fell asleep thinking how the outside world and my

dreams were so much alike, vivid and frightening to experi-
ence, then softer as if veils began to drop, more veils after more
time, so that the reality of my experiences and the illusions of
my dreams were one and the same creature. Already I felt like
I was waking up from the dream of college and the pink waitress, because this was another day, another place, another
world. And, like dreams, you always wake up from memories.

Indian
Love

Turtle Belly

One time Carver Hill told me the definition of Indian love was a hickey and a black eye. My cousin Tom laughed at that. He said no truer words were ever spoken. I don't know how he knew that, because in all the time he was married to Ellie, I never heard a cross word between them. They were married for fourteen years, and after she died Tom said he didn't think in all that time she was mad at him for more than five minutes. Total.

It sure wasn't that way with Anne and me. She could get mad at the drop of a hat. Sometimes you didn't even have time to drop your hat. She'd just knock it right off your head, coming in the door, without warning. That's how much she loved me. I told her, "STOP hitting me in the face like that!" But she had turned her back on me, and when I reached out for her shoulder she spun away and drove her elbow back with so much strength that I heard my ribs pop. She broke two of my ribs, but it was hard to blame her. She'd never been anywhere. She'd never left the rez, and I had been away to a college and had taken up with an older white woman. That's just how she saw it, and I think she figured she couldn't measure up. She was wrong, of course. Anne was a great gal, but I couldn't convince her she was just as good as the waitress who gave me the car. I guess I figured she'd kill me one day, or else I'd snap and kill her first.

All I really wanted was to get through each day, and I was trying to make life work. Ever since old Jonas had died, his tar-paper house across the road from our place sat empty. It wasn't so bad—a couple of leaks in the roof, but it had a sink, and a toilet set off in the corner of the kitchen behind a curtain, and some wires were run in off the electric pole, so there were lights. The woodstove worked fine, and it was pretty warm. Jonas's grandson told me he didn't have any use for the old place and said I could use it if I wanted, so I carried my clothes and a few other things across the highway and set up house. Then Anne moved in with me. Actually we never discussed it. She just came and sort of never left. So that after awhile, as spring came up green all around us and I was getting strength back in my shoulder and arm after getting out of the cast, we were a couple of angry lovebirds, getting up every morning, going to bed at night, fighting in between. She just wouldn't let go of anything. There was something about that gal, Anne. She had an imagination for evil. She remembered everything that ever pissed her off and then made some up to fill in the gaps.

"I know you really wanted Ima Jean!"

"I don't think about Ima Jean. She has two kids. She and Larry got back together."

"But if they hadn't got back together, you'd be after her."

"She's not my type anymore. I used to like her, you know, in that way, but I don't anymore."

"I don't believe you. I know you think about her. I know you think about that waitress who gave you the car. All you do is think about other women."

On one point she was right—I did think about Judy. I kept thinking that one day I should give her a call on the telephone. It was April already, and the last time I saw her was at Christmas. Then I came home. I guess she must have thought I dropped off the rim of the world.

The longer I put off calling her, though, the harder it got to do it. Then one morning, as I was standing at the sink with the sun streaming in the window, a razor in my hand and my face all lathered up, Anne said, "If you weren't half white, you wouldn't have to shave so much. I never knew a guy with such rough skin."

I put down the razor and wiped my face with a towel. I

buttoned up my shirt and stuffed the tails into my jeans and went for the door.

"Where are you going?" she asked.

I turned and looked at her. "I'm going over to Tom's to use the phone."

"Who are you calling?" she asked. Then she narrowed her eyes at me. "You're going to call that woman, aren't you?"

"Her name is Judy," I said.

Anne said, "If you call her I'm leaving."

"Leaving what?" I asked. "An empty shack?" Then I went outside. It was a chilly morning, with frost on the grass in the shadows of trees. I hurried across the road, and Tom's new dog greeted me with its tail wagging. It was a Doberman and black Labrador crossbreed with ears that winged out like he was going to take off flying. Tom was at work and Eddie was at school, and I slipped inside the house. I flopped down on the sofa and lighted a smoke and just leaned my head back. I felt like I was tired all the time. I didn't even know why I was still alive. I guess that's why I let Anne hit me so much. Sometimes I didn't even feel it, and I just didn't care.

When I finished my smoke, I picked up the phone and dialed Judy's number from memory. It rang about a dozen times.

I heard Judy say, "Hello." Her voice was real quiet and sleepy.

I said, "Hi. Sorry if I woke you up."

She said, "Who is this?"

"It's me, Sam."

Then she was silent, and I waited a long time for her to talk to me.

I said, "Maybe I shouldn't have called. Bye—"

"No, don't hang up," she said. "Let me wake up a little bit."

"I knew it. You were sleeping."

"It's alright. Where are you?"

"I'm at home, the rez."

"You sound really close."

"I guess they polished the wires."

"How are you, Sam?"

"Still alive. How you doing."

"Still alive," she said.

"I should have called you sooner," I said. "But I had my mind on a lot of things."

Judy said, "I'd just about forgotten you. What have you been doing?"

"Well," I said, "I got shot for one thing."

"You got shot?"

"Yeah, my cousin Tom took me down with a shotgun when I was climbing in the window. He didn't know it was me, or else he wouldn't have done it. It happened the day after Christmas, right when I got home."

"Are you alright?"

"They put a stainless-steel ball in my shoulder. I'm a robot. How about you? You alright?"

"I'm alright now. I didn't know what was going on. I didn't know what to think. It was a real mess. I really screwed up."

"I'm sorry I left like that—"

"No, it's not your fault. I didn't even know you were gone until the end of February, when I came home. I found your note."

"I left that on Christmas, after you went to work."

"I didn't know when you left it. I sort of ran into a problem."

"What kind of problem?"

"I fucked up. I gave a guy a ten-dollar blow job, and he turned out to be a plainclothes trooper. The son of a bitch didn't arrest me till I was wiping my chin. Then he booked me for prostitution. I spent the night in jail, and the next day I was up before a judge, who gave me sixty days in the county jail. When I got out and came home, I found your note. I figured that's why you left, because it was in the newspaper, me going to jail."

"I didn't know," I said. "I just had to come home for a while. You doing better now?"

"No," she said. "I'm all fucked up. They threw me in jail for selling sex, and while I was there they wanted to buy it. It doesn't make sense. Life doesn't make sense."

"I've got a girl with me now. I know what you mean. She says she loves me, but she keeps hitting me in the face. A month ago she broke two of my ribs. I still wake up at night trying to catch my breath. But she says she loves me. When I first got home she said she hated me. I can't figure it out. It seems like the more she loves me, the more she hits me. I guess I wish she hated me a little more."

"I thought you were a smart boy," she said, "coming to Dartmouth and all that, and you still haven't figured out that everything has a price. Anything you want, anything, is gonna have a price on it just because you want it. It's only the stuff you don't want that comes free. Everything good in the world costs, and everything bad is free. It's set up that way so we spend all our time and money trying to feel good. We do all the things we hate, just to feel good for a few minutes in between all the bullshit."

"This woman, Anne, the one who keeps hitting me, wants to get married, but I don't love her. Not like I loved you."

"You said that in the past tense. You don't love me now?"

Suddenly there was a loud pounding on the door, and I

knew it was Anne before she even spoke. "I swear to God I'm leaving!" she yelled. The dog was barking, not angry but all excited, and Anne kept banging on the door.

"Just hold on a minute," I told Judy.

I went and opened the door, and Anne stood right up to me.

"I'm on the phone," I said. Then she slapped me real hard.

"I told you I'd leave if you called that whore!" She barged right past me, saw the phone receiver lying on the sofa, and grabbed it up. "Who the fuck do you think you are giving away cars—"

I grabbed the phone away from her and tried to talk into, it but Anne started wrestling me for it. I dropped the phone and pushed Anne hard, and she came right back. I don't know what came over me—yes, I do know—I hated her, and when she came back at me with her teeth flashing, I hit her so hard she spun around and hit the wall beside the TV set. Then she didn't move. I was ready for her to come back at me with her claws out, like always, but she didn't move. She just lay there like a rumpled blanket. I stared at her for a long time, and then I heard the crackly static voice on the phone. "Sam! Talk to me! Sam! What's happening?"

I slowly reached for the phone and brought it up to my ear.

"Sam, are you alright?"

"I'm alright," I said. I was still staring at Anne. She was twisted up beside the TV set. I never saw anyone look so still before. "She's not moving," I said.

"Who's not moving. What'd you do?"

"Anne. She grabbed the phone, and then she came at me, and I hit her and she fell down beside the TV, and she's not moving."

"Sam, listen to me. You just knocked her out. Go and give her a little shake. Wake her up."

I put down the phone, and I went over to Anne. I pulled her up by her shoulders, and her head flopped over like a dead cat. There was blood coming out of her ear, and it had seeped through her long black hair and left a smear against the wall. I let go of her, and when she fell back, one of her eyelids jarred open. She lay there, with one dark, dilated eye sightlessly staring into the room, her mouth hanging open. I slowly picked up the phone. "I don't know what happened," I said. "I think she's dead. All I did was hit her once. She was coming at me, and I hit her."

My heart was pounding fast, and I felt suddenly sick, my stomach rolling back against my spine. Judy's voice was trembling when she spoke, "You didn't kill her. I don't believe it!"

"I think I'm gonna throw up," I said, dropping the phone and rushing to the kitchen sink. I leaned over the sink, and my stomach heaved so hard and long I couldn't breathe or see. Everything was all blackness and pain like the world had closed in on me. My stomach kept punching up, over and over, until I didn't have anything left to give. Slowly the waves subsided, and I hung limp against the sink, trying to ease my breathing, wiping tears out of my eyes.

I hauled myself back to the sofa, my legs heavy, and fell back against the cushions. I picked up a smoke, then the phone.

"I couldn't help myself," I said. "I'm better now."

"What are you going to do?" asked Judy. "If she's really dead you gotta get out of there. Will anybody believe you if you tell them what happened, that it was an accident? Will anybody help you?"

"I don't know," I said. "Let me think a minute. I gotta clear my head."

"You can come back here. No one would think of looking for you with me, or we could go somewhere else."

"Just shut up!" I yelled. "I'm trying to think." But the only thing that came to me was how alone I was in the world. No one, not even the Creator, if one existed, or the spirits of my dead ancestors, looked out for me. Nothing I could do would save me from myself, from accidents and nightmares, or all the forces between heaven and earth that somehow conspired against people like me. Nothing I could do would prevent me from ending up like Carver Hill, drunk all the time in a turquoise-blue house trailer, or Larry Killdeer, broke with two kids and not even twenty years old, or Tom, who spent his whole life breathing gypsum dust in a Sheetrock factory, who'd die coughing and alone. Tom's son, Eddie, was already smoking and drinking at thirteen, and Ima Jean was a fat cleaning woman in a nursing home, changing putrid bedding and wiping soup off old people's chins. This was the way it had always been for us, thinking back, and this was the way it would always be, unless I became some fat professional Indian with blue eyes, skimming the people's pot till I got caught.

"No, Judy," I said. "It wouldn't do me any good to run away. It'll always follow me. I'd bring all the bad luck with me and dump it right in your lap."

"My lap's already full, in case you didn't figure that out. It's worth a try, starting over."

I was staring at Anne, and my pulse began racing. "I think I saw her move!" I said, dropping the phone. She let out a small moan and slowly fluttered her eyes open. She stared at me with a blank, dazed expression and slowly whispered, "You son of a bitch."

I sat back, now feeling sick that she was alive, seeing a dark hatred in her eyes, a loathing made up of jealousy and envy that slithered out of her, uglier than any other animal I could imagine in the human spirit. Her whisper was like a cruel hissing, and I backed away from her until I got to the couch. I carefully picked up the phone and said, "She's alive."

Anne said, "You were trying to kill me! The two of you wanted me dead!" She rubbed the side of her head and felt the sticky blood, then looked at the scarlet stains on her fingers. She tried to stand but lost her balance and sat back down. She grabbed the edge of the doorframe for support and pulled herself up on wobbly legs. She rolled around the edge of the open door and fell out into the yard.

"Judy, I gotta go. She's just fell out the door." Then I dropped the phone.

When I looked out the door, Anne was weaving down the driveway like a drunken person. She was yelling, "I'll call the goddamned cops! I'll have you locked up!"

She stumbled along the line of trees and bushes up to the highway.

"Anne, NO! STOP!" I called.

She looked back, "You ain't talking me out of it." Then she turned right onto the highway, stepping out from the tall bushes. And that was when the green pickup truck hit her, so hard she flew over the hood and the cab, landing like a bag of broken shells in the bed of the truck. The driver braked so suddenly the truck screeched, then turned sideways before flipping over on its side, dumping its lifeless cargo onto the middle of the road. He must have been going seventy when he hit Anne, and he slid over fifty yards in front of the house. While I'd watched the whole scene, it had seemed to happen in a strange slow motion that abruptly became motionless, with only by the sound of steam escaping from the radiator. The only thing I could think was that no one was immune, not

Anne or even the unsuspecting driver of the truck, who was now banging both fists to escape through the cracked windshield.

A station wagon coming from the other direction made a fast stop in the gravel by the side of the road, and I suddenly found my feet, running as fast as I could with Tom's dog barking at my heels. A woman with two scared little kids got out of the car. The little kids stood silent and openmouthed, looking at the busted figure of Anne and the streaks of blood, like sloppy red graffiti, on the road. Tom's dog licked the blood and gravel. I stood back and made a big lunge, kicking out the windshield of the truck, and the woman and I pulled out the driver. He was a middle-aged Cayuga man named Gerald James. I'd seen him at the community center. He knew Tom. He stood up, shaking, but he wasn't really hurt, just jostled around and bruised. The woman looked at her kids and said, "That girl is dead. Say a little prayer."

Gerald James said, "I don't know what happened. All I saw was her flying up over the truck. I don't even know where she came from!"

"It's alright," I said. "I saw it all. She was in a hurry crossing the road, and she just ran out from those bushes down there. It wasn't your fault."

Two more cars stopped beside the road. "I'll go inside and call the cops," I said, pausing to stare at Anne while grabbing the dog's collar.

I had a strange sense about life when they planted Anne in the ground. It was the same time of year the old people were watching the stars and the moon and readying their gardens for planting other women—the Three Sisters who sustain the people—corn, beans, and squash. I don't remember anyone sitting me down and telling me these things, so I guess a lot of it just soaked inside my brain, listening to people talk when I was young. They said the time to plant was with the new moon in May, so things would grow as the moon grew full and fat. Another sign was when the baby oak leaves were as big as a raccoon's paw and the Juneberries were in blossom. Some people even said you ought to pull down your pants and sit on the earth for a while, and if a chill didn't rise out of the ground, it was OK to plant.

I never much listened to all that stuff when it was going on around me, but when I was alone it sneaked up on me like a nagging conscience. I mean it's hard to put crap outta your head when it's been cooking in there your whole life. I tried to put it out of my head, because it just didn't make any sense, like some old guy with his bare ass pressed into the damp earth. It was like the whole world was blown apart into a bunch of jigsaw puzzle pieces—all those little bits stuffed into my pockets to carry around and worry about. I did a real jigsaw puzzle once, and the one thing I learned from it was that you wouldn't get anywhere without four corners and a border. Only then could you fill in the center and get a clear picture. The problem was that in real life the picture seemed to change when there were only a few pieces left.

So after a while, with things like Anne getting hit by a truck, you didn't even try to put the puzzle together. You just turned the pieces over and over in your hand. I still had no idea about life. I didn't know why bad things happened to good people, or why bad people had so much to smile about. All I knew was that voices came to me in memories—my mother laughing, Ellie cooing to her horse, Aunt Bess loud in her deaf-ness, Uncle Lewis's saliva slurring—all of them, and others, gone. All of them planted like corn and beans and squash, and their words coming up in me the way life bursts out of the earth every spring.

Outside my tar-paper house, I could see all this life com-ing up around me. The corn slipped up quietly in the flat acres along the highway. The tractors had come and done their work, and now the corn struggled above and below the earth, setting deep roots to hold on and waving pale green spears in the face of the sun. The squash and the beans were slow and shy, like closed jade eyelids, hiding among their sister, corn. These sis-ters seemed to have voices, too. They said to me, "How short we live."

I didn't know what I was doing, but I burned some to-bacco and prayed one morning before the dew burned off.

Corn, you live.
Beans, you live.
Squash, you live.
The people live,
The people die.
I am afraid of what
Exists between us.
Help me understand.
Is the meaning of my life
Fertilizer?

The Three Sisters answered only, "How short we live."

Hangman

Larry sat slumped down in old Jonas's favorite soft chair, drinking a beer, picking shreds of horsehair stuffing from a frayed hole in the arm. His feet were propped up on an old wooden crate with the words *Cream of Wheat* embossed with black ink on the sides.

I was working on a painting. The stretched canvas was hung from a nail on the wall, and before me on a rusty folding card table was an array of oil paints in wrinkled tubes, brushes in mason jars of turpentine, rags, and a palette of muted colors. Larry said, "It's coming along." It was a painting of a guy in blue jeans sitting on the bumper of a truck, leaning over a bottle of beer he was holding between his knees. It didn't look like the guy had anywhere to go, anything to do. I called it *Waiting*. The background was all flat land with a distant tree line and wide blue sky. I did a lot of paintings like that one— people alone in places they knew best—in a rocking chair, on the edge of a bed, leaning on a fence, holding a hoe—because it seemed to me that every honest person knew exactly what their station in life was, and if you looked you'd find them parked in that spot their whole life. It was like when you thought real hard about a person, and one image stood out in your mind that seemed to sum up everything about them. I had a painting of a young Indian girl—I guess it was Ima Jean— with a baby held on her hip. Because that was Ima Jean's lot in life, and no matter how old she got, she would never grow up. She'd always be that young girl, saddled with babies. Carver Hill would always be standing behind the screen door of his trailer with the shadow of his woman over his shoulder. Larry would be that guy waiting on the bumper of his truck. On the surface we all seemed different, we all carried a different burden. But I saw it as a similarity, just different faces, like masks. I saw us all, rising out of an earth, a land, filled with generations of pain and longing, as dispossessed people from whom each newly born child inherited a legacy of blank expressions. That's what I saw, and that's what I painted, in soft colors, as if each subject was caught halfway between this world and that other world that was timeless, being both a place we had come from and a place we were going to.

Larry nodded his chin at a group of other paintings leaning along the bottom of the wall. "I like that one, too. It reminds me of Ima Jean."

"It's a little like her, I guess." I didn't talk very much to Larry, or anyone, about my paintings. I really didn't care to hear their opinions.

"If you really want to be famous you gotta start painting naked ladies. I saw a book that was full of famous artists, and they were hot for naked ladies. But don't do that abstract stuff, four eyes and three tits, like what's his name did—"

"Picasso."

"I guess so. Who cares, anyway? Just do a few naked gals if you really want to be famous."

"Maybe someday. I'll think about it."

"But none of Ima Jean!"

"I promise. None of Ima Jean." I swirled my brush in a jar of turps and wiped it clean on a rag. I looked around the tar-paper shack. It was full of paintings, stretched canvas—I used old window frames from abandoned buildings to stretch canvas I cut from an old tent-and pictures, torn out of magazines, tacked to the walls. It was a good little studio.

"You never done any paintings of Anne," said Larry.

"She was always so angry and jealous. I can't get that picture out of my mind," I said.

"It's been three months," he said. "I think the least you could do is one painting of Anne."

"Someday," I said.

"Goddamn, she liked to fight, didn't she?" said Larry. "I don't know how you put up with her. I think I would have coldcocked her."

One thing Larry never knew, nobody did, was that Anne might have had a clear head, crossing the road, if I hadn't coldcocked her. I sure didn't want anyone to know that.

"What day is it?" I asked.

"I think it's Tuesday," said Larry.

"Can you come over tomorrow with your truck? Help me take some paintings to the cultural center?"

"What for?"

"There are some people coming from museums. They want to see some art and meet the artists."

Larry drank down his beer and tossed the bottle near a garbage can. It missed but didn't break, spinning like a top for a few seconds. "I'm sick of that shit, man," he said. "All the time they's coming here, poking old Grandma for her silver brooches and moccasins, picking through our lives and taking all the good stuff. It pisses me off!"

"I might sell a few paintings. Just bring your truck, man." I got a couple of beers out of a small fridge and sat on the floor beside Larry. We stared at my paintings for a while, and Larry said, "I hope you make some money. I need a loan."

When we drove up to the cultural center, we passed by the small cemetery where Anne was buried. The earth still hadn't settled on her grave, and there was no grass growing above her. A guy was driving a tractor with a brush hog, and he was cutting back the field to make the cemetery bigger. Larry saw it too. He said, "People tripping over each other to get buried. That's the only way some of us will ever own a piece of land."

Then he raised his palm and slapped my hand.

"Sooner or later they'll figure a way to evict the dead out of their graves," I said.

"What are you, stupid?" he said. "They already done it. It's called archaeology! College didn't teach you nothing. Archaeology is just another word for eviction."

Then we drove quietly until we arrived at the center, and Larry parked the truck near a side door. We each grabbed a couple of paintings out of the back of the truck and went inside the center into the big gym. There were a lot of people milling around. Some other artists had tables set up with pottery or soapstone carvings. We leaned the paintings against the bottom row of the bleachers and slipped outside for the rest. When we came back to set up the last of the paintings, there were already quite a number of people standing in front of the first four paintings. The director of the center—a small man with thick glasses—came up to me and whispered, "Your paintings look real nice. There are some people here from galleries in New York and Montreal."

Larry finished setting up the paintings. He was standing right beside them when a man started taking his picture. A well-dressed woman—grey skirt and scarlet jacket with a big gold pin—circled back and forth in front of the paintings. Then she asked Larry, "What are they priced?"

I couldn't get up to him in time. He said, "I dunno. Maybe five hundred?"

"Each?"

"I guess so," he said.

"Three fifty," said the woman.

Larry said, "Sure, why not?"

I just turned away and took a deep breath. Then, looking back over my shoulder, I nodded at Larry to come over to me.

"Jesus Christ!" I said. "I was only asking a hundred bucks each."

"I'll split the difference," he said.

"You got it," I said, turning back to see the woman writing a check. The photographer was waving at us. We went up to them, and the woman spoke to Larry. "I want you to stand against this one for a promotional shot." She handed him the check. I squinted. It was a bank draft for cash, a lot of cash. I never saw so much money in my life!

"Sam, get in the picture with me," said Larry.

"That won't be necessary," said the woman.

When I came up beside him, Larry looked puzzled. "Don't you want some pictures of the artist?" He put his arm across my shoulders.

The woman looked at me. "*You* painted these?" She called over the director. "What's going on here? I thought this was supposed to be Indian art only?" She was accusing him, with her gold pen pointed like a dart at his heart.

The director said, "Sure, Sam lives down the line. He was raised here. He's Mohawk.

The woman put one hand on her hip and cocked her head.

"Listen to me," she said. "I can't sell ethnic art from someone who doesn't *look* ethnic. How do I know he's a damned Indian?"

The director said, "Because I'm telling you so."

"Fine. And are you going to stand in my gallery and tell all my customers the same thing?" She reached over to Larry and said, "Give me back my check!" Then she said to Larry, "Who the hell are you?"

Larry said, "I'm his friend."

The woman tore the check in two and stuffed it in the pocket of her scarlet jacket. She grabbed the photographer by the arm and walked away.

"I'm gonna kick her fucking ass out the door!" said Larry.

"Just let it go," I said.

"Man, I just lost a thousand bucks. Eight paintings times a buck and a quarter!"

"I lost, too. And I'm just gonna let it go."

Larry said, "Why don't you get lost for a while, and I'll stand here and sell them. There's still a lot of people hanging around."

"And what are you gonna say if someone wants you to talk about them? I can hear you now: 'None of that abstract shit here folks. No extra tits and all the eyes on the front of the face!'"

Larry shuffled his feet. "Goddamn it! I never figured you'd make money just for looking like a Skin."

"You oughta go to Hollywood," I said.

Larry jerked up. "No shit! Kick John Wayne's ass big time! Big Bucks!"

"Would you just fucking shut up!" I said, sitting down on the bleachers beside my paintings. Larry sat down beside me, and we lighted some smokes and waited.

It could have been worse. I sold three paintings for a hundred fifty bucks a piece. I gave Larry fifty bucks just for keeping his mouth shut all day.

When we were driving back to my shack, I told him to stop at the feed store. I bought a pound of grass seed, and we went by Anne's grave. We each scattered the seed on the bare ground.

Then we bought four cases of ice-cold Molson's Export

Ale and five cartons of smokes, and when we finally got home, we lay in the cool shade of the shack and drank beer till it was dark. The stars began to emerge, bright and restless in the inky sky. I was feeling pretty good for a change, even though I was wondering about my mother and Ellie and Anne, flung out into all those stars.

Larry said, "I heard something this morning before I came over. I forgot to tell you."

"Oh yeah, what's that?"

"I don't know why I forgot. I guess I was thinking about all that money and the phony bitch in the red coat."

"So what is it?" I saw a shooting star dash across the heavens and instantly thought that someone had been born somewhere.

"Remember I told you Alvin Cloud took up with that Sioux girl from South Dakota and joined the Marines with her brother while you were at college?"

"Sure. You hear from him?"

"Ima Jean told me this morning, his mother got a telegram yesterday. Said he got killed in Viet Nam."

I stared at the sky and picked at the label on my bottle of beer. I closed my eyes and tried to remember what Alvin looked like. "That dumb son of a bitch," I said. "I bet he dragged his balls over a land mine."

"He was our friend!" said Larry.

"And we're sitting here drinking beer and counting our money. Tomorrow you or me will go, and whoever is left will still sit here drinking beer, counting money. What do you want me to do? Spend my whole life crying over every dumb son of a bitch who doesn't make it to the next day? I'm nineteen fucking years old, and I feel like a god Damned old man. I don't wanna hear about death anymore! Do you understand that? There isn't enough of me to go around!"

"Alvin was our friend. We ought to do something!"

"Fine. Alvin was our friend. Let's open two more beers and drink to Alvin's big dick."

Larry popped some beers open and gave me one. "Here's to Alvin," he said, lifting his bottle against the sky.

I raised my bottle. "Alvin! If you're listening, you dumb son of a bitch, watch out for Annie. She'll kick you when you're down!" I looked at Larry. "How's that?"

"Fucking good advice!" He clinked his bottle against mine. Another shooting star zoomed towards earth. "Look! He heard us!" said Larry. Then he sighed and leaned back, resting against the tar-paper shack. Across the highway, I saw a light come on inside the log house where I grew up, and I knew that Eddie was taking a midnight leak. A few minutes later the light went off. It was a quiet, windless summer night, made peaceful by the rhythmic clicking insects and the lonely calls of night birds seeking companionship in the dark.

"Larry?"

"What?"

"I don't know what to do anymore," I said. "I feel like I'm drowning."

"The trouble with you is that you think too much," said Larry.

"The trouble with *you* is that you don't think enough," I said.

"Where would it get me? Thinking just breaks your heart big time. Stop thinking so much, and you'll slide through life a happy bastard," said Larry.

"You don't understand. When I'm here, I'm not Indian enough for the outsiders. And when I'm outside, I'm not white enough there. Where's the middle ground?"

"At least you got an outside chance," said Larry. "Remember once I played a hockey game in Toronto? I went out walking after the game—I guess to get a pack of smokes, see the city—I tried to get a cab when it got late, and none of them would stop. Finally one did, and the guy looked at me and said, 'No Spics,' and he drove away fast. Right here on the rez is the only place for me."

"No place is right for me," I said.

"Fuck, if I felt like that I'd kill myself."

"Would you really?"

"I'd get tanked up and hang myself. A strong rope and a stout beam. Why, are you thinking about it?"

"I had a great uncle who hanged himself in Aunt Molly's barn, right down the road. I don't know if I could do it."

"It's supposed to be an easy way to go, but I heard that if you drop a long way your head can come off, and if that doesn't happen you shit your pants."

"I heard that, too. There's gotta be a better way."

"What about in the cowboy movies? They slap a horse out from under you. You don't drop, so your head doesn't come off and you don't shit your pants. You got a horse, don't you! Star Blanket!"

"That was Ellie's horse. I can't just let him go riding off alone. He'll get busted up in the woods or hit by a car."

"Yeah, I see what you mean. What about kicking out a stool? They do that in prison movies."

"You think that would work?"

"If you don't want to lose your head, shit your pants, or kill the horse, it's the only way. Trust me."

"Wait a minute. You'd have to cut me down."

"Why me?"

"You want Eddie to find me and have to do it? He's only

thirteen. It wouldn't be a big shock for you. Not like for anyone else, say Tom. He's gettin old. He might have a heart attack."

"Sure. I mean if you want me to, I will," Larry said.

"Who else? You're my best friend."

"Alright, let's do it."

When we tried to stand up, Larry stumbled into me and we both fell down. Larry said, "I guess we'll have to crawl inside. I'll lead the way."

"How can I hang myself if I can't stand up?"

"We'll do it sitting down. Trust me," he said.

Larry pulled himself into the doorway of the shack, and I followed. "It's dark in here," he said. "How are we supposed to find a rope?"

I rolled into the big main room, and the light from Grandmother Moon smiled after me through the open door, bathing the floor in a pale silvery wash. "There's a rope around here someplace," I said, trying to remember where I had left it. I moved across the floor in the darkness and suddenly cracked my head against something hard. "Goddamn it!"

"What happened?" asked Larry.

"I hit my head on the fucking woodstove."

"Do you have any aspirin?"

"What do I need a damned aspirin for?"

"You don't want to hang yourself with a headache, do you?" said Larry.

"What difference does it make?"

"The least you could do is feel good when you kill yourself," he said. "You oughta feel fucking great when you die! I'm sorry for trying."

I found a coil of old rope near the stove. "Here's the rope!"

"It's about time," said Larry.

"Are you late for an important damned meeting?" I asked.

"Just tie up the rope."

It was an open ceiling with bare rafters and a small storage loft with a ladder. I flung the rope up, and it came back down on top of me. Larry grabbed it. "Let me do it." The rope sailed over a rafter and came down the other side.

Larry said, "Tie the end to the leg of the woodstove."

I stretched out the rope and wrapped it around the iron leg, knotting it.

Larry shoved the wooden box across the floor, right in the light of the moon. "Here, sit on this crate." I sat on the crate, and Larry held the loose end of rope up to my shoulder, measuring the bottom of the noose. It wasn't a fancy, long coiled noose, just a slip knot, which Larry tightened around my neck. Then without warning he yanked away the crate, and I lurched down, the rope jerking up my head. I grabbed the rope, then rolled up onto my knees.

"What the hell did you do that for!" I said, loosening the rope and breathing deeply. "I didn't say ready, set, go!"

"I didn't know you wanted to say ready, set, go! The least you could do is tell a guy what you want!"

"Maybe I want a last cigarette?" I said, lighting a smoke and sitting back down on the crate. "Go get some more beer."

Then we sat and thought it over some for a while. "This isn't such a good idea," I said.

"Why not?" asked Larry.

"Because you can't hang yourself *sitting* on a box. You have to stand on it. It's the only way."

"Then we have to do it all over again." Larry stood up slowly, holding the rope for support. He put the noose over his neck. "You go and shorten the rope on the stove leg when I stand on the box."

I crawled over to the woodstove and fumbled with the

knots. Larry mounted the box and stood with his arms out for balance. "I'm flying," he said. "Pull up more."

I shortened the rope and wrapped it tight with a couple of knots, and then I heard a splintering crash. When I looked up, I saw Larry's arms flailing in the air, his feet stuck through the broken bottom of the old wooden crate.

"What happened, Larry?" I looked at him for a few seconds. "Come on down!"

Larry started clutching at the rope around his neck, and he was thrashing to untangle his feet from the box. His face was purple in the moonlight. Suddenly I understood what was happening, and I wrapped my arms around his knees and boosted him up. He choked out the words, "Untie the rope," and I let go of him and scrambled to the woodstove.

"Larry, it's all tightened up!"

Now he was thrashing again, and I thought I should just cut the rope.

"Hold on, Larry. I'm gonna get a knife!"

I had to think where I'd put my hunting knife, then I remembered it was in a sheath in the top drawer of the bureau. I got up and rushed to the bureau and pulled the whole drawer out, dumping everything on the floor. "I'm coming, Larry. Just hang on a little longer!" Then I rummaged for the knife, found it, and went back to begin sawing on the rope. Larry was starting to slow down a bit. I figured he was just being patient. After all, I had the knife and was working on getting him down. Jerking around wasn't going to help. The rope snapped when I was halfway through it, and Larry came crashing down with a deep grunt and a sudden gush of air. He lay with his head almost out the door, and I helped him get the rope off his neck. He stared up at me and gasped, "What the fuck did you mean, *just hang on a little longer!*"

"That was a close one," I said. "What was it like?"

A strong odor rose in the air.

"I shit my pants, that's what it was like," he said, his breath wheezing in and out.

"What about your theory about dropping from a high place?" I asked.

"I was goddamned wrong, alright!"

"You don't have to be so touchy," I said. "It wasn't my fault."

Larry rolled over onto his hands and knees, holding his head at a cocked angle. "Just give me another beer."

Larry turned over with his beer and sat in the open doorway, as though the moonlight covered him with warmth.

He said, "The crate's ruined. You'll have to use a chair, and we better tie the rope together."

"Are you fucking crazy?" I said.

He gave me a crooked look. "You mean I went through all that, and now you *aren't* going to hang yourself?"

I smiled at him. "I wouldn't be caught dead with a load of shit in my pants."

He smiled back. "Shotgun."

"Poison," I said.

"Razor blade," he answered.

"Drive off a cliff."

"Lie down in the middle of the highway," he said.

"Jump out of a plane without a parachute."

"I've got it!" he said. "Dynamite!"

"No, I think I'll let the Creator decide. The way my life's going, I'm sure the Creator will think up something pretty fucking nasty."

I looked at him in the moonlight, and he had a bright purple-and-red burn all around his throat, like a snake under his skin. He must have come down on the side of his face, because his right eye was beginning to swell up. I thought: "A hickey and a black eye". In a strange kind of way, I guess I loved Larry. I never would have let anyone else hang me.

"What are you gonna do now?" he asked.

"I don't know. I got the money from the paintings, and the car still runs pretty good. Maybe I'll drive around. I sure would like to see Judy again. When the money runs out, get a job somewhere, scrape some cash together, come back here once in a while."

"I got nothing to hold me here," said Larry, "and I still got forty bucks to chip in. So what if people think I'm a Mexican? Fuck 'em."

"You saying you wanna go?"

"I guess I better change my pants first, pack a few things. I could be back by nine in the morning, and we could take off," he said. "We could take on the world together!"

"You got a deal," I said. "But first take a damn bath."

Larry slapped my hand and got up, staggering out to his truck. He fired it up, pulling away with grinding gears.

I leaned my head in the doorway and listened to the insects clicking across the night. Then I slept until the sun coming over the trees burned against my eyelids. I didn't feel too bad as I stuffed some clothes, my paints, and a few personal things into the old army duffel bag. I drank a soda and smoked a cigarette, and I waited for Larry.

By ten o'clock he hadn't arrived, so I drove up the line, cut over on a side road, and swung south past Ima Jean's trailer. I slowed down as I came close, and I saw Larry sitting in the uncut grass, playing with his two kids. One kid was wrapped around his neck, hanging down his back, and he was helping the little one stand up and walk in front of him. The little one was holding onto his forefingers with both tiny fists. Ima Jean was hanging wet clothes on a rope stretched between two trees. She looked up and smiled at me. The baby rolled down in the grass, and Larry waved at me. He tried to smile. He really couldn't leave, and he really tried to smile. He nodded at me, and I nodded at him. He looked pretty beat-up with the side of his face bruised and his head cocked over. He always did talk big when he was drinking.

What I saw then was something I hadn't realized—that Larry was exactly where he belonged, doing what he was supposed to do, and he had something I wanted. I wondered if I could have had that with Anne, and if it was possible to try again with someone, anyone:

I shut off the car, opened the door, and swung my legs out. I sat there, with my elbows on my knees, watching those little kids playing with their dad, possibly the biggest loser in the world and my best friend. Larry couldn't do a damned thing except bum smokes, beer, and money, but he sure as hell loved those kids. I guess that's what kept him from leaving.

Ima Jean put down her wash basket by the trailer door and slowly walked over to where I was parked.

She kneeled down and looked up at me, with a sadness in her eyes.

"You ain't got no business leaving again. Didn't you learn enough already?"

"Larry told you, eh?"

She nodded at me. "You never done a painting of me," she said. "If you go, who will paint my picture?"

"There are plenty of artists here. One on every corner it seems like."

"But they ain't you, Sam."

I smiled and put my hand on her shoulder. "Maybe I just keep running away from things I can't have."

Ima Jean took my hand and pressed it against her cheek. "No, Sam, you keep running away from yourself. We all see it. I'm surprised Tom don't kick your butt for you."

"Tom's getting like the old-timers, he just lets you figure out life on your own. He never gets in the middle."

"Maybe you outta go talk to him."

I thought about it for a moment. "When I was a kid I used to go talk with old Jonas. . . . You remember that guy?"

Ima Jean nodded, "Yep, I remember his funeral. He was buried the old way behind the longhouse. I remember walking to school and seeing his body in the backseat of the car. It was February, and they kept his body cool until the feast."

"I didn't always catch a lot he said back then, but it's funny how those words come up again when you need them."

"You ain't alone, Sam. Not really. Can't you see that?" She leaned up and gave me a gentle kiss on the lips. It was warm and moist, and she smelled like laundry soap. She stood back from me. She still had the blackest hair on any gal, shining almost blue in the sunlight. It was strange, though. She didn't take my breath away anymore. I still loved her in a way, but she and Larry had too much going.

"Whatcha gonna do, Sam?"

"Not exactly sure."

I swung back into the car seat and closed the door, started it up, and gave her a wave. Larry waved, too, when I headed down the road.

Five minutes later, I drove across the imaginary line that separated the rez from white-man's land, and I stopped the car. I got out and stood straddle-legged on the border, with a foot in each of two worlds. The sun was straight above me, casting an equal light on those worlds—no shadows, no place to hide. I felt in full view of the Creator and all the spirits. I

294